*To Cody... You put your hands on my sister like a little bitch. Let this book be your warning.*
*XOXO - Cassie*

# content warning

- Sex
- Drug Use
- Murder
- Torture
- Graphic Violence
- Death of Parent (on page)
- Parental Rejection due to Sexuality
- Sexual Prejudice
- Hate Speech
- Stalking
- Kidnapping
- Cheating (not between the MCs)
- Attempted SA
- Sexuality Gaslighting
- Attempted Conversion

If you believe you are the victim of a hate crime or that you witnessed a hate crime dial 9-1-1 or call your local police station. If you need someone to talk to about it, the Justice

# Steel

HELL'S MAYHEM MC
ILLINOIS CHAPTER

## CASSIE LEIN

Cover by ShayBabe Designs

Formatting by Cassie Lein

## one

### IGNATIUS

IT'S DECEMBER. I can officially dress for the season at work and not get written up. I've only been waiting since the day after Halloween; the second-best holiday. If Susan wasn't such a bitch and her daughter, Nancy, the biggest snitch and ass kisser, I would have just said fuck the rules and started my Christmas ensembles early. But I got written up last year when I wore a Christmas sweater on Black Friday.

I button my black dress slacks around my waist before slipping the Gucci belt through the hoops. Flipping through my closet rather quickly, I pull my Santa short-sleeve button up from the hanger, deciding to start with a bang. It's styled like a sports jersey but is sky blue and covered with large Santas. I smile as I tuck it into my slacks and brush my hands down the front to smooth the wrinkles.

God, Susan will shit a brick if she sees me today, but the Howards' employee handbook states in strong bold letters that as of December first, employees may dress as holidayish as they want.

*Is holidayish a word? Or is it Christmassy? But what if they don't celebrate Christmas per se but a different winter holiday? Focus, Ignatius. It's almost time for work.*

There are only two ways Susan would know what I was wearing. She either actually looked at the cameras, which is laughable, or her daughter Nancy cried about me breaking the rules, which she does every chance she gets. She used to leave me alone, but when she asked me to dinner and I turned her down, she's been a bitch ever since.

I thought it was pretty obvious that I wasn't into women, but Nancy either didn't care or thought she would be the woman to make me straight. Ha! Fat chance of that happening. I love the dick, the masculine smell, the rigid muscles, the rough hands. Just the thought of a strong, rugged man has a shiver coursing through my body.

Now, if only I could find someone who checks all my boxes. It's not even that many; employed, don't live with their mom, not still in the closet. I'm rather easy to please, but after many blind dates, Meet Males meetups, and even a Men2Men speed dating event, I'm twenty-eightand single as hell.

Don't these men know what a catch I am? I own my house all by myself; I own a car, and work a full-time job. Plus, I know I'm easy on the eyes and I'd like to think I'm funny and smart. But it seems while everyone else is finding their one true love and settling down, I'm just here living the bachelor's life.

Fuck! I need to stop the pity party or I'm going to be late. Scrambling to put my shoes on, I grab my keys and run out the door.

Hitting the button on the key fob, I unlock my car and

climb behind the wheel. The drive to Rockford isn't so bad. It's all highway and minimal lights, so before I know it, I'm pulling into the parking lot and shutting off my car.

THIS SHIFT HAS BEEN DRAGGING ass and my sales are nowhere near what I need them to be if I want to get the promotion I've been working for. Howards is looking for a new Philanthropy Manager, the job I've wanted since I started. I know they always fill the position from within the company, so I needed somewhere to start. I've enjoyed my time as the children's department manager, but it's not what I want to do for the rest of my life.

"Ignatius! Where are you?" Nancy's voice is like nails on a chalkboard.

"Over here!" I roll my eyes as I put away a basket of toys people discarded and set the last doll back in its proper place.

"I need to go on break and Tom went home sick, so you're covering my department." She steps closer and runs her hand down my chest.

"Who will cover here, then?" I ask, pushing it off of me.

"Quinn. Not that it matters. This place is dead," she purrs.

"Why doesn't Quinn just cover for you, then? That makes more sense than her covering me, covering for you." I raise a brow.

"Mom gave the order, not me. So you can take it up with her or just come with me." She stomps her foot like a child; fitting since we're in the children's department. "Do you really want to risk her finding out you didn't follow her orders? She's already going to write you up if she sees that shirt."

"The handbook says I can dress in holiday wear as of December first, so she can't write me up," I argue. She goes to open her mouth to fire back at me, but I don't want to argue with her. It's like trying to get a preschooler to share their favorite toy. "Fine," I sigh. "I'll head over there now." I leave Nancy standing by the dolls and head toward the men's department.

I hate this part of the store. Everyone who comes into the department is a judgmental asshole, it seems, with only a few good eggs that don't act like it's a hardship being helped by me. It's why I like the kids' department. Kids don't care that I'm overzealous or love to wear fun outfits. Their parents appreciate my spirit when helping little Tommy or Tina pick out the perfect toy to spend their allowance on.

Not wanting to stand too close to the register so I don't have to ring anyone out, I settle on refolding the table of jeans instead. At least it will be ready to go when it's closing time. I personally don't wait until the last minute to get my shit done for closing, but Nancy doesn't care. It's not like she's opening and will have to deal with it. Mommy always gives her the closing shifts so she can sleep in.

I'm fixing the last stack of Silver jeans when a tall figure steps beside me. "Are you able to help me find something?" a deep, yet raspy, voice asks.

I straighten up from leaning over the table and see possibly the most gorgeous man I've ever laid eyes on. His tattooed, muscular arms look like they're about to rip the white T-shirt he's wearing to shreds. Over the shirt, he has a leather vest with two patches on the left, one says Steel, and under that President.

My gaze trails up his firm body to his light brown hair that is cropped close to his head, minus the top that he has slicked back and to the side, making his deep chocolate eyes even more stunning.

"Y-y-yeah sure. What are you looking for?" His presence throws me off.

"My club's got this dinner thing coming up and we gotta dress up, they say. So I want to get all the guys new jeans. Nothing with holes or grease stains," he says, but seems unsure of what he's asking.

"Okay. Do you have their sizes?"

"Yup. Had one of the old ladies track them all down for me." He digs in his front pocket for a second before pulling out a piece of crinkled notebook paper.

*Old ladies?* So he had someone's grandma get the sizes instead of asking himself? Of course, all the hotties have to be assholes.

I take it from him and open it. *These are names?* Who named their kids these things? No matter, I guess, all I need are the sizes and they're written in pink next to each name.

"Do you want dark, light, or medium wash? Any distressing at all?" I start firing off questions, but stop when his eyes widen.

"Umm. No distressing, they'll get enough of that when this dinner is over with. I don't know about the wash, so just give me a variety, as long as they're the right sizes."

"Okay, well, do you have a budget in mind? We have these here that are ninety dollars or so a pair, but we do have some more budget-friendly options too," I tell him and bite my bottom lip as he steps closer to me to inspect the jeans on the table.

*Christ.* He smells like motor oil and musk. As he leans over the table, I see the back of his vest has a large skull wearing a bandana over its mouth with the words Hell's Mayhem Motorcycle Club around it.

Oh, so he's like the president of a motorcycle riders club, like in that movie with Tim Allen and his buddies who ride bikes. *That's fun.* And now he wants to get his buddies new jeans for a dinner. He's philanthropic too. *Just my type.* I mean, the old lady thing is kinda a red flag, but I can't expect perfection.

"Price doesn't matter. These look fine to me." He grabs a pair of jeans, holding them up.

"Okay, well then, let's get started. It says here Viper is a 34x42, so you find those and I'll find Pistol's 40x48." I flip through the stack in front of me while he does the same. Every time his biceps brushes against mine, there are tiny electric zaps.

I hope Nancy takes her sweet time, so I can be the one who rings up biker boy. No one has to know if I also add my digits on his receipt where I write my name for the customer service survey.

First, though, I need to see if he plays for the same team as me. No more chasing straight men. That was the old Iggie. I'm a new Iggie now.

*two*

## STEEL

I CAN'T BELIEVE I'm in this fucking store shopping for jeans like some high school girl buying her first prom dress. Department stores are not my thing; I get my shirts from Amazon and one of the old ladies buys my pants if I need 'em. But I wanted to do this for my brothers, since we're going to this fancy dinner to raise money for the Angel Tree Organization.

The whole club is going minus the prospects and well, I wanted to get my members all new pants, so we look good. It's hard enough to be a one-percenter in this town, so I don't want us showing up looking like scrubs.

This sexy little thing tucked in the corner, folding jeans, made the trip so much better. I stood back, hidden behind a display for a while, just watching him work, my cock twitching every time he bent over the table. Visions of him in the same position on my bed, my cock slipping between his plump ass cheeks, fill my mind. It's a no-brainer that he's gay, or at the very least bisexual like me. No straight man would have the courage to wear such a fun and festive shirt. They'd be too worried about what everyone else would think.

Once I've got my fill of watching, I head his way. It's time I make my presence known. He doesn't pay me any attention as he continues to fold, none the wiser to the predator approaching him. "Are you able to help me find something?" I ask as I step up behind him.

He whirls around to face me, obviously surprised, and his eyes widen as his gaze roams up and down my body. Bingo! Oh, naughty boy, you're going to be mine.

I take in his innocent green eyes behind a large, thick-rimmed pair of glasses. His blond hair looks like he rolled out of bed and ran his fingers through it before calling it a day.

"Y-y-yeah sure. What are you looking for?" he stammers, running his tongue across his puffy lips.

As I'm explaining what I'm looking for, he doesn't bat an eye at the club lingo. He must know about MC life or know someone in a club somewhere.

I hand him the paper Goldie wrote the sizes on and watch as he unfolds it, his eyes scanning the page. He looks back at me and smiles. Without missing a beat, he asks something about distressing and wash. I have no fucking clue what he's talking about. Distressing must mean holes and stains, but I don't need to buy jeans pre-torn. Me and the guys will mess them up plenty after the dinner.

"Okay, well, do you have a budget in mind? We have these here that are around ninety dollars a pair, but we do have some more budget-friendly options too." He motions toward them, chewing that sexy bottom lip.

I step closer, acting like I need to inspect the pants better. Really, I just want to touch him any way I can. "Price doesn't matter. These look fine to me." I grab a pair, holding them up. He reads the first name and size on the list and I start to dig through the pile, searching for what I need while he does the same. I don't miss his little gasp as my arm brushes against his. "Got 'em." I chuckle as I throw Viper's over my shoulder.

"Okay, next is Rubble, and he's a 40x42." He hands me a pair of jeans I'm assuming are for Pistol, and I get back to searching.

After about thirty minutes, I have sixteen pairs of jeans and I'm ready to check out. "Do you need anything else?" he asks, handing me the last pair.

"No. That's it for me. You were great—uh, I didn't catch your name."

"Ignatius, but my friends call me Iggie," he murmurs, his cheeks reddening.

"And is that what we are already? Friends?" I step toward him, so he's almost completely boxed in between my body, the table, and a shelf of shirts.

"I-I-I don't know. It's just something I say." His breath hitches. I chuckle as he fumbles before he quickly ducks away and heads toward the cash register.


I FOLLOW CLOSE BEHIND with my arms loaded with jeans. The entire way, my eyes are locked on his ass and the way it moves in those slacks. I can't wait to see them on my bedroom floor, and mark my words, they will be. My gaze never leaves him as he scans the jeans and removes the security tags. I smirk as his soft hands pick up each pair, folding them and tucking them into the bags.

"One thousand five hundred fifty-one dollars and sixty

cents is your total." He smiles. God damn, if that smile isn't one I want to see again and again.

I hand him a wad of hundred-dollar bills and his eyes widen as he takes them before entering the amount in the register and handing me my change. "You're all set—"

"Steel. My name's Steel. Iggie, tell ya what, you were a lot of help today. Every year, my club donates a good amount of gifts to a charity for underprivileged kids. We ain't very good at picking them out. We get a list from each family of what they need and want. What do ya say, me and my brothers come back another day and you be our shopper?"

"This isn't my normal department, so it's a one-off I was able to help you. I'm normally in the children's department. But I'd happily set you up with an associate in this department," he tells me, setting my bags on the counter.

"That's even better. While we do buy for the adults in the families, it's mainly kids and we like to get them the toys on their lists, but we also get them essentials like clothes. Give me your number and I'll text ya to set it up," I tell him bluntly.

He looks up at me, his eyes wide, and a blush creeps across his cheeks. His lips part and I can tell he wants to, but there's also some apprehension—there's no room for that here. "Give me your number, Iggie."

"O-Okay." He grabs a pen from the cup on the side of the register and writes his number on the back of the receipt. "There's a survey link on the back, too. If you take it, mention my name and it will enter you to win a ten thousand dollar shopping spree."

"I will," I rasp. "Expect my text, Iggie. I don't like to be kept waiting." I take the receipt, my calloused hand grazing his, before I shove it in my pocket and grab the bags from the counter.

Even after I've left the building, I feel his eyes follow me to my truck, watching as I throw my bags in the passenger seat.

*Don't worry, I'll be back for you.*

My lip curls slightly as I get behind the wheel; I hate driving this damn thing. I feel like I'm locked in and can't get out. My bike is my preferred mode of transportation, but I knew I couldn't get all the bags home on just my Harley Wide Glide. Plus, living in Northern Illinois means that driving my bike all year round just isn't an option. We get only about seven or eight months of good riding weather, if we're lucky.

Twenty minutes later, I'm pulling into the clubhouse, nodding to the prospects as I cruise slowly through the gates. Parking in my designated spot, I turn the truck off and grab the bags to head inside.

Loud music greets me as I pull open the door. My brothers are all sitting around drinking beers as they watch a MMA fight on the TV. Why they need the TV and the music on I don't know, but whatever. I stride to the stereo and turn it off. They throw shouts of anger and annoyance my way. "Listen up, you ungrateful fucks! I went to Howards and got us all something for the Angel Tree dinner."

"You went to Howards? No fuckin' way, man," Viper shouts.

"Yeah. Were they running a sale on carburetors and whiskey?" Rubble jests.

"Fuck off, the lot of ya. I got us all some clean jeans to wear. Now come find your size and shut the hell up." I dump the bags out on the pool table with the list of names and sizes, so they can make sure they get the right pair. There are a few that are the same size and they can fight over who gets what one. My job is done.

"Thank you!" Pistol claps me on the back with a huge smile on his face.

"You're welcome. Finally, someone who appreciates my generosity." I roll my eyes as I grab my jeans and head off in the direction of my room.

I don't realize Pistol is following me until I go to shut my door and his booted foot prevents it from closing. "You seem way too happy for a man who just spent the afternoon in some hoity-toity shop downtown."

"That's because I met someone there who made the experience not too bad," I admit. Pistol has been my best friend since we were kids, and he's my VP now, so I trust him with my life.

"Who is she? Why isn't she here and bent over the dresser? Lost your touch?" He crosses his arms over his chest and quirks a brow.

"He. His name is Iggie, and he works at Howards. I got his number, so I can text him when we're ready to shop for the Angel Tree. He's going to be our shopper," I tell him, opening my closet and hanging my jeans up.

"He, huh? It's been a long time since a male has caught your eye. It's why I assumed it was a she. What's different about this guy?" He leans against the door, now fully invested in my new obsession.

"Pistol... man, he's sexy as hell, and I don't think he even knows it. Totally innocent and unaware of how close he was to a killer today. I even mentioned the club, and that Goldie helped with the sizes. He didn't bat an eye. My cut was on too, of course, and he looked me up and down multiple times and wasn't scared," I tell him and I can feel my cock hardening at the thought of Iggie.

"Lots of women have had that same response and you

weren't looking like a kid who saw Santa come down the chimney. What gives?"

"I don't know, man. When I saw him, something in me just called to him and I knew he had to be mine. He will be mine. I only know he's hot as fuck, works at Howards, his name is Ignatius and I'm obsessed." I pull my cut off and hang it on the back of the chair next to my bed.

When Pistol stops giving me the third degree, I need to take a shower. We have church tonight and then I have to go to the club and take care of some business.

"Tread lightly, Steel. I know how you can get, and I'm not sure Ellie can get you out of another stalking charge," he warns as he pulls the door open and steps out, leaving me alone in my room.

Bastard. Ellie has only had to get me out of two stalking charges and they were both years ago. Alisha and Bre didn't know how good I would be to them. They saw my cut and bike or witnessed one little law get bent and they freaked out.

Iggie won't be like that, I can tell already. He knows I'm president of an MC club and he still flirted and gave me his number. He wants to be mine.

# *three*

## IGNATIUS

"IGNATIUS! I need you in my office right now," Susan bellows, nearly causing me to jump out of my skin.

"Be right there!" I call back, grabbing the bank bag and slamming the register shut. Fuck, she nearly made me piss my pants when she shouted across the store like it was a playground or something. I thought I was one of the last ones here tonight. What in the world does she want now? Lord knows it can't be anything good. It's Susan.

Stepping into the main office, I hurry to the safe, type in the code, and toss the bank bag in. After making sure it's locked tight, I blow out a deep breath and head to the door on the right—Susan's office. I can already smell tuna fish and her musky old lady perfume seeping out from under her door.

"Hey, Susan. You wanted to see me?" I give her a fake smile as I step inside. From the corner of my eye, I make sure that my chair moves just enough so the door can't close behind me. Not only do I not want to be in the room alone

20

with her because she gives me just a bad vibe all around, but her office could use a good airing out or a Febreze shower.

"Yes. Why did you leave your department for almost two hours today? The men's department is not where you belong. So, would you like to explain why you spent most of the afternoon there?"

I hold back from rolling my eyes. What does she want me to say? Her fucking daughter sent me to menswear and when I asked she said 'Mommy told me so'. Okay, maybe not those exact words, but close enough. "Nancy came and got me so she could go on her break. She said you approved of me going to menswear and Quinn to kids."

"I know that, Ignatius. Of course, I approved of her break and you covering. However, her break is only thirty minutes, and you were in men's for..." she pauses, grabbing a paper from her desk before her beady eyes are back on me. "One hour and forty-three minutes."

"Oh. While I was covering, a customer came in and required help to find jeans for an event. So I helped him, rang him out, and then went straight back to my department," I tell her, relieved that I can explain my actions. Customers are always right and always come first. That's Howards' way, so she can't get too worked up.

"Why didn't you hand him off to Nancy when she returned? Instead, not only did you leave Quinn in a department she is clueless in, but you also took a sale from Nancy. It's my understanding it was a rather large sale, which means a nice commission." She looks at her paper once more. "An over one hundred dollar commission. On top of what you make an hour in kids and your three percent per hour over there. Does that seem fair to you?"

"Umm. Yes? I was the one who helped him find all the jeans and rang him out. Also, Nancy never made me aware that she was back, so I just continued to help him. If she wanted to step in, she could have approached us." I'm so sick of her and Nancy's shit. Why Roman Howard continues to employ the two of them, I have no idea. But every six months when Susan's review comes up, we all pray for her to get canned.

No matter. I'm on my way out of here, hopefully. On my lunch break, after I helped Steel—*which is still a crazy name for a guy, but it's also kinda fucking sexy*—I applied for the Philanthropy Manager position. I have everything crossed; mind, fingers, toes, even my damn eyeballs.

"You think Nancy needs to track you down like some sort of coon hound? To what? Tell you how to do your job? How to have manners? I'm tempted to write you up for this act of total disregard for your fellow associates."

"That's your prerogative, Susan," I murmur, watching as she pulls Tupperware from her desk and puts it in her bag.

"You got that right, it is my prerogative. I'm going to take the high road and not write you up. But your shirt is a different story. How many times must I tell you that you cannot be so over the top during the Christmas season?" She pulls the main offender of the air quality out—tuna casserole with broccoli and sauerkraut—and shoves it in her bag.

I swear to God, if Scrooge and the Grinch were to have a baby, Susan would be it. It's a department store, for Christ's sake. "Well, Susan, as you know, today is officially the day that the handbook states I can get as festive as I want until after the new year. So you could write me up, but I'd go above you and have it expunged."

Her face morphs from fake pleasantries to pure rage. Her eyes narrow at me and she takes a deep, harrowing breath. "I suppose you're right. But you should watch how you talk to your superiors, Ignatius. I'd hate for you to get a bad recommendation for that position you applied for."

My stomach sinks at her words. How the hell does she know about that already? She's only the retail manager for the store. I'll be damned if she prevents me from moving up the ladder and forces me to a life of selling Polly Pockets and Legos.

"Is that all, Susan?" I grind out through clenched teeth.

"Yes, that is all. You may go."

I stand from my chair and hurry from the room. I refuse to stay in that bitch's presence any longer than necessary.

She turned a perfectly good shift and day into shit in a matter of thirty minutes. I had plans to go home, curl up on my couch and watch the new Hallmark Christmas movie that premieres tonight, but I'm not in the mood. Good thing I have it set to record on the DVR.

No. I know what I need. A good old-fashioned night out. Pulling my phone from my pocket, I text my best friend.

> Me- Hey! What are you up to right this minute?

> Draco- Nothing, why what's up?

> Me- Shitty day at work. Wanna hit Slick's and get drunk?

> Draco- Dude, it's a Thursday.

> Me- So? When did you become a pussy?

> Draco- Fine. Meet you there in thirty minutes.

> Me- Love you! Byyyeeeee

As I tuck my phone back into my pocket and get into my car, I can't wipe the grin off my face. I get in my car and turn the heat as high as it will go and wait for my window to defrost. Living in the Midwest is trash in the winter; I swear if I wasn't terrified of hurricanes or earthquakes, I'd move somewhere it was warm all year round.

The radio plays *Vampire* by Olivia Rodrigo, and I smirk at the fact I just survived a meeting with a bloodsucker myself. Once my window is clear enough, I put the car into reverse and back out of my parking spot, heading toward Slick's.

A night out with my bestie is just what I need.

━━━━☠━━━━

"YOU KNOW that movie where the girl gets hit by a bus for being a cunt?" I slur and set my drink down on the bar.

"*Mean Girls*?" Draco asks, his brows raising at my random thought.

"That's the one! Susan and Nancy should take a page out of that movie. I hate them both. They're creepy and give me major cat lady in the basement with a serious doll collection vibes."

My friend barks out a laugh as he raises his hand, waving the bartender over. "Can we get our tab?" He turns back to look at me. "So tell me about this hottie you helped at work today. I can't believe you gave him your phone number!"

My stomach flutters at just the thought of Steel. "He wasn't just hot. He was seriously sex on a stick. A sex-ka-bob!" I burst out laughing, only stopping when a hiccup frees itself from my throat. "Oh god, I drank too much," I whine. "I didn't give him my number for a hookup. He asked for it, so we could arrange a shopping trip thing he needs help with. It's a work connection, nothing more."

"Suuuure, whatever you say, Igg. Have you messaged him yet?" He purses his lips and quirks a brow.

"No. He texted me earlier, just a quick 'It's Steel', but that's it. I'm working for the next few days. Plus, I don't even know if he's into men. My New Year's resolution was to not flirt or fall for straight guys anymore.," I remind him.

"Yeah. I remember. I also remember you broke that resolution like four times."

"Rude! Well then, I made it my end-of-year declaration, and I've been good since September, so don't be mean," I pout.

"Well then, text Mister Kabob." He wags his brows at me. "And see what kind of vibe you get. The worst that can happen is he isn't interested and you just schedule a day to do the shopping. Easy way out."

"Fine!" I grab my phone from the bar and scroll to his contact I saved earlier.

Me- Hey it's Iggie from Howards

I WATCH as the bubbles pop up and disappear repeatedly before I sigh and set the phone down. "He's obviously thinking of a way to let me know this is business only. I have to pee. Be right back." I wobble a bit as I stand and make the trek to the bathroom.

After taking the piss I've been holding for ages now, not

wanting to break the seal, I wash my hands and splash some water on my face. *Get it together, Ignatius, one sexy biker boy won't have you losing your shit. You are a sexy, strong, independent man.*

When I get back to my stool, Draco is giving me a mischievous look. Cocking my head to the side, I stare at him as I sit down. What is he up to?

"Don't be mad." He smiles.

"What did you do?"

"Well, the sex-ka-bob was taking too long, so I went ahead and just sent another text. You're welcome."

"You bastard. What did you say?" I grab my phone and hurry to unlock it.

> Me- So tell me Steel. Do I make you horny, baby?

DEAD, he's fucking dead. I'm going to murder my best friend. Then bring him back to murder him again. "You asshole," I hiss.

"Come on, the Austin Powers' line is a classic and a great way to break the ice." He cackles.

"I'll never be able to do the shopping assistant thing now. Fuck, Draco, you're an asshole." I drop my head to the bar with an audible thump.

"You know you love me. Now, let's get you home. I'm glad I took a Lyft, so I can drive your ass home." He helps me from my stool and grabs my elbow, leading me outside to the parking lot.

As soon as we're in the car and it's moving, I lean my

head back and close my eyes, thinking about all the filthy things I'd let that motorcycle man do to me. While I come across as bubbly, innocent, and maybe a tad flamboyant on the outside, I love to be bossed around and degraded in the bedroom.

You'd never know that by looking at the pristine front and my serious obsession with the most cheerful holiday of the year, but even Santa has some kinks in his closet; I'm sure of it.

"We're here," Draco interrupts my filthy thoughts.

I push the door open and stumble out in the crisp night air. Luckily, Draco comes around the car, grabbing my elbow and helping me into my place. I gave him a key years ago and I'm thankful for it at this moment because I have no clue where my set is.

"I have them. It's how I drove the car home, babe."

"Shit. Did I think out loud?"

"Yeah, you did." He laughs. "Come on, let's go. To the bed with you, mister." He escorts me to my room, where I promptly collapse into the bed. My eyes close instantly and I groan as the room spins. Reaching over, I put a hand on the nightstand to secure myself, and as I knew it would, the room stands still. Draco lifts each of my legs, removing my shoes before pulling my slacks gently down them.

"Nice briefs, Igg," he teases.

If I were sober and cared, I'd tell him to fuck right off, but I'm too tired and intoxicated to deal with him right now. Plus, who wouldn't want to wear gray briefs with cute little snowflakes all over with a waistband that says 'Snow Cute'? It's practically a crime to not buy something so fun when you see it.

"Alright, babe. I put your phone on the nightstand, charging next to your glasses. Your keys will be on the kitchen counter, and I'll lock up when the Lyft gets here to take me home. Call me in the morning, so I know you didn't die in your sleep."

"Fuck you," I mumble.

"Love you, too!"

The bedroom goes dark, and I hear the door close. Dammit! Why did I take so many Christmas Cookie shots? Thankfully, tomorrow is my day off.

I WAKE the next day with a pounding ass headache and my mouth is drier than the Sahara. Blindly, I fumble around the nightstand for my glasses and slide them on. I unlock my phone and squint at the bright screen. Fuck, it's almost noon already.

With a sigh, I roll out of bed and stumble to the bathroom. I seriously need to brush my teeth.

Swishing some water in my mouth, I spit and drop my toothbrush back in its holder before trudging back to my room to throw on some black joggers. I find an oversized hoodie and remove my Santa shirt, slipping into it. This will have to do. I'm not doing anything but lounging around today and watching Christmas movies, anyway.

I flop onto the couch with a humph and turn the TV on, flipping to my saved recordings. A Royal Christmas is the first one on my list. I hit play and lay my head back, pulling a blanket over me off the back of the couch. My stomach decides to growl at that moment and I groan. I'm way too lazy to cook right now. Oh, I know. I've been wanting to try that new place Lung Fung so ordering it is. Slipping my phone from my pocket, I pull up the Grubhub app.

Thirty minutes later, I'm wrapped back in a blanket on my couch eating Chinese food, living my best life. Stephen Hagan and Lacey Chabert are wrapped in each other's arms, kissing passionately, and I feel myself deflate a bit.

Why can't I have that? Someone to love me unconditionally. Without time, distance, or anything getting in the way. A handsome, strong hunk to come home to every night— shit, they could come home to me. My phone beeps, interrupting my pity party.

> Steel- Horny, huh? Are we asking for real or just quoting ridiculous movies?

OH MY GOD! I forgot my asshole bestie sent that text last night. What do I say back? Fucking hell.

*four*

STEEL

I SIT at the clubhouse bar and watch as the little text bubbles appear and disappear, waiting for Iggie to respond.

> Iggie- I am so sorry. I went out last night. Left my phone on the bar unattended and my BFF hijacked my texts.

> Me- Ha! Happens to the best of us. I figured something was up.

> Iggie- Yeah we'll blame all the shots I took. I hope this doesn't affect you wanting my help with that shopping trip.

MY GRIP on my phone tightens. There were shots, more than one. He was out drinking, without someone watching over him. I can feel my anger building. He said his friend was with him, but he let him drink too much. And how did he get home? He better not have driven, or he'll be getting an ass beating when I see him again. Hell, he might still get one for being irresponsible.

I take a swig of my beer, feeling my cock twitch at the thought of his creamy, bare ass over my knee. He'll cry so beautifully for me, and then I'll kiss it better before bringing him more pleasure than he could ever imagine. First things first though, I need to see him again and the way to do that is to get this shopping trip set up. I'm going to make him mine, whether he likes it or not.

"Another beer, baby?" Daria asks, leaning across the bar so her tits look bigger and perkier.

"Yeah. Get me a shot of brandy, too."

She nods and turns around, reaching inside the cooler, grabbing a Busch Lite before snatching the bottle of E&J, and pouring it into the little glass in front of me.

"You seem tense, Steel, baby. Wanna go to your room and work that out?" she purrs, rubbing her hand up and down the handle of brandy like that should turn me on.

"Nope."

"Boo. Well, I could send Cody or Gabe in, if that's what you're in the mood for."

"No. I'm a taken man, Daria. So I won't be needing you or the other club whores." I stand, throw my shot back, and grab my beer. I'm not in the mood for her to throw herself at me. She's always thinking she's one cock away from being a permanent fixture here—she's not.

Our club is a bit different from others when it comes to the whores. No whore can ever become an old lady. The last time one of the brothers got attached and married a club whore, it caused nothing but issues. Drunken arguments about who fucked her better, a few guys forgetting she

31

wasn't a whore anymore, and then there was the time she forgot she wasn't one, either. Dory was caught with her legs spread and Gunther balls deep in her. She's a whore elsewhere now and Gunther... he's buried out back. Viper wasn't too thrilled and got a little trigger-happy when he saw his wife with someone else.

We also have two male club whores, which is almost unheard of. I'm not the only brother here who likes the same sex, so when I became president, we took a vote and the motion passed that we would hire a few males. Cody and Gabe came to us after knowing one of the girls; we laid out the rules and expectations and they were on board. They're fucked by sexy biker men, and get the protection of the club, and a stipend, since they help with chores around the clubhouse.

"I didn't know, Steel. I'm sorry," Daria whispers.

I ignore her and head inside the room where we hold church. Of course, she didn't know; I haven't made an official announcement yet. I need to be sure that Iggie is on board with club life. He saw my cut, and I told him about the club and he was cool with it. But knowing and not being judgemental and living it are two different things.

Realization hits me I haven't messaged him back. I need to call church, but I want to assure him his text did not deter or change anything first. My fingers glide across the screen.

> Me- It didn't.

> Me- Shopping, can we do it Wednesday? The dinner I told you about is coming up and I wanna take the stuff with us if I can.

> Iggie- Yeah. I work 10-5 so I'll be there.

Me- See you then. And don't make plans for after your shift.

Iggie- Okay? Why?

Me- I'm taking you out.

HE DOESN'T RESPOND and I start to worry that I came on too strong, but I don't have time to get torn up about it. We have church. The date is set and I'll just show him I'm exactly what he needs and wants. Tucking my phone into my pocket, I toss my now empty beer into the trash and open the door.

"Let's go! Time for church!" I holler and head back inside to sit behind the table and wait for everyone to arrive.

"You look like you're up to something. What did you do?" Pistol asks, taking his seat next to me.

"Nothing. Iggie just agreed to go out with me after we finish shopping for the Angel Tree gifts."

"Why do I feel like you didn't give the guy a choice to say no? Did you ask or just tell him?" Viper and Zero choose that moment to walk into the room, still fixing the buttons on their jeans.

"What did I tell y'all about fuckin' before church?"

Viper rolls his eyes, taking his place in the back of the room so he can watch the room, and Zero sits in the chair at the far left end of the table. "Sorry, Pres. Won't happen again."

Once everyone is inside and seated, I bang my gavel on the table. "Alright! I'm calling church to order. First, we have the minutes from our last church. Go ahead, Hawk."

Hawk gives us a rundown of what we discussed the last

time. We spoke about donating even more this year to the Angel Tree and who would be attending the dinner.

"Alright, I have it set up to have a personal shopper help us on Wednesday with the Angel Tree shopping. I'm taking Viper and Zero. You two can pick a prospect or two to come to carry the bags and load the truck."

"Aww, come on, Pres, don't make me go to the fancy store and shop. I fucking hate that shit," my enforcer groans.

"You're going and that's final. Next time don't come in with your cock still dripping cum and you won't have to go shopping," I snap, shutting him up.

"We have a run next weekend, so where are we with our shipment?"

"We have all the product and Trucker is supposed to have the route finalized this afternoon," Pistol informs us, directing his eyes to our road captain for confirmation.

"I'll have the route ready in a few hours. I wanted to make sure we took an alternative one this time. On the last run, we had to detour after Viper spotted that Hellhound, so I'm taking no risks. Michaelov wants MK6s, Magnums, and ARs, so he's gonna get them. But I'll be damned if my route is the reason we have a run-in with the Hellhounds," Trucker seethes as he clenches his fists.

"Where are we with the Cockpit? Any issues with the girls or customers?"

"No, Pres. Everything has been running smoothly over there as of this morning, according to Brian. He said there have been no issues since we hired that new bouncer, which I'd like to ask him about prospectin' for the club. He's a little older than our usual prospects, but the guy is huge and I like him and his morals. Brian did say he wants to hire a few more girls to waitress and go-go dance, but not strip. I told him to go ahead," Tex pipes up.

"And what about our progress on the bar? Where are we on that?" I ask. We've had the strip club up and going for a few years now and it brings in a good chunk of our 'legal' revenue. We're working now on opening a regular bar so some of the people we help get out of dangerous situations can work to earn some money to get back on their feet.

"Element is still set to open in two months. Gabe brought up an interesting idea, so I said I'd pass it on the next time we had church. He suggested a ladies' night either at the Cockpit or Element, where one night a month we would have male dancers come in and perform," Tex rattles, his knee bouncing anxiously. Not sure why, though. From where I'm sitting, it sounds like a smart plan.

"I like this idea. I don't want to limit it to ladies only though. Men can come in if they stay respectful to the performers. Any remarks or touching, though, and they're banned from both establishments. Let's vote because this isn't just my money we're talking about here." I stand so I can see all the brothers and count the votes, and Viper does the same from the back of the room to make sure we both come up with the same number. "All those in favor of having one night a month at Element be ladies' night, but open to the public, raise your hand."

All hands go up except for Pepper and Combo. "All those opposed say no." Theirs go up. "Motion passes."

After that, we discuss who is going on the run next weekend and who is staying behind to watch the clubhouse. Once we are done, I adjourn the meeting and head back to my room to see if my new obsession has messaged.

# *five*

## IGNATIUS

MY STOMACH IS in knots as I watch the clock tick. Steel should be here soon for our shopping spree. He's obviously into me, so I'm not sure why I'm more nervous than normal, but I feel like I'm going to be sick. It's like a swarm of bees buzzing around in my belly. Sweat is dripping down my back and beading on my forehead even though it's not hot. I should have asked what time he is coming, so I'm not jumping to look at the door every time the buzzer dings.

"Hi, is there anything I can help you find today?" I ask the elderly man who just walked in.

"Yeah. I'm looking for a gift for my grandson. He's fifteen and not really into toys anymore, so I'm not sure what to get," he tells me as he walks with his cane down an aisle of Legos.

"Okay. Well, kids his age are into games over toys. Do you know if he has any gaming systems?"

"I know he spends a lot of time on an Xbox of some sort. My daughter is always yelling at him to get his chores and homework done and get off of the damn thing." He chuckles.

"An Xbox. Perfect." I clap my hands together. "Let me take you over there to the case with all the games and you can pick one out. I can even show you which ones are newer, so we can make sure he doesn't have the game." I walk toward the electronic section slowly so he can keep up. When I get to the case, I stop and turn to him with a smile. "Okay, everything on the first shelf is new this week."

"Well, how do I know what he doesn't have? My daughter spoils the hell out of him ever since his dad died," he mutters, talking more to himself than me. "I'll call her and ask. She should know." He fumbles with his phone as he pulls it from his jacket pocket and clicks the buttons a few times before he holds it to his ear. "Blair. It's Dad. I'm here at the store and I need to know what games Landon has for his box." He pauses for a minute, nodding his head. "Now hold on honey, I can't remember all of them. Does the kid even need another game if he has all those? Okay, start again."

I motion to get his attention and he pulls the phone from his ear. "May I?" I ask, holding my hand out for it. "Hi, Blair, was it? This is Ignatius from Howards. I'm helping your dad today find the perfect gift for Landon. Mind if I just ask about the new ones and you tell me if he's mentioned wanting any of them? And it is an Xbox, correct? Perfect." I rattle off the five new games we got in this week and once I know which one to pick, I hand the phone back and unlock the case.

"Thank you, young man. I'm Keith, by the way."

"You're welcome, Keith. I'm happy to help. Now let's get you checked out so you can get home, huh? Unless you have more shopping to do." I move to the register with the game still in hand.

"No." He laughs. "Just the one grandson for now. I hope Blair gives me more, but she's not found someone since the boy's father passed."

"I'm sorry to hear that. Love always finds you when you least expect it though, right? So I bet her time is coming." I scan the game and remove the anti-theft device. "Alright, Keith. Your total today is sixty-two dollars and five cents." He hands me a credit card and I process his payment before bagging up his purchase and handing him the receipt. "Thank you. Merry Christmas!"

I go over to the Barbie aisle and begin to straighten the dolls. Ever since the movie came out, this has been our busiest section and dang, all the little girls and boys tear up my displays multiple times a day. Lost in the music pumping through the speakers and putting all the little Kens, Barbies, and Skippers back where they go, I don't notice anyone entering the department.

"Iggie," a low voice calls and the hairs on the back of my neck stand up as a shiver rolls through me.

Slowly, I straighten and look up into Steel's piercing eyes. "Hi, I'm glad you made it." A smile takes over his face as he looks at me. "I see you brought friends." I look behind him at the four men watching us curiously. Two have the same leather vest as Steel, the only difference is one has an Enforcer patch, and the other a Treasurer patch. The other two are younger; fresh in their twenties it looks like, wearing black shirts and jeans.

"Yeah, there was no way I could shop for all the families alone, even with your help. So Viper and Zero are here to help with the shopping, and the other two are Nate and Chad. They're here to be bag boys and to cross shit off the

STEEL

lists as we find it. Our assistants, you could say." He chuckles and the sound goes straight to my cock. A tingle in my balls moves its way up my body and I shiver.

Clearing my throat, I pull myself together.

"Well, let's get started then. Who is first on your list?"

"We don't get names, it's all anonymous, but first up is an eight-year-old little girl. She wants the Barbie movie, a skateboard, and a purple winter coat," he tells me and my heart breaks. I can't even imagine being eight and wanting a winter jacket. Something so basic that most people don't think twice about having, and it's what this little girl wants as a gift.

"We're gonna head out and get our stuff. We have a couple of older people who want candles, robes, and blankets," Viper grunts. "Prospects, you stay here and help Pres. We got our end handled."

Prospects? I know the dictionary definition of the word, but why would these two guys be called that? Why not just call them Nate and Chad? I'm missing something, but it's not my business; I'm here to help find gifts and that's it.

"I can see the wheels turning in that pretty little head of yours. They're prospectin' to be in our club. We call them prospects, but since you're not a member of the club, you call them Nate and Chad. That's why when I introduced them, I told you their legal names. Same as they'll call me Pres and Viper and Zero by their road or club names and not our legal names," Steel informs me.

My eyes widen and I reach a hand out to the shelf next to me to hold myself up. I feel like a total moron right now. A giggle bursts free before I slap a hand over my mouth.

"What?" Steel asks.

"I thought Steel, Viper, and Zero were all your real names. I was questioning why all your parents named you

39

such... umm... interesting names." I laugh at how silly I feel. "So, I call them Chad and Nate. I call you Steel, but since I'm not in the club, do I call the others by their club names, or do I need to learn their legal ones?" I ask.

He looks at me with a brow raised and then a deep barking laugh comes from his mouth. "You call them Viper and Zero. To call them anything else, including the names their momma gave them, would be disrespectful since they're in Hell's Mayhem. If the prospects become full-blown members, they'll get a road name like the rest of us and we won't call them their legal name anymore."

"I feel like an idiot," I groan.

A growl comes from Steel before he has me pressed against a shelf. "Don't ever call yourself an idiot again. You can't be ignorant of something you don't know. I won't have you talking or thinking about yourself like that again, you hear me?"

"Yes," I murmur, looking up at him and seeing how serious he is.

"Yes, what?"

"Yes, Sir?" I squeak and my cheeks heat at the sound that just came out of me.

"Good boy," he praises, and sweet lord, if my dick doesn't jerk in my pants at him calling me such a thing.

"Now, we better get back to shopping. We haven't even crossed one name off our list yet." He smirks.

"O-o-okay." He releases me from the shelf and I spin, heading down the aisle to grab a few Barbies before making my way to the movies. The whole time I'm trying to discreetly adjust my dick so my erection isn't so pronounced and easy to see.

"Why Barbies?" Steel asks as he follows close behind me.

"Well, I know you said you like to get a few extra things for each kid. So I'm guessing if she wants the new movie, she'd like some dolls too."

"Smart and pretty, I see."

Yup. That's it. My cock is never gonna be soft again. I've never heard anything sexier than this man and his gravelly voice calling me pretty and good. Who knew I liked that? Who knew I liked to be called pretty or good? I'm learning new things about myself today as well.

IT'S close to the end of my shift and I've just run the last item over the scanner, smiling as the register beeps.

"Alright, that's the last of it. Umm, I have to admit I've never seen a total this high. Should I even read it out loud?" I ask as I place the baby doll I just scanned into a bag.

"Yeah. The guys will ask tonight when we have church, and Zero will hoard the receipt." He rolls his eyes and gives Zero a pointed stare.

"Ten thousand five hundred seventy-one dollars and thirty-two cents."

I gasp as he pulls a stack of money from his pocket and hands it to me while undoing another stack and counting out six more. The corner of his mouth turns up as he hands me the six hundred dollars.

Quickly I count it and put it in the drawer, making a mental note that I'm going to have to call and schedule a pickup before I can cash out my drawer. I hand him his twenty-eight dollars and sixty-eight cents in change and watch as he and the other guys haul all the bags and boxes out of the store.

"I'll see you in a bit, Iggie. Just gotta get these guys squared away and then you and I are going to dinner. Yeah?"

"Yeah," I whisper.

He nods as he grabs the last six bags and turns. I watch as he walks out of my department and a few seconds later, the door beeps as he leaves the store. I rush back over to the phone by the register and call Susan so she can come to do a cash pickup before I have to balance my drawer and clock out for my shift.

Weirdly enough, she gets to me in no time and my stomach rolls at her stinky fish smell. My God, does the woman ever think to bring something else for lunch? Have a fucking PB&J or spaghetti? I don't know.

"Ignatius, I'm so glad I was free to head over here right away. I'd hate to leave such a large amount of money in the drawer. That is just screaming for someone to rob us, huh? It must have been busy over here today. Look at you, playing Santa's elf and making sure all the gifts are bought." Susan smiles, but her tone is dripping with sarcasm. "And you even dressed the part. Adorable."

Today's shirt is a red Hawaiian print shirt, but the whole front is covered in an elf with no head. My head is its head. I think it's hilarious, cute, and still dressy when I pair it with slacks and my dress shoes.

"It's been pretty slow today. That money was all one transaction," I tell her with a shit-eating grin.

"You're telling me you had an over ten thousand dollar transaction in this department?"

"Yes, ma'am. A local club came in and did some charity shopping and got everything they needed," I tell her truthfully.

"Interesting. Is that whose phone is on the counter?" she questions, pointing at a black iPhone lying face down. Shit! Steel forgot his phone.

Snatching it up, I hurry away from Susan and toward the exit, hoping to catch him before he leaves the parking lot. I burst through the doors and onto the sidewalk at the front of the store, but see no sign of any of them.

Hurrying around the corner to the side street where there is more parking, I stop short when I hear shouting in the alley. Turning to see what is going on and to make sure no one is being robbed or mugged, I suck in a sharp breath of cold air when I see Viper with his hands around another man's throat while Steel is yelling in his face.

The guy is gasping for air and shaking his head back and forth rapidly. I drop the phone in shock and the sound of it hitting the pavement has all six pairs of eyes snap my way.

"Iggie. I can explain," Steel calls.

I don't give him time to say anything else, simply just turn and run back to the store. I need to clock out and go the hell home. I can't believe I was going to go to dinner with him. He's a bully, a thug. I'm so fucking stupid.

## *six*

### STEEL

"GOD DAMMIT!" I shout, pulling at my hair. Fuck! Iggie wasn't supposed to see this. We didn't plan on seeing Butch out today, but we have been looking for him. He owes the club money and he's been avoiding us. He's been a ghost at all his normal hangout spots, so running across him randomly as we were loading the truck with the donations was a one-off.

"Maybe this is a good thing, Pres. Better he finds out now than later, right? Then he can't claim he didn't sign up for this when things get tough." Viper puts a hand on my shoulder.

"I thought he did know. I've had my cut on every time, mentioned the old ladies and the club. He didn't bat an eye," I hiss through clenched teeth. "I need to fix this."

"Go on. We got this. Butchy here is gonna go get us our money, ain't he?" Viper teases before punching Butch in the gut. "Matter o' fact, we're gonna follow him home to get it."

"I want that money. Don't care if you gotta take shit to

sell or pawn. We get paid back today and part ways," I tell my guys. "Butch." I turn my head to look at him. "Our business ends after this. If we see you again, I'm gonna let Viper here take you to his playroom, ya hear me?"

"Yes," he sobs.

Pussy. I don't waste any more time thinking about him. Iggie is all I can think about; I need to find him and clear the air. He's not exactly innocent in this either, letting me think he was in the know about Hell's Mayhem and acting shocked when he sees us in action. It's a little too late, though. Ignatius is mine and I won't let him walk away.

Sprinting back to Howards' entrance, I rip the door open, burst into the uppity department store, and storm toward the children's department. Eyes wild, I scan the area for my man but come up empty. Where is he? I see an older woman behind the register and make my way toward her.

"Excuse me," I call, since her back is turned to me as she reads a magazine. My Iggie would never read on shift; he's far too good of an employee for that.

"Can I help you?" she sighs like I've inconvenienced her. When she turns, I almost laugh that I thought she was an older woman. She sure is dressed like one, but now that I've seen her face, she's definitely younger, probably around Iggie's age.

"I'm looking for Iggie. He helped me earlier, and I just wanted to thank him," I lie.

"Ohh. Iggie just clocked out. I think he parked out back today, though. Might wanna hurry. He was headed home to get ready for later," she says huskily while licking her lips.

"And what is later?" I ask, since last I knew, he had plans for me to take him out. What could he possibly have set up in such a short amount of time?

"Heard he had a date tonight. Lucky snot. I've been

trying to take him out since he started here, and he won't budge. Guess I'm just too much woman for him," she purrs. "But you, baby? You busy later? I get off at nine."

"Not my type, lady." I curl my lip in her direction. Quickly, I turn and head back out in the cold winter air and jog to the back parking lot. I'm taking my man to dinner, whether he likes it or not.

As soon as I get to the back lot, I see Iggie beside his car, a fancy cup on the roof while he digs in his bag for, I'm assuming, his keys. Not wanting to waste another second and risk him getting in his car and pulling away, I stride over to him briskly.

I rest a hand on his car on either side of him and he whirls around to face me. "Where you going, Iggie? I thought we had plans."

"I saw you beating that man. You're not a good guy, Steel. I was a fool to think some random stranger could be different just because you're sexy and give back to the community." His lips quiver and I don't miss the way his chest is heaving.

"He's not a good man either, babe. Owed the club a lot of money, we were just having a little chat about getting our funds." I step closer to him so he's pressed against his car.

"So call the cops or go to small claims court!" He stomps a foot at me, causing me to chuckle.

"And what would I tell 'em? Hey, Officer Doe, it's Steel down here at Hell's Mayhem MC. Yeah, the one percenter club. So we have a guy out there named Butch Debaroy who owes us six grand and won't pay up. Oh, it was for the strippers and blow we got him. Can you arrest him?" I snicker even thinking about it; that would go over about as well as a pregnant pole vaulter.

"So you're in one of those MCs like Ryan Hurst played in that biker show? Fuck! I just keep running through red flags."

"Iggie!" I interrupt his tirade. "You knew I was in a club, even knew I was the president. You've seen the cut and the logo. We talked about church, old ladies, and brothers. What did you think all that was for?"

"Christ, I'm so fucking stupid! I knew brothers were your friends, but I thought old ladies were literally old ladies. Like, you know, you had a grandma get the guys' sizes. I saw your vest, but I thought you were in more of a Wild Hogs type club. Not tie me up and kill me type." He's breathing heavily, and I can't help the smirk on my face.

I run a hand down the side of his face and smooth my thumb over his lips. "I won't kill you, but I'd love to tie you up for much sexier and fun things."

He whimpers, and the sound has my cock standing at full attention. He's upright and saluting his general. "I can't."

"You haven't even tried. One date. Let me take you out tonight and show you how much of a gentleman I am. I'm a callous bastard, Ignatius, but I swear I'd never hurt you. I'd kill anyone who did. I want you to be mine. I'm not the type to beg, baby, but I'm beggin' now. Give me tonight to show you what it would be like to be mine."

Iggie's sexy eyes dance back and forth behind his glasses as he sucks his bottom lip between his teeth. He's warring with himself on whether he should take me up on my offer or not. He looks up at the sky and blows out a breath. "Fine. But only because I think I need to get you out of my system."

"Baby, if only it was that easy. No way could I ever get you out of mine," I growl before kissing his temple. "Put your stuff in the car, lock up and let's go."

He unlocks his car door, drops his bag inside, and moves the cup from the roof to the holder between his seats. "I should probably grab my wallet," he murmurs to himself as he snatches it from the bag and shoves it into his slacks' pocket.

I grab his hand and pull him toward the front of the store where I parked my truck. "Come on, I have a reservation at Century House and don't want to be late."

⊹⊹⊹⊹💀⊹⊹⊹⊹⊹

## IGNATIUS

I can't believe I agreed to this, but I'm certain one date will get the sexy bad boy out of my system and I won't crave him anymore. Even as I repeat the mantra in my head, I know it's a lie. Don't get me wrong, seeing him roughing up that guy in the alley was a shock and while I want nothing to do with that lifestyle, if he doesn't treat me like that, then is there an issue? Is it possible to date and be serious with someone who's president of a biker gang and not be fully immersed in that lifestyle?

Will they even accept me? His other brothers? I know Zero, Viper, Nate, and Chad didn't bat an eye at our flirting today. Would they be the only ones, though? I don't exactly scream hardcore biker boy. I love fashion, iced coffee, and Christmas. Well, the latter is more like an obsession. The sparkly lights, the pretty wrapped gifts, and just people giving back have always made me feel more alive than at any other time of the year.

I'm snapped from my thoughts when Steel opens the door to his truck for me. I climb inside and he reaches over and buckles me in before squeezing my thigh. With a wink, he shuts the truck door.

When he gets behind the wheel, he immediately buckles up and turns the truck on before turning to look at me. "You can change the station to whatever you want or hook up your Bluetooth. I only drive the cage when it's cold and icy out. Otherwise, I take my bike, so I'm not controlling the radio."

"The cage?" I question.

"It's what we call our cars or trucks. Our bikes are our preferred way of getting around; after riding for so long, being in a vehicle is like being in a cage."

"Oh. I've never been on a motorcycle," I tell him absent-mindedly as I look out my window and smile at all the pretty holiday decorations that line the streets.

"When the weather changes, we'll fix that. I think you'd look good on the back of my bike."

Why does the thought of straddling his bike, pressed tightly against him, make me so hot? Do men even ride together? I don't think I've ever seen two guys ride together like he's talking about, but I've also never paid that much attention. If he says it would be hot, it must not be that uncommon.

We pull into the parking lot at Century House. Steel is out of the truck as soon as he shuts the ignition off and walks around, opening my door. He grabs my hand, helping me out, but even when my feet are on the ground, he doesn't let me go, just laces our fingers together and leads me into the restaurant.

"Hi, how can I help you tonight?" the bubbly teen hostess asks as soon as we enter. She's wearing a Mrs. Claus dress and I can't help but be jealous that I couldn't wear an actual costume to work. I'd show up as Santa every day, no questions asked during the holiday season.

"Reservation for Steel."

"I got you right here. Follow me and I'll take you to your booth." She grabs two menus and heads deeper into the restaurant. She stops when we get to the back in a dimly lit corner close to the kitchen. Steel holds a hand out, gesturing for me to take a seat, then takes one across from me. "Here are your menus. Erica will be your server tonight and she should be by momentarily."

We're both quiet as we look at the food options. I can feel my eyes bulge out when I see the prices. Holy hell! Some of the fancier entrees like filet mignon and lobster don't even have prices. It just says market price. What the hell does that even mean? I've never been here before because I knew it was out of my budget, but fuck, I didn't know it was this far out of it.

"Hi, I'm Erica. I'll be taking care of you tonight. What can I get you to drink and do we want to start with any appetizers?" a shorter, thick woman asks when she steps up to our table.

"I'd like a Busch Light on tap and we'd like a spinach artichoke dip," Steel tells her, and my mouth waters at the thought of that creamy goodness.

"And for you, sir?"

"Umm. I'll take a Moscato and whatever this Christmas Polar Bear Dip is."

"Okay. I will be back with those drinks in a flash and your appetizers should be out soon." She smiles and steps into the kitchen briefly before heading toward the bar for our drinks.

"So, tell me, Iggie, do you like working at Howards? Is there a long-term goal?"

"Yes, I love working at Howards, but I don't like my position. My goal is to be the Philanthropy Manager. I knew they only hired from within for that position, so I started at the bottom and hoped to work my way up. I just applied for the position I want, but haven't heard back yet. I also loathe my manager and her daughter. They live to make my life hell, I'm sure of it."

"Philanthropy, huh? No wonder you jumped at the chance to help us with the Angel Tree donation." Steel chuckles.

"Well, it's a proven fact that thirty-four percent of all charitable giving happens in the last three months of the year. Eighteen of that is during December, which is one of the main reasons I adore Christmas so much. I love the cheer, the sparkly light and decorations, and the giving. We are all more human during the holiday season, I think. So I'd like to be the Philanthropic Manager to spread that cheer throughout the year and not just October through December." I slap a hand over my mouth when I finish because I just rattled off facts and information like I was in an episode of Jeopardy.

"I'm sorry. That was probably a whole lot of shit you didn't wanna hear. I just get lost in anything Christmas and giving," I tell him.

"No, I love it. I love that you have something you're so passionate about. That gets you so excited. We should all have something like that. For me, that's Hell's Mayhem. I love those guys like they're my blood. We may not be above the law, but we aren't bad people. I know that sounds crazy, but it's true," he tells me, and I can see how much he believes that in his eyes.

"Here are your drinks," Erica says as she sets our beer and wine down on the table. "Are we ready to order?"

"I think we are. Iggie, you go first."

"I'd like the beef wellington, rare, the twice-baked potato, and the side salad." I smile and hand my menu to her.

"And for you, sir?"

"I'll take the prime rib, medium, with mashed potatoes and whatever the soup is tonight."

"Alright then. I'll get that order put in for you and be back with your appetizers." She takes Steel's menu and heads back into the kitchen, only to reappear minutes later with both dips. "And here we are."

"May I ask what's in the Christmas dip?" I look at the bowl and see it's pinkish in color, but it smells amazing.

"It's just the owner's play on the holiday. A fun name change for the salmon rillette. It's skinless salmon and smoked salmon, white wine, shallots, chives, and seasoning. Delicious and fresh."

"Thank you," I tell her before she nods and hurries off to her other tables. I grab a baguette and dip it into the spread. Bringing it to my lips, I bite off a small bit. The moment the flavors hit my tongue, my eyes close and a moan escapes. "Fuck, this is good."

"Damn, Iggie," Steel groans. I open my eyes as I swallow. His tongue glides across his bottom lip as he stares at me like he's about to climb over the table and have me for dinner. My belly heats at the thought and I kind of hope he does.

"Sorry. You need to try this, though. It's amazing." I hold a baguette out to him.

"If you make any more of those noises, this dinner is going to be cut short and we're going to get back to that tying up thing. I can think of a lot more reasons for you to make a noise like that, and all of them involve my cock."

I feel my face heating, but I won't apologize, or say anything for that matter, because I'm not sure how one responds to that. I do, however, continue to eat my rillette and steal a few bites of his spinach artichoke dip.

## *seven*

### IGNATIUS

THE REST of dinner flew by as we talked and ate. I had another glass of Moscato, but then switched to water. I don't need alcohol clouding my judgment. I'm already teetering on the edge of wanting to be Steel's.

Erica brings us the check and I reach for it, but Steel is quicker, snapping it out of her hand. "I asked you to dinner, so I'll take care of the bill."

"That's not necessary. I can pay my half, just tell me what it is."

"Not happening, baby. This is a date and a gentleman always handles the bill. Didn't I tell you I'd treat you right? That includes paying when I take you out." He puts a card in the book with the check and slides it to the edge of our table. Erica grabs it on her way to the kitchen and returns with it moments later. Steel uses the pen she left and scribbles on the receipt before slipping his card back into his well-worn leather wallet.

"Come on, Iggie." He holds a hand out to me when he

stands from the table. I lace my fingers with his and let him lead me toward the exit.

"Hey! Wait up!" a female voice calls out from behind us.

We stop and turn around to see Erica walking briskly toward us, determination shining on her face. "Is everything okay?" Steel asks. She looks at him like he just told her the grass is pink.

"I think you have an error on the receipt. You left a two hundred dollar tip. I think you added an extra zero on accident, so I just wanted to let you know I caught it and will only run it for twenty."

"No error. Merry Christmas, Erica." He smiles at her and we turn, leaving the restaurant.

As we get to the passenger side of the truck, Steel presses me against the door and steps closer so our chests are touching. "Tell me you don't want tonight to end. That you aren't scared of me," he whispers.

"I'm not scared of you, Steel. I'm scared of how you make me feel. The life that you live isn't meant for someone like me. It'll chew me up and spit me out." It's the truth. I'm not worried that Steel will hurt me like he did that guy back at Howards, but I am worried about his lifestyle.

His club is dangerous and I'm not even willing to dip a pinky toe in the criminal life. I want to help people, work at Howards, and do their charity. I have so many goals and none of them involve joining a gang or learning to drive a motorcycle.

"You don't have to join Hell's Mayhem or even partake in anything I do with them. Some of the guys have old ladies–or wives, as you'd call them. They aren't part of the club. Sure, they come to the parties if they want to, and a few even help out around the clubhouse, cooking or cleaning, but otherwise, they stay at their own houses. Have jobs, the whole normal life thing. They're just madly in love with a member of my club."

"Okay," I whisper, looking up into his eyes.

His coffee-colored eyes bounce back and forth between mine. "Okay, what, Iggie?"

"I don't want this night to end," I admit. A low grunt-like noise leaves his throat and his lips slam down on mine, his tongue demanding entrance. I open up and it instantly slides inside, gliding over mine like a sensual massage. He tastes like mint and citrus, a combination I can't get enough of.

Steel groans as he sucks on my tongue and the sensation goes straight to my cock. I can feel he's just as affected by me, his hard length pressing against my belly. One of his calloused hands cups the side of my face as he continues his attack on my mouth.

"Let's go for a walk," he breathes heavily when he pulls away, my hand clasped in his.

He doesn't let go as we walk down the street, looking at the holiday displays in the store windows. I wish Howards had a pretty display, but all Susan puts up is one shittily decorated tree and a sign that says Happy Holidays. It's pathetic and when I get the promotion I applied for, I'm going to change that.

You can't expect others to donate during the holidays if the store doesn't scream holiday cheer. We don't even have a box set up for toy drives or clothing for the local homeless foundation. It's ridiculous.

I'm so lost in my inner bitchfest, I'm not paying attention to where we're headed until I'm jerked to the right into the mouth of a dark alley.

"Whaaa..." I start as my heart begins to beat faster in my chest. I lick my lips nervously. What the hell is Steel doing?

Why are we in the alley? He says nothing, just pushes me roughly against the side of one of the buildings encasing the alley, and puts his mouth on mine once more.

"I couldn't stand not having my lips on you," he murmurs against my cold, wet lips.

A groan sneaks out at his words. I've never felt as wanted or desired as I have by this man in the short time I've known him. He's lit an inferno inside me that I'm not sure how to put out.

"Do you trust me?" he asks, peppering sweet, soft kisses down my neck.

"Yes." I lean my head back and feel the roughness of the bricks bite into my scalp.

Without another word, he drops to his knees in front of me and cups my cock through my slacks.

My eyes widen as I look down at him through my lashes and shiver. This large, strong man is on his knees like he's about to worship at my altar. He rubs my dick before reaching up and unbuckling my belt and slacks. Agonizingly slow, he pulls them down my thighs just enough that my cock can spring free.

He groans when he sees I'm sans briefs today, but I was running late and forgot. He places a kiss on the slit of my swollen, red tip and I close my eyes briefly before remembering where we're at.

"What are you doing?" I gasp.

"I want the taste of you branded on my tongue as a reminder of what I'm working toward. Told you I'm not a saintly man, but I want to be when it comes to you. I want to give you the world, baby. Now, I'm going to taste you. Let your cum be a reminder of how good you can be for me and how fucking wild you drive me."

There's no time for argument or even for me to push

him back and pull up my slacks. His mouth opens, and he devours my cock, sliding it to the back of his throat instantly before swallowing.

"Fuuuck," I moan.

Steel bobs up and down my shaft like it's fall, and he's trying to get the best apple from the tub. Up and down, repeatedly, at a steady pace. His tongue swirls around my mushroom head each time he pulls back, but he never fully releases me from his warm mouth.

One of his hands glides up, sneaking between my legs and two fingers stroke my perineum. Fucking Christ! I can't believe I'm getting a damn blowjob in an alley where anyone could see. I can also feel pre-cum dripping from my tip like a leaky faucet, but Steel doesn't seem to be turned off by it.

He looks up at me through his thick lashes and I almost come undone at the vision of my cock down his throat. He works me more, increasing the pressure of his mouth around my shaft.

The hand that's not rubbing the sensitive flesh between my balls and asshole wraps around the back of my right thigh and squeezes hard. I'm going to have bruises and I honestly can't be bothered to care.

"Come for me, baby. Flood my mouth with your sweet taste," he orders when he pops off my cock for the first time since he started. Instantly, his warm mouth envelops my dick again, and my hips thrust of their own accord. I'm so close that I'm chasing my release right along with Steel.

When his left hand squeezes my thigh roughly and his teeth graze my shaft, I'm done for. My hips snap forward one more time, lodging my erection into the back of his throat as I spasm and shake. Cum shoots out in ropes and Steel swallows every last drop.

We make eye contact as he pulls off, dragging his tongue along the underside of my length. He licks his lips and gingerly tucks me away, buttoning my slacks as if nothing happened.

He stands to his full height and I notice the knees of his jeans are soaked through from the cold, wet ground of a Midwest winter. He kisses me softly and I can taste myself on him, which has my dick twitching like it's ready to go another round.

I'm not stupid. I know it's my turn to repay the favor. Nervously, I reach down to the button of his jeans and begin to fumble with it.

Steel removes his lips from mine and pushes my hands away. I look at him with a raised brow and push my glasses up my nose. Does he not want me to suck him off now? Everyone else I've been with has always wanted reciprocation.

"Nuh uh, baby. This was about you. About getting a sample of my sweet boy, so I know he's worth being good for. To show you I'll treat you like a king whenever I can. But mark my words, Iggie, sometimes when we're alone in the bedroom, you'll be my little whore instead."

I swallow hard and whimper.

"You like that don't you, Iggie? You wanna be a king in public, but a dirty whore for me in private?"

"Yes," I tell him, loving how he's speaking to me. I've never been talked to like this, but I better get used to many more firsts if I'm going to be with Steel. He's unlike anyone I've ever been with before. I just hope this doesn't bite me in the ass later.

# *eight*

## ????

BILE RISES in my throat as that scumbag drops to his knees in front of Ignatius. He better be looking for something he dropped or tying his boot. Those thoughts are shot to shit as soon as his hands drag Ignatius' slacks down and he sucks his cock.

That is my cock!

How dare that filthy biker scum put his hands on my soul mate. Ignatius is mine and has been since I laid eyes on him. I stand at the mouth of the alley behind a dumpster watching as that... that... that felon puts his lips where they don't belong, where only my lips should be.

It takes everything inside of me not to storm over to them and drag my knife across that bastard's throat. Then, as he lays there dying, I'll drag Ignatius to my place and teach him that he belongs to me. Only me. No one else will ever be good enough for him. It's always been us.

This is pure torture, watching them kiss and hearing my man moan as if he's feeling pleasure. I know it's fake because I'm the only one who can bring him to the cusp repeatedly before pushing him over the edge.

I thought watching them shop and flirt at the restaurant was bad enough. But this? This is pure agony, and rage fills my icy veins.

Ignatius will pay for this betrayal. I will have to teach him that I don't like to share.

Reaching into my bag, I rifle around blindly, not willing to stop watching this horror in front of me. Finally, I find what I need and pull out my Nikon camera.

I glance at it briefly to make sure the flash is off before I bring it up to my face and snap a few pictures of Iggie's infidelity happening in front of me. Once I'm happy with what I got, I drop the camera back in my bag.

After Ignatius has been drained of his—or shall I say my —cum, I tiptoe away from my hiding spot and head home to print these pictures.

Time is now of the essence—no more waiting and planning.

Ignatius will be with me where he belongs very soon.

*nine*

## IGNATIUS

"THANK you for shopping with us and have a Merry Christmas!" I tell the woman and her son as they grab their bags and leave. She turns her head slightly and flashes me a half smile. I know it's because my tone isn't very convincing.

This is my favorite time of the year and I'm just feeling *meh* today. It's not just today honestly, I've felt like this for almost a week. Five days ago, I went on the best date of my life and got the soul sucked out of me in a dark alley, and yet I can't find it in me to text or call him.

It's not for his lack of trying, either. He's called and texted every day since that night, but I've been avoiding him. I know that makes me a shitty person. I agreed to be his, to let him treat me like a king, and I want that, I really do. But I can't seem to forget how that man drew back and winced in fear of Steel, or how easily Steel just explained it away.

I know I'm risking him showing up here and demanding an explanation, but I don't have one for him. That might even push me farther away. My mind is a mess and I don't know what I'm going to do.

"Hello, Ignatius," a male voice interrupts my inner panic.

I look up and see Barron Howard himself standing on the other side of my register and take a deep breath. Holy shit. The owner and CEO of Howards is here greeting me. My stomach churns and I can feel the clamminess in my hands already.

"Mr. Howard. How can I help you? Is everything okay?"

"Please, call me Barron. Mr. Howard is my father. I took it upon myself to comb through the applicants for the Philanthropy Management position and I saw that you applied. If you have a moment, I'd love to speak to you about it. That is, if you're still interested?"

This would happen today, of all days. The day that I'm having the hardest time figuring out what I'm doing with one Mr. Steel. Speaking of him, I should have asked what his legal name is. Surely it can't be Steel. Probably something super mainstream like Ryan or Theo.

"Ignatius. Are you alright?"

I shake my head and chastise myself for losing track of my thoughts again today. "Yeah, I'm fine. Sorry. I'm just in shock that you came to speak to me yourself. I'm still interested and as long as I have coverage, I'm free."

He smiles. "Well, this position is very important to me now that I'm in full control of the company. So I wanted to go over and interview the applicants myself. I already have Susan here ready to cover your department while we chat." He waves his hand over to the entrance and I see one very pissed-off-looking Susan glaring at me.

"Are you sure?" I ask him, trying not to gain any more of Susan's wrath. "I could ask another associate to cover."

"No. It's fine. Covering is part of Susan's job description if the department head needs to leave or take a break. Didn't you know that?"

"No, sir, I didn't," I tell him truthfully. I've never seen Susan on the floor working a day since I started here. I always have to get another associate to cover my breaks, which has always been odd since I'm the head of the children's department and the people who cover for me are just retail associates.

"Follow me, please." He gestures for me to remove myself from behind the register.

I give him a small smile, close my drawer quickly, and sign out of the POS system. No way am I letting that bitch near my money. Not when she looked *thrilled* to be covering my shift.

We go to Susan's office and he sits behind her desk while I take the chair by the door. The same one I sat in not that long ago when she scolded me for selling Steel those jeans.

Barron wrinkles his nose. "I hate to be unprofessional, but does it smell funny in here to you? Maybe I should call someone to come check the room over for any issues."

My right hand covers my mouth as I try to contain my laugh. "Yes. It smells funny, but you don't need to call anyone. It's Susan's lunch. She brings tuna and sauerkraut casserole every day for lunch."

He says nothing but his lips downturn just slightly. "Okay, so tell me about yourself and why you want this position. Also, why, with the qualifications you have, are you only the head of the children's department?"

"Well, I wanted the Philanthropy position when I saw it open before I started. I knew that you only promoted from within the company, so I started as an associate and worked my way up to department head. I've been biding my time until there was an opening once more."

"That's drive. I respect that you saw what you wanted and went for it no matter that you had to start at the bottom, as we say. You are more than qualified with your history and qualifications. Why this job? Why is philanthropy so important to you personally?"

I smile because this is the easiest question he could ask. "It's the start of social change. I think of it this way. If we donate a wardrobe and money to the local homeless, they might be able to go out and get a job themselves. They become successful and do the same for someone else needing help. Charity has a ripple effect, and I want to be the one who creates that first wave."

When I make eye contact with him again, he has a huge smile that crinkles his eyes at the corners. "Well, Iggie, I think I found the right man for the job. Also, I must admit I love your holiday spirit with your outfit choice. Do you dress for every holiday or just Christmas?"

"Just Christmas. Susan has made it very clear that no other holiday has rules about it in the handbook, so we can't dress up. She's very firm on the December first start date for Christmas wear."

"We might have to change that. I'd like you to start right away if that works for you. We have charities lined up already for donations on the national level. I, however, would like to do more right here in our own town. Do you think you can throw something together locally before the holiday?"

"Yes, Sir... I mean Barron. I have ideas ready to go. I just need to implement them." I bounce slightly in my seat. I'm so excited that I'm getting my dream job and I will get to start right away.

Oh God, Susan and Nancy are going to flip their shit when they find out I'm no longer under their thumb. I now answer directly to Mr. Howard and I couldn't be happier.

***

When I get home, I hurriedly change out of my work clothes and into something more comfy. I'm still so thrilled about my promotion. I pretty much skip to the kitchen. Like Thumbelina dancing in the window of her cottage, I move from the pantry to the stove and back again, making some simple nachos for dinner.

Sitting on my couch with my plate of food on the table in front of me, I grab my remote and hit play on Heartland. I'm on season ten and I'm addicted. I need a sexy man who owns a ranch and rides horses to take me away and teach me to be a country boy. Or maybe I just need a biker that treats me like his dirty whore.

My phone dings and I pick it up.

> Mom- Hey, Darling. We got your message on the machine but we're headed out of town for vacation. Talk soon. Love you.

I DON'T EVEN BOTHER with a reply, tossing the phone back on the table with a thud and rolling my eyes. Heaven forbid they call back and speak to me. I called their house earlier to tell them my news and got the answering machine.

We've not had the greatest relationship since they think

I'm wasting my life's talents by not having some fancy doctorate, but I'm happy. My dad hasn't spoken to me since I turned twenty and officially came out of the closet. Not sure how he didn't see that coming after my entire childhood, but then again, he was gone a lot. Servicing his mistress was hard work and really, why wouldn't he when my mom lived in denial the whole time? To this day, she still won't admit that he was cheating on her. It wouldn't surprise me if he has a whole other family hidden somewhere.

How pathetic is it that I have this awesome news and no one to share it with? Draco is on a work trip so I don't want to bother him. I know how seriously he takes his job. He has a degree in fashion merchandise and freelances for big corporations. I think this time he was headed to Kansas to help some department store whose numbers are trash.

I should tell Steel, he knows how badly I wanted this position. He'd be happy for me and maybe we could celebrate.

*No! I am not calling him. He is bad for me.*

I don't care that he gave me the best date of my life or the best blow job ever. He is a violent man and I can't risk my heart with someone who could quite literally break it. This fucking sucks.

Solemnly, I finish the episode of Heartland I'm on and take my plate to the kitchen, setting it in the sink to deal with later. I head to the bathroom, hoping a hot shower and a good sugar scrub will help my mood. If Amy could love Ty even though he had known criminal charges but was still a good man to her, then maybe, just maybe, I should give Steel an actual chance.

*ten*

## STEEL

THIS CAN'T BE HAPPENING AGAIN. No way did I put myself out there with a guy, suck Iggie's dick in an alley, and now he's ghosting me. It's been a week of me calling and texting with no response, not even a go fuck yourself. Who lets someone suck them like a hoover, agree to be theirs, but as soon as they're given the chance, act like they don't fucking exist?

Pistol and Viper have been my anchors, giving me reasons I shouldn't just show up at his house or work and demand answers. I haven't told them about how I've been in front of his house every night, watching to make sure he's not with someone else and that he's safe.

Ellie talked me off the ledge from following him to and from work. I know his whereabouts and can be there instantly if something seems off, thanks to the tracker I installed on his car. According to Ellie, if they can't prove I'm the one who installed it, then I'm in the clear. A pair of gloves and no cameras made that easier than getting a club whore to suck me off.

A knock on my door has me sluggishly getting off the bed and heading to see who has the balls to disturb me in my room. Ripping it open, I see Trucker standing there with a shit-eating grin on his face and his left brow cocked. "Ya alright in there?"

"Fine. What do you want?"

"We're all loaded and ready to hit the road. Just waitin' on you, our fearless leader." He wags his brows at me.

This bastard has always been playful and can't read the room to save his life, or maybe he can and just doesn't give a fuck. Either way, he's already on my last nerve. "Let me get my boots on and I'll be there. I want everyone armed and ready for anything. I don't trust those Hellhound bastards for a minute."

"Yes, Prez." He salutes me, throws a wink my way, and saunters down the hall to do as he was told. He may be an annoying fuck, but he's loyal.

I put on my boots and take my piece from the top drawer, slipping it into the inner pocket of my cut. Grabbing two knives, I sheath them inside each of my boots before tugging my jeans down over them so no one is the wiser. When I'm armed and ready, I lock my door and head outside, where everyone is waiting.

"Listen up! I'm goin' to say this once, and you better have your fuckin' listenin' ears on. This run is important. It's one of the largest for the year. We need this to go off without a hitch. Trucker has found the best route. If any of ya spot a Hellhound or anything out of the ordinary, I wanna know ASAP. If we run into Hellhound trouble, we shoot first and ask questions later. And if I find out any of you have been rattin' us out to the enemy, I'll cut your fuckin' eyes and tongue out myself. Are we clear?"

A chorus of *yes, Prez* rings out, and I nod. "Let's fuckin' get it done, then!" I climb into the driver's seat of my truck and fire it up. Trucker revs his Jeep as he passes me. Viper and Pistol are behind him, leadin' us out of the compound. After Rubble's semi passes, I follow with the rest of the guys close behind.

During runs like this, Hawk and the prospects remain behind to protect the compound. The old ladies stay home and the whores fend for themselves. Gives them a few days of 'me' time. The rest of us are on the road making sure these guns get to Michaelov. I'm not wanting to get the bratva on the club's ass. We've been on good terms and I intend to keep us there.

We've been on the road just shy of two hours when my phone vibrates and I glance down at my watch.

> Trucker: Trouble ahead. 2 guys on each side of the road. They're in cuts but can't see the logo.

I GRIT my teeth so hard I swear I hear one of my molars crack. Fucking cocksuckers! We have a rat, and this proves it. We discussed this route exclusively among the men on the run, and solely in church. With one hand on the wheel, I swiftly swipe a finger across my watch, giving the signal to go to route B.

I then hold my free hand out the window and make a fist, before pointing up to the sky with a finger gun and shaking it twice. The men behind me know to be armed and ready. I see Rubble in one of the semi's side mirrors cock his shotgun, just in case anyone gets too close to the eighteen-wheeler.

We go over a small hill. To them it looks like we're playing a game of chicken, one we could win, but Trucker and I made a contingency plan in case this happened. In a split second, the three vehicles ahead brake and Rubble skillfully maneuvers the truck onto the side road.

Once the semi is on the straightaway, Trucker, Viper, and Pistol gun their engines, following him. The remaining men begin firing at the two men on the road. They go down in a rain of bullets and don't even see it coming. I'm sure just down the road behind them is the rest of the Hellhound MC. It would be their style to leave two men on the road-side, all foreboding and shit. Too bad for them, it got them killed.

I holster my gun and press on the gas to catch back up to Tex, ready to be done with this run already. What more could possibly go wrong?

THE REST of the trip was smooth sailing. Despite the detour, we arrived at the meeting point only an hour later than expected and are currently waiting for Michaelov and his men. Once we were in the clear, I sent him a quick text about the delay so he could prepare.

We're sitting in the parking lot of this creepy abandoned high school, twiddling our thumbs. I despise tardiness, and Michaelov knows this. So either he got caught up as well, or he's about to fuck us over. Neither eases my anxiety. The school sits back from the road, surrounded by fields, and looks like it could collapse any minute.

Three stories, all brick with boarded-up windows, like something straight out of a horror movie. I survey the place, my mind whirling with possibilities. The spacious grounds, the huge building, all seem to give me the same thought.

*This would make one hell of a compound.*

Enough space for all our current members to stay if they need to. Plus, room to grow since we have had an influx of prospects recently.

Twenty minutes later, two silver SUVs pull up, followed by a semi and two more SUVs. Michaelov steps out of the backseat of the second vehicle. With a grin stretching across his features, he slides his sunglasses from his eyes to the pocket of his suit jacket. "Sorry for the delay, my friend. It seems someone has loose lips."

"We had an interruption as well. You wouldn't happen to know anything about that, would you, Michaelov?" I question. It's slightly foolish to provoke the head of the bratva, but no one ever said I wasn't a tad bit deranged.

"Ha! You are a funny one, Steel. I like you. You're not scared of me like you should be." He chuckles, closing the gap between us. "Now, I came here for my guns. Let me see them."

I turn, signaling Rubble to open the trailer to reveal the product. He obliges and in seconds we're standing inside the semi looking into the crates that house Michaelov's merchandise. "I see MK6s, Magnums, and ARs, but where are my RPG 18s? I noted them in the order."

"You didn't ask for no RPGs," I snap at him. I'm not sure what game he's playing, but I'm not falling for it. I personally handled the order, and he didn't mention anything else.

"Yes, I did, young biker boy. I sent in a change order and added four of them. I believe I spoke to someone who calls themself Snake."

"I ain't no boy. You'd be mindful to remember that. We also don't have anyone named Snake in our club. So I don't know who you called and talked to, but it wasn't us. If you want to place another order, I can have it ready for you in three weeks."

A creepy smile takes over his face, and a split second later, he has his pistol directed straight at my face. "I want what I ordered."

I pull my gun and point it back at him and we stand there in the semi at a standoff. I hear the rest of our men all cocking their weapons, and I know if one motherfucker gets a twitchy finger, it's gonna be a bloodbath.

"Michaelov, I ain't ever done you dirty. I'm tellin' you, there ain't no one called Snake in my club."

"I'm telling you, I know who I contacted and talked to. I'm sure you didn't send those other filthy bikers to interrupt my convoy either, huh?" His eyes narrow and the vein in his neck throbs.

"Their cuts have a wolf's head surrounded by a gaudy ass orange flame?" I ask.

"Yes."

"That's who delayed us as well. They call themselves the Hellhounds. We have nothin' to do with them, minus them bein' a pain in my damn ass," I answer him honestly.

"Well, it seems one of us has a leak. I don't like leaks. They cause damage and I don't care for the cleanup. So what do we do?" He taps a finger on his chin with his free hand.

My phone rings, startling me. I kept my phone on silent, except for Iggie. Call me crazy or fucked up. I don't care. I've been called far worse. I reach into my pocket and pull my phone out, hitting the answer button before holding it to my ear.

"Iggie. Is everything okay? I haven't heard from you."

"Yeah. I feel stupid now that you actually answered, but I have news and no one to share it with."

"What did I tell you about calling yourself names?" I growl.

"Are you talking on the pho—"

"Ssshhh." I hold a finger up to my mouth, shushing Michaelov. "I've been waitin' for this call and you ain't fuckin' it up."

"Crazy, fucking American biker," he murmurs.

"I'm sorry, Steel, are you busy? I can call back later or you know what, just forget it."

"No! I'm not busy. Not with anything important, anyway. So tell me your news."

"Well, today, Barron, the CEO of Howards, came and spoke with me and I got that position I told you about. The philanthropy manager? I got it!"

"That's amazin', baby. I'm so proud of you. We should celebrate," I tell him, and an idea begins to form in my head. "Will you let me celebrate with you?"

"Y-y-yeah."

"Okay, let me handle what I'm doing and I'll text you. This time, answer me, Ignatius, or I'll be forced to take more drastic measures." He doesn't respond, just sighs, and I hang up, sliding the phone back into my pocket. "Now where were we?"

"You really took a call while I have my gun aimed at your skull? While my men have theirs on you and your men? Krāzē."

"It was important. Plus, I heard you loud and clear. One

of us has a leak. I agree, especially since two runs involving you have been interrupted. I'll get you your RPGs and we will clean up our organization. Sound fair?"

"Indeed." We drop our guns and slip them back into their hiding spots. Our men follow suit. "As always, Steel, it's been fun. I'll be in touch."

Michaelov whistles for his men to load the product onto their truck, while my men and I stand guard. When they finish, I shake hands with Michaelov and we head to our respective vehicles, leaving the school grounds.

I drive for about twenty minutes before using Bluetooth to call Pistol.

"Steel."

"We have a rat and I wanna know who it is and fast," I bark.

"I know. Anyone you can rule out right away to help me investigate?"

"Trucker, Viper, Zero, and Hawk. We vetted them ourselves and they've been with us since the beginning. I trust them. No one else. If we need eyes and ears where we can't go, ask Kiki. Don't tell her what's goin' on, just ask her to keep her ears on the ground and report back to you."

"And what are you gonna do?"

"I have a plan to put into motion." I smile at the mere thought of it.

"This have anything to do with the call you took with a bratva pistol in your face? Quite the move, Steel. You crazy fucking bastard."

"Sure does. Now find me my rat. I made a promise I'd take their eyes and tongue and I intend to stick to that." I hang up and floor my truck. I have a list to make, some errands to run, and only a week to pull everything together.

# *eleven*

## IGNATIUS

I CAN'T BELIEVE I called Steel in a moment of weakness. The more I think about his response, the more I question my perception of him. How can he be so violent and bad, but still be so tender anytime it comes to me?

Today my focus is on my new position and everything I want to do to improve the company's image; no time for personal thoughts. Grabbing my keys and the bag that holds my lunch, I hurry out the door.

The drive to work consists of me being a karaoke star, and scream-singing *Back to You* by Selena Gomez. Before I know it, I'm pulling into a parking spot and getting out of the car, ready to kill it today. I pull my suit jacket down and rub out any wrinkles the drive may have caused. I'm wearing my favorite plum jacket with a lavender shirt underneath and black slacks. A power outfit, one that makes me feel strong and that I'm about to rock this shit.

Butterflies swarm in my belly as I step through the doors and head upstairs to the offices. It feels odd not turning left for the children's department like I normally would. I momentarily wonder who they got to fill my spot, but then I realize I don't care as long as it gets me away from Susan.

I stride into my office—my own damn office—drop my bag and keys on the desk, and do a slow spin, absorbing every detail of the room. As I settle into my chair, I immediately spot a stack of papers on the desk with a post-it note reading 'Fill me out'.

It seems HR wasted no time getting me the forms I need to complete to make them happy. I grab a pen and get to work with this mundane task so I can move on to what I really wanna do. Which is to figure out an event I can throw together in the short time I have before Christmas.

An hour later, I feel on top of the world. Howards is the designated shopping destination for Shop with a Cop starting next year. I agreed to give them a discount on all purchases in exchange for a ten-year contract. Barron was ecstatic when I told him the news. I kinda worried he'd be upset that I locked us in for such a long period, but he loved it.

I'm determined to launch something for this year, despite Christmas creeping closer. I tap my pencil on the top of the desk as I wrack my brain, trying to think of a plan. What can I throw together quickly that would have a decent impact, since we're only weeks away from Christmas?

Shit! Two things come to mind, but I need to make sure the one is doable, since it would require Howards footing the bill. Standing from my chair, I leave my office and head to Barron's. I hope the two visits I've already paid him today won't give him a needy vibe from me.

He doesn't even let me knock as he waves me inside. "What can I do for you, Ignatius?"

"So, I know I spoke to you about Shop with a Cop and

that's a go starting next year. But I have an idea for this year, well, two actually, but I wanted to get the green light from you on one of them."

"Okay. Shoot," he replies, folding his hands on his desk.

"Every year, Goodwill puts a program together where companies can sponsor a family for Christmas. We'd pay for a Christmas tree and decorate it, then the weekend before Christmas the public can walk through the community center to view them all and can put change in a jar for their favorite tree. The money from voting goes to buy more gifts for families in need. That Sunday we'd deliver the tree to the family along with gifts we bought for them and a full holiday dinner."

"I love it! What do you need from me?" He smiles, and it covers his face almost ear to ear.

"I need your approval and a payment method. I will do everything else," I reply.

"I can get you the funds in two different ways. One, you pay for them upfront and keep your receipts. Submit them to Polly in accounting and she'll get you reimbursed within minutes. But the second option means I'm prepared to take a leap of faith for you, despite the potential consequences from the board. I like you, Ignatius, and you've shown me already you're a go-getter. So, I'm willing to give you a company card. I'm trusting you to use it only for business expenses related to your position. You'll have to submit your receipts weekly to Polly still so she can make sure everything lines up."

My stomach somersaults as I stare at him, blinking in surprise before I pull myself together. "Thank you, Barron. I appreciate your trust a great deal. I'll take the card, I swear to account for every penny."

He smiles before bending in his chair and searching

through one of the lower drawers. Seconds later, he straightens and hands a black Amex to me.

*Holy shit!*

I give him my thanks and practically prance back down the hall to my office. I'm so excited. First things first, call Goodwill and get our name on the list for a family. They let me pick how big of a family we want and I tell them to give me the largest one they have left. While on the phone with her, she sends over an email with all the family's information. A family of nine; mom, dad, six kids, and grandma all live together.

I wish I had siblings growing up. My life might not have been so lonely. No point in getting lost in the past. My therapist can deal with that shit at our next session. Right now, I need to get some help in decorating and delivering the tree. Pulling up my browser, I send a company-wide email looking for volunteers to help me.

Once I'm done for the day, I head down to my car and drive home with a smile and a warm feeling buzzing through my veins.

———✦💀✦———

IT'S FINALLY Friday and I'm exhausted. Who would have thought a desk job would be more draining than retail work? It won't stay like this forever. With everything being new, I've been networking and shopping nonstop. I have almost everything in order for the Adopt-a-Family and I set up boxes by every register in the store that are wrapped like presents but open on the top for people to donate anything they want. I will make sure everything goes where it fits, whether an animal shelter, a women's shelter, or the local foster care agency.

I've just sat down on my couch with a glass of Moscato and a takeout container of baked mostaccioli when the doorbell rings. Dammit! I'm not expecting anyone. Who is trying to ruin my plan to veg out on my couch and watch Hallmark all weekend?

Setting my less-than-stellar dinner on the coffee table, I walk to the door, making sure my robe is securely tied around me. I don't need to be giving anyone a show. There might be some residual PTSD from the one time I came to get a package and when I bent down to get it, the wind blew my robe open and the delivery driver saw my ass.

Upon opening the door, a young man stands before me, his face looks familiar, yet I can't recall where I might know him from. He's holding a large box with an envelope tied to it and a big red bow. I take the box from him, and without a word, he turns and heads down the path to a Ford Mustang, climbs inside, and speeds away.

What the hell?

Stepping back inside, I shut the door and carry my box to the couch. I grab the envelope and open it. Inside is a handwritten note from Steel.

*Ignatius,*

*I'm sorry I'm not the picture of perfection or fit the mold for what your perfect man may look like. But I promise that no matter how gritty and violent my job might be, I won't ever bring it home* to you. On the outside, I may give off hot-tempered and aggressive vibes, but when it comes to those I care about, I'm the total opposite. Please, give me the chance to prove this to you. Take a leap of faith, Iggie, and let me catch you. I promise not to let you fall.

P.S.- I'm not this pretty of a talker. But Kiki helped me write this and said I just needed some flowery words. You'd like her. She's a real bad bitch.

P.P.S.- That was all Kiki.

Steel

I LAUGH as my heart pounds in my chest. I untie the ribbon and open the box, revealing a neatly folded pile of clothes. Quirking a brow, I hold up the contents to see what he's sent. It's a pair of dark green dress pants, a gray sweater with a teddy bear in a Christmas sweater on the front, and a red and black plaid jacket. It's fucking adorable, trendy, and something I would totally wear.

*But why send it?*

Underneath the jacket is another note. This one just says call me if and when you're ready to jump.

With a deep breath and a few second guesses, I pick up my phone and call him. He answers on the first ring and I stay silent, trying to remember how to speak or what to say.

"Hello, Iggie, are you there?"

"Yeah, I'm here. I got your gift," I whisper.

"Good. And you called, so that's fucking fantastic," he

replies.

"I did. How did you know my size? What is this for? Your letter didn't say."

"Don't be mad, but I had one of the guys look up your call records the night you sent me that Austin Powers text and saw you messaging with a guy named Draco so I called and explained myself to him and he gave me your sizes. I now owe him a ride on the back of my bike when it warms up," he mutters the last part, clearly not too happy about my best friend being on the back of his bike.

"I'm not mad, but uhm, that is pretty intense, so maybe just ask me next time."

"Well, I would have, if you'd take my calls or texts," he growls.

Touché.

"Yeah, I guess I was a bit of an ass. I have my reasons and when I'm ready, I'll tell you. But tell me what this outfit is for."

"I want you to go to the Angel Tree dinner with me tomorrow night. A bunch of the guys are goin', and I want you to be my date. I'll pick you up at six," he tells me.

"O-o-okay. I guess I'll see you tomorrow night. Thank you, Steel, this was nice, and you really did a good job picking out something I'd like. I'm surprised." I chuckle lightly.

"I may not have known ya long, Iggie, but when I like someone, I make it my business to be the best I can be. I intend to prove that to you, I just need the chance. Don't run away again, baby."

"I'm gonna try not to," I murmur.

"See you tomorrow."

"Steel!" I call before he hangs up. "Tell Kiki I said thank you."

"Oh, for fuck's sake." I hear before the line goes dead.

I drop my phone down onto the couch next to me and grab my forgotten pasta, turning on the TV as I lean back and take my first bite. Guess I have a date tomorrow night and while I'm nervous as hell, I'm also feeling energized and breathless. It's time to stop making excuses on why I shouldn't give Steel a chance and at least let him try to prove that what he says is the truth.

# *twelve*

## STEEL

I SWALLOW HARD, my tongue sticking to the roof of my mouth like glue. A nervous flutter dances in the pit of my stomach. I've never had these types of feelings before when taking someone out. Iggie brings it out of me. He makes me feel things I can't recall feeling before. Sure, I've had obsessions, but eventually, after some forceful intervention, I moved on. Bre and Alisha are a thing of the past. I hardly remember what caused my obsession with them.

But Iggie. He makes obsession feel like child's play. He consumes me in ways that I didn't think were possible. I'm determined to prove to him that he is *mine*, no matter what.

I park in front of his house and walk to his front door. Like one of those douches in a movie, I straighten the black polo shirt under my cut and knock on the door. It opens and my breath gets caught in my throat, causing me to choke. His ashy blond hair is messily slicked back, and his glasses are perfectly perched on his nose. I stop myself from reaching up and cupping his jaw, which is masked in the slightest five o'clock shadow.

I knew the outfit I sent would look good on him, but picturing him in it and seeing the real thing doesn't compare. I want to drop to my knees and worship his body once more. Again, something I'm not used to feeling. Sex for me is usually all about *my* gratification. I get in, come and get out. This man, though, has me wanting to give him all the pleasure.

"You ready?" I hold my elbow out like Kiki told me to while I wait for his answer.

"Yeah," he replies softly. He hooks his arm in the crook of mine and I escort him to my cage. Once he's inside, I reach around him, buckling his seatbelt, and shut the door. Strolling around to the driver's side, I climb in.

"Where are all the gifts?" Iggie asks while looking in the backseat.

"The old ladies wrapped them with some help. We loaded them into our van and one of the guys drove it over so they'd get there safely."

"Smart," he responds, staring out the passenger window as we pull out onto the road.

"So how has work been? You likin' the new position?" I ask.

"Yeah. I love it. Limited time made the start of my week challenging, as I wanted to do something for Christmas."

"I'm sure you figured somethin' out. You're smart."

"Your faith in me means a lot." He chuckles. "I figured something out, the company is sponsoring a family through the Goodwill program. We will provide a fully decorated tree, Christmas dinner, and gifts galore."

"See. I didn't doubt you were about to tell me something

amazin'. Your passion and problem-solvin' abilities are clear."

"It's the glasses, huh? They give the impression I'm super smart and nerdy, but I promise you I'm not. I had a solid 3.0 GPA all of college and high school." He pushes his glasses up his nose.

"The way you talked at dinner about your passions told me you're smart. The glasses give you a librarian look with a sexy twist. It's an image I very much can't get out of my head and has starred in every filthy, depraved thought I've had since we met." I look at him out of the corner of my eye. He rubs his hands down his thighs, the bulge in his pants very noticeable.

For the rest of the ride, we talk about the week and what shows we like. Stupid first date shit that we didn't cover at dinner because I was too busy stuffing his cock down my throat.

"We're here," I tell him, stopping the truck in the banquet hall parking lot.

I jump out and hold his door open for him, grabbing his hand and escorting him to the entrance of the building. Once I help Iggie out of his coat, I hang it up, and we head into the dining room, where I can hear the crowd chatting loudly. I spot Pistol and the guys right away and lead Iggie to their table with two empty chairs waiting for us.

A round of whistles greets us as we step up to the table and I pull Iggie's chair out. "Knock it off, you bunch of assholes. You'll scare him off."

"I think you did a fine job of that yourself in the alley that day," Viper teases.

"Fuck you," I spit at him. Then turn and look at Iggie. "Don't listen to them. They're a bunch of barbarians who don't know how to act."

He says nothing, just gives me a small smile. "Let me introduce you, though. Guys, this is Ignatius. Some of ya met him at Howards. Iggie, this is Viper, Pistol, Rubble, Trucker, and Zero," I tell him, pointing to each brother as I go clockwise around the table.

"Nice to meet you all. I hope to remember all your names," Iggie tells them. "They're a bit out there, so I think it'll be easy enough." His eyes widen and his mouth gapes as he slaps a hand over it.

His embarrassment over what he just said and the bright red taking over his cheeks are cute.

"Ha! I like this one, Prez. He's not scared to say things. I vote you keep him." Viper laughs.

"I like him too, and trust me, I plan on keepin' him." I reach over and lay a hand on Iggie's thigh, squeezing it. "If he'll let me."

The head of the Angel Tree organization, Tina, clears her throat and we all turn her way, seeing her standing on stage, microphone in hand. "Welcome everyone to the annual Angel Tree dinner. Tonight will be filled with joy, good food, and hefty checkbooks. So without giving a long-drawn-out speech, I declare that dinner be served!"

The crowd claps and cheers while the doors to the dining room open and wait staff flood the room holding trays of food. Bartenders walk around taking drink orders and when they get to our table, we order a round of Busch Lights except for Iggie, who asks for a Strawberry Moscow Mule.

They set our plates in front of us while another waiter dishes our portions onto them. Upon completion, they place the remaining trays on a buffet table at the front of the room. I look down at my food and hear my stomach rumble. Filet mignon, crispy potatoes with gravy, green beans, and a salad. My mouth waters as I pick up my fork and dig in.

We eat and chat like old friends. The guys are keeping Iggie entertained with their endless stories and banter. He's holding his own with them, though, which surprises me. He's it for me, and this is just more proof.

As we finish, the servers clear our plates away before setting a plate of strawberry cheesecake in their place.

"Ladies and gentlemen, it seems we are starting dessert, which means it's time to reveal this year's auction items. You all know the drill. My assistant will hold up the item and, after a brief description, we'll start the bidding. The one with the highest bid takes it home." Tina steps away from the microphone as the auctioneer steps forward. "Oh! I almost forgot. We have a few last-minute gifts that need to be brought in. So if you have any, let's do that now."

I nod to Pistol, who glances down into his lap momentarily before giving me a thumbs up. The doors open and the prospects file in with wagon after wagon full of our gifts. Ten thousand five hundred seventy-one dollars and thirty-two cents' worth, to be exact.

Once they're all inside and I've made my point to these pompous assholes, Tina smiles with a wink and retakes her place on stage. "The Hell's Mayhem MC made this huge donation and we thank you deeply for it."

Her assistant steps forward and holds up the first item while the auctioneer describes it. It's some fancy wine tasting and not anything we'd be interested in. The bidding begins, and the thing sells for almost ten grand. Iggie chokes on his drink and I smack him on the back.

The night continues in the same manner. Stuck-up dicks flashing their money around trying to prove to each other who's the richest. It's ridiculous, but it's for a good cause, so who am I to judge?

The last item of the night is a trip to Las Vegas for a long weekend. It's an all-inclusive stay at the Bellagio minus spending money while you're there. I see Iggie perk up when the bidding starts.

"We'll start the bid at one thousand dollars. Do I have one thousand?" the auctioneer calls.

Iggie raises his hand, and I smile. "You wanna go on a vacation?" I chuckle. "Didn't you just get a promotion?"

"I've never been to Vegas. It's on my bucket list," he murmurs.

"I'd be interested to know what else is on that bucket list," I flirt.

"Two thousand! Who'll give me two thousand?"

My man's hand inches up again.

"Two thousand! Going once. Going twice." Iggie is practically bouncing in his seat. He's so excited he's about to win this trip. "So—"

"Five thousand," someone calls from the crowd.

Iggie immediately deflates. "No worries, babe. Bid again," I assure him.

"I can't afford to," he whispers as his cheeks flush and he plays with his collar.

"Six thousand," I call and Iggie's eyes snap to mine. "What? I like Vegas. I could go back."

"Seven," the asshole calls again.

"Eight," I bark.

"Nine," he volleys instantly.

"Fifteen thousand dollars," I reply, unwilling to back down. I see Iggie in my peripheral and he has tears in his eyes as his head shakes in denial. Not sure why he's so surprised, he wanted this trip and if I can give it to him I'm going to.

"Do I hear sixteen? Going once. Going twice. Sold!" The auctioneer bangs his gavel on the podium. "That ends our auction for the night and we end on the night's high. Congratulations to all of those who won tonight and thank you to everyone who donated."

"Let's go." I grab Iggie's hand and pull him away from the table. Dragging him from the room, I pay my auction bill, grab Iggie's coat, and head to the cage.

When we're back on the road, I look at Iggie and squeeze his hand.

Iggie sits in the passenger seat, his fingers tapping lightly on his knee as he glances out of the window. He turns with a grateful smile, his eyes bright with excitement.

"Thank you for buying that vacation for me."

I grin, feeling a warm sense of satisfaction at his appreciation. "It was my pleasure," I reply, my tone laced with sincerity. "And maybe we could go together," I add, giving him a playful wink.

Iggie's cheeks flush a rosy hue, and he looks away, a shy smile playing on his lips. "I'd like that," he says softly, his gaze meeting mine again with a hint of anticipation.

Not wanting to push the issue further just yet, I change the subject.

"Do you want me to take you home? If not, I'd like to invite you back to the clubhouse. And I'm hopin' you say yes."

"Umm, sure. We can go to your clubhouse." He smiles.

"You don't have to. I just want you to see and understand everything that I am, so you can decide if you're in or out. I don't want you disappearin' on me again."

"Okay. Show me your club," he breathes.

"Good. You're mine, Ignatius, and I plan on showin' you just how good being mine can be."

# *thirteen*

## IGNATIUS

TONIGHT HAS ALREADY BEEN INCREDIBLE. I don't know what got into me, bidding on that weekend trip to Nevada. But I had an empty credit card and was fully prepared to almost max it out to cross Vegas off my bucket list. The bidding went too high, though, and I didn't want a huge monthly payment, so I called it quits.

I wasn't expecting Steel to pick up the bidding where I left off. Buying the trip for fifteen grand. My stomach plummeted, leaving me staring wide-eyed at him, utterly dumbfounded, while he smirked. I've never had someone do something that big and thoughtful for me.

My heart is pounding as we pull into a short drive and slow down by a small guard shack. Steel waves, gives them a curt nod and they watch as we roll past. "We have two people guardin' the drive at all times. Not that we've had any issues, but we want to know the comings and goings of people. It gives the old ladies and kids a sense of security."

"Like a gated community, but only for your members. I

like that. The world is changing and people are so vulnerable," I admit.

Steel parks the truck and hurries around to my side of the vehicle to open my door. Taking my hand, he leads me through the front door of what looks like an old warehouse. As we walk in, I notice they have redesigned the inside to resemble a massive rec room.

A long bar dominates the left wall, while a pool table, dartboard, and couches are scattered around the room. Near the entrance, a jukebox stands, and a large TV screen displays a hockey game.

"So this is the main area of the clubhouse where we hang out and party." He leads me into another room, a sprawling kitchen that would make any chef drool. Connected to it is a dining room with a table big enough to accommodate twenty guests.

"This is incredible, but where do you sleep or do you not live here?"

"I live here. Not all the guys do, but any of them who are single and want to can. The married members have their own places, but a room is always open for them in case they need it."

"Am I going to see your room?" I ask, my breath hitching at how brazen that question is. This isn't like me, but Steel makes me feel like I'm flying, and I have a hard time controlling my thoughts when I'm around him.

"Do you wanna see my room?" he rasps.

"Maybe." I lick my lips. The word lingers in the air, filled with indecision. We stand there staring at one another. His eyes are dark, filled with desire.

"Later," he murmurs, breaking the tension. "Let's go get you a drink."

I follow him as we head back into the main room and

straight to the bar. Chad is behind it making drinks, and I raise a brow at him. "Hey, Chad. Nice to see you again. Can I get a Corona with salt and a lime?"

"Get me a Busch Light," Steel tells him. Chad turns to the beer coolers behind him and grabs our drinks, setting them on the bar, and popping the tops. He then opens a small fridge and grabs a lime.

"Thank you," I tell him when he slides the salt and beer over to me with the lime wedge shoved down the neck of the bottle.

"No problem," he replies, moving to another club member.

I slide onto a stool, and Steel moves in behind me, his chest pressed against my back. I look up at him and smile. "Do we pay or tip him?"

He laughs before kissing my forehead. "Nah. The prospects take turns bartendin' as part of their service to the club."

A door in the back of the room slams open and three people I haven't met come strolling in.

Two men wearing black jogging pants and white t-shirts along with a woman wearing a short as hell skirt with a little crop top. The woman and a guy with hazel eyes and a face tattoo come our way.

"Steel, baby! You told me he was a looker, but he's hot as fuck!" the woman squeals.

"Iggie. Kiki. Kiki this is Ignatius. And this is Gabe," Steel introduces us, and I extend my hand. She shakes it firmly before I hold it out to Gabe, who copies her actions.

"Hey. I'm glad to put a face to the name that helped Steel with his letter." I smile at her and she laughs as she nods her head.

"I couldn't let him write it alone. The rough draft was scary," she teases.

"Kiki! Baby, I got a little something for you!" some guy calls from a chair by the pool table. He is thin with fluffy brown hair, reminding me of that vampire that glitters in the sun.

"Duty calls. I'll talk to you later." She waves her fingers before sashaying over to the man and straddling his lap, kissing him.

"Is that her boyfriend?" I ask, wondering how a guy like him snagged a girl like her.

Gabe chokes on a laugh and Steel shoots him a glare. "Well, I better make the rounds," he says. "It was nice meeting you, Ignatius."

I turn to Steel, my brows furrowing and my lips parting in confusion. "Did I... say something?"

"Baby," he whispers, turning my stool so we are face to face. "Kiki, Gabe, and Cody, the other guy who walked in with them, they're the club whores. There's also another female, Daria, but I don't know where she's at right now."

"Club whores?"

"Yeah, their *job*, I guess you could call it, is to service the members of the club in any way asked. If you catch my drift. In return, they get to stay here and are under the protection of the club," Steel informs me. His voice is unsure and his eyes aren't focused on me, so I can tell he's nervous.

"What if they don't want to *service* a member?" I ask using air quotes when I say service.

"They're never forced, if that's what you're askin'. If they're asked or made to do anything they don't wanna do, they know to come straight to me and I'll handle it. We do not stand for violence." He winces. "Okay, we don't stand for sexual violence."

"Have you slept with them?" I ask, even though I don't think I really wanna know the answer.

"Kiki, yes. Gabe has sucked me off. I've never touched Daria or Cody. But I haven't even looked at any of them in that way since the day I laid eyes on you."

"Okay," I whisper. What else is there to say? I didn't expect him to be a virgin, but I am shocked that he told me without a second thought.

# *fourteen*

## IGNATIUS

I'M DRUNK. Not fall over, I don't know what I'm doing drunk, but enough that I can let loose and not be so anxious. Maybe this could work? Steel has been nothing but nice to me, more than nice, actually. He's gone above and beyond to show me he's not who I saw in the alley. Those two parts of him are separate.

"Do you want me to take you home, baby, or do you wanna stay here tonight?" Steel mumbles against my ear as he licks and nips at my lobe.

"Mmmm, can I stay here?" I ask.

"I was hoping you'd say that. I can't imagine anything better than wakin' up to you beside me. Let's go."

He leads me from the main area of his clubhouse to a door I haven't been through yet. He told me earlier in his tour that the bedrooms were back here, but didn't show me. I turn my head to call goodbye to Kiki and Gabe, but my eyes widen when I see them involved in a full-blown orgy in the middle of the room. Kiki is bent over a stool getting fucked by Zero while Gabe is in the same position, but Trucker is driving into him. Kiki and Gabe are passionately kissing over the barstool.

Holy shit! I know Steel said they were club whores, but I wasn't expecting to see them fuck right there in front of everyone. When Steel said he and his brothers weren't modest, he wasn't lying. "You like watchin', baby?" Steel purrs and I jump, forgetting he was there.

"I-I-I don't know. I've never done it before. Live porn wasn't what I was expecting when I came over tonight." I turn to look at him and lick my lips.

"Babe, you must have been lost tonight." He laughs before ushering me down the hall. "It's not the first time they've gotten off with you here."

"Seriously?"

"I'm gonna take it as a compliment. I was such good company you didn't notice the whores fuckin'." He unlocks and pushes open the door at the very end of the hall. I follow him inside, our hands still intertwined.

His walls are white but his bed, nightstands, and dresser are black. The room is clean, minus the messy forest green bedding, which isn't a big deal. I never make my bed either. "The bathroom is there if you need it, otherwise this is it. It ain't much, but I really only sleep here, so it serves its purpose."

Steel shrugs his arms out of his cut and folds it neatly, setting it on the dresser. He grabs his shirt from the back of his neck and pulls it over his head. Fuck, that's hot. He has defined abs and a sinful Adonis belt I want to explore. His pants go next until he's left in nothing but his boxer briefs. My eyes bounce between his noticeably huge package and his face. I'm not sure where to look. My cheeks grow hot as I realize I'm acting like a teenage boy.

"I usually sleep in just these, but I can slip some sweats on if you're uncomfortable."

"No. You're fine. I don't want to inconvenience you more than I have," I murmur. He growls as he steps toward me until he has me pressed against the door.

"You could never inconvenience me, Ignatius. I prayed you'd stay the night. Now get in bed so I can hold you while we sleep."

My cock jumps at his words, but he didn't say fuck, he said hold. Being brazen, I pull off my pants along with the sweater and leave them in a pile on the floor before crawling into bed.

The mattress dips as he climbs in beside me. He pulls the blanket over us, removes my glasses, then leans over and sets them on the nightstand beside me.

"What about the light?" I ask, wincing at how lame that sounded.

Steel claps twice and the room goes dark. I chuckle at him having a clap-on light, like an old lady. "I got fed up with gettin' comfortable and noticin' the light was still on. Problem solved. Now roll over so I can hold you." He wraps an arm around me, pulling my body tight to his and I close my eyes, willing my now fully hard cock to go away and not make things awkward.

We lie like that for a while, just cuddling. I love how safe I feel in his arms.

"Can I ask you something, Iggie?" Steel breaks the silence.

"Yeah," I whisper.

"When I told you I've fucked Kiki and let Gabe suck me off, you only said okay. Are you sure there isn't more? That you're not upset that I'm still friendly with them or around them daily?" His voice is breathy and nervous.

"You said you weren't sleeping with them now and haven't since we met. Despite the short time we've known each other, I feel like I can trust you. Do you plan on sleeping with them?"

"Fuck no!" His arm tightens around me.

"We all have pasts, Steel. I can't be mad at you for being with someone before me. Plus, I like Kiki and Gabe, and from what I gather, there are no feelings involved with them and your members. It's more like a job without cash pay." I chuckle.

He places an open mouth kiss on my shoulder blades and the back of my neck. His lips touch every inch of skin he can reach with the position we're in. I roll slightly so when I turn my head, my lips can find his. We kiss, slow and deep, our tongues savoring one another.

As we continue, one of his hands trails down my body to my briefs, and he rubs his hand over my bulge. Our movements turn more urgent, our tongues tangling as I chase his hand with my hips, wanting more.

His body shifts so he's above me, looking down. I'm flat on my back, staring into his brown eyes. His lips find mine again, but only for a second before he trails them down my chest to my belly and then to the waistband of my briefs. Taking a hold on each side, he gives a gentle tug and I lift my hips so he can slip them down my legs and throw them onto the floor behind him.

Instantly, his mouth wraps around my crown, and he takes me to the back of his throat. I moan and he pulls back, only to bob up and down on my cock. His forehead touches my pelvis with each movement.

With his eyes locked on mine, he pulls off my dick, only to replace his mouth with his hand. He jerks me as his tongue flicks at my slit, collecting all the pre-cum that is leaking from my tip.

"Fuck, Steel," I gasp, my hips arching slightly off the bed.

He smiles up at me and releases my dick from his sinful touch. "You wanna come, Ignatius?"

"Yes," I cry. "Please."

"Please what?" he teases me.

"Please, fuck me. I want us to come together," I admit.

He chuckles, but then growls. "Earn it."

Looking at him, I blink and raise a brow, not quite knowing what he means. "What? How?"

"Wrap those pouty lips around my cock, baby. I want to know what your throat feels like." He scoots to the end of the bed and pushes his boxer briefs down his thighs. His huge dick springs free and my mouth waters at how pretty his cock is.

I bite my bottom lip as I get up on all fours and crawl slowly over to him. When I reach him, I wrap my hand around the base of his shaft, positioning his tip at my lips. Painfully slow, I part them and take him farther into my mouth. I feel his mushroom head hit the back of my throat, silently thanking whoever's upstairs that I don't have a gag reflex, and then swallow around him.

"Fuck. Yes," he cries, his voice thick and husky. I swirl my tongue around him as I move up and down his dick. He lightly touches my hair without guiding or pressuring me. Just sets his hand there and watches me with lustful eyes as I suck him.

I let him pop from my mouth and trail my lips down his shaft, licking and nipping at his tender flesh.

"I need to fuck you," he breathes.

He cups my chin in his hand to guide me as I straighten up on my knees. Our eyes are level and I part my lips slightly as he leans forward to kiss me. Except he doesn't. A sharp slap echoes through the room as his hand comes down on my bare ass cheek.

"Don't be a brat. Brats use teeth, but brats also don't get to come." There's a grit in his voice that demands I submit. "Now lie back and put your head on the pillow." I hesitate until he presses his hand on my chest. My arms fall behind me to catch my balance as he gently, but firmly, nudges me backward. As he crawls forward, I scramble to straighten my legs.

Once my head rests on the pillow, he leans across me and opens the nightstand drawer. "Just in case," he says as he holds up a small bottle of lube. With all the pre-cum covering my dick and hole, I doubt there'll be a need for any. He lowers his head to kiss me, and before I can respond, his lips are trailing kisses along my jaw to my ear.

"Roll to your right a little," Steel whispers, and I do as he says while he moves behind me. When he tugs me back to him, he grips my left thigh and pulls it over his to spread my legs apart and places his tip at my entrance.

A mewl leaves me as he pushes past the first ring of muscles.

"Shhhh, baby, it's okay. You feel so good."

A strangled gasp escapes as he plunges the rest of the way in. "So fucking tight."

After pulling back halfway and surging back in, he adjusts our positions, sliding his right leg under mine, spreading my legs even further, until my right asscheek is almost on top of his thigh.

He forcefully thrusts once more, fully seating himself in my ass. I moan in response to the overwhelming sensation of fullness. My legs fall wide open as he begins to pound into me. His left hand once again circles my dick and jerks me in time with his thrusts.

I'm a mess, panting and groaning as he fucks me. We only have to add lube once, and his speed never falters as he keeps me right at the edge, my orgasm just out of reach. "Oh, fuck me," I grunt.

"You look sexy as hell wrapped around my dick, Ignatius." He picks up the pace, fucking me harder and faster, if that is even possible. "Come, Iggie. Come while my fat cock fills you up."

I detonate. My hips arch off the bed as my eyes squeeze shut and rope after rope of hot cum covers my belly and his hand.

He releases my dick and swipes his fingers through my cum before holding them up to my mouth. I look up at him as I wrap my lips around his thick fingers, swirling my tongue around them.

Steel freezes and his dick twitches inside of me. His teeth dig into his bottom lip before he roars his release, and I feel his hot seed filling my ass, coating my inner walls.

He pulls out and I can feel his cum following him, dripping down my ass. "God damn, baby. That was even better than I imagined."

"Same," I whisper.

Steel gets up and heads to the bathroom, returning with a warm washcloth, and cleans me up. He tosses it in the hamper by the door and crawls back into bed, holding me.

I lie there with a smile on my face and a pleasant soreness in my ass. As I close my eyes, ready to sleep and hoping this high is still there in the morning, a thought hits me, causing my eyes to fly open.

Fuck! Holy shit! We didn't use a condom. I've never been so careless.

"Steel!" I panic.

"Yeah, baby?"

"We didn't use a condom," I tell him and I feel his body tense up behind me.

"Fuck," he hisses. "I get tested every few months. We all do since, umm, ya know, the whores and all that. I'm clear."

"Okay. Yeah, that's good," I stutter. "I'm clear too. I've never not used a condom."

"I'm sorry, baby. I got caught up in the moment. From now on, I'll use one. I promise. And I'll get tested again if you want." He places a soft peck on my neck.

"You think there's gonna be a next time?" I tease.

"Baby, I'd live in your tight ass if I could. It was heaven."

I'm not sure what to say to such a compliment. So I close my eyes and snuggle closer into him, drifting off into a deep sleep.

# *fifteen*

## STEEL

I WAKE UP, and I can't stop the smile from spreading across my face. Iggie's head is on my chest, his legs tangled with mine. I'm so glad he stayed the night. As I remember our night of passion, I shut my eyes and revel in the pure happiness this man embodies, easing me back into a peaceful slumber.

A while later, the need to pee forces me awake. I panic when I don't feel Iggie beside me. Reaching out, the bed is still warm, so he couldn't have left the bed that long ago. Where did he get off to? The sound of water turning on in the shower answers my question.

I slide out of bed and head to the bathroom. As soon as I open the door, I'm met with a wall of steam, and through the glass wall of the shower, I see Iggie. Wasting no time, I quickly relieve myself and hastily step in behind my man. He doesn't acknowledge me, so I decide to make sure he knows he's no longer alone. My arms encircle him from behind, and I press a tender kiss to his exposed shoulder, savoring the moment. "Morning, baby."

"Morning." He turns to face me and I lean down to press my lips to his.

"How do you feel this mornin'? I was a little rough with you last night," I ask, my words tinged with remorse as I remember how I treated him. I intended to be soft and slow with him, so he knew I'd never hurt him, but I lost myself in the moment.

"It was amazing. I'm a bit sore. But nothing that would deter me from doing it again," he teases, looking up at me as water beads on his thick lashes.

"I wanted to take it slow and show you I'm not that rough and violent man you saw in the alley. At least not with you."

"Steel. You don't have to prove that to me. I'm seeing it all on my own."

I crash my lips to his and kiss him like he's the oxygen I need to breathe.

He whimpers when I bite his bottom lip, and I smile into our kiss. Picking him up, I press him against the shower wall, forcing a gasp to leave him. I move one of my legs between his to help hold him up, positioning us so our cocks are at the same level.

Wrapping my hands around both, I squeeze them together and stroke, creating a pleasurable friction. Our eyes connect, and I maintain the contact, skillfully pleasuring both of us with every stroke. "Fuck," I whisper, enjoying how good we feel together.

"I'm gonna come, Steel," Iggie pants, his eyes closed and his head leaning back against the wall.

"I'm almost there, baby. Don't come. Not without me," I growl.

"Oh, God," he murmurs.

I pick up the pace, not wanting to push him over the edge without me, but also pushing toward my release. My hand moves up and down our shafts furiously and when I get to the tips, I swirl it around our crowns.

I groan, "Come, Iggie."

Like I hit the go button, he cries out, his body quivering as I continue to jerk him through it. The first wave of his cum barely coats my cock before my own is erupting, mixing with his. Thrusting my hips slightly, I shoot cum all over my hand and our dicks.

"I'm gonna need to nap for a while after this sleepover," Iggie teases, and I chuckle.

"You can nap in my bed while I'm in church. Shouldn't take long but I have to go. I can have Kiki bring some breakfast to the room for you."

"Can't I go to church with you or are you not ready for that step yet?" he asks, and I can see the hurt in his eyes, like I'm trying to keep him a secret.

"No, baby. It's not church like that. Church is what we call club meetings. They're for members only. Where we discuss business."

He covers his face with his hands. "Ugh, I'm such an idiot. I don't know any of these club terms. First the old ladies and now this."

"Hey." I pull his hands away from his face. "I think it's sexy that you don't know everything about my world. It means the world hasn't totally tainted you yet. It also means that you're still too good for me, but I'm goin' to keep you, anyway."

Leaving Iggie in the room in bed while I handle club business is maybe the stupidest thing I've done. I could be balls deep in his ass or have my mouth on his long, curved cock. Instead, I'm going to go hold church with my brothers about the run.

When I enter the main room of the clubhouse, I see Kiki sitting on the couch reading a book. "Hey, Kiki, any chance you wanna do me a huge favor?"

"Sure." She closes her book and looks up at me. "Not like I really have a choice though, Prez."

I glare at her cause she knows there's always a choice. While I expect her to tell me no if I ask too much of her, she also knows I respect her as a person. I'll always ask because I want her to know she has the right to say no.

Being a club whore isn't about just a warm hole to sink into. At least not for Hell's Mayhem. They do a service for the members of this club by choice, in exchange for protection. So, I want them all to know they have autonomy over their bodies. We don't force; we don't rape. It's about as lawful as we get.

"Can you take Iggie some breakfast? I don't want him wanderin' the clubhouse without me and we have church, so I don't have time to do it myself."

"I wonder what the two of you could've been doing that'd have you running short on time?" She playfully taps her finger on her chin like she's thinking.

"Smartass," I grumble as I turn to head back to the room we hold church in.

"You love me anyway!" she hollers to my back.

"SHUT THE FUCK UP!" I bang my gavel on the table. These assholes have been chatty ever since they got in here and I got shit to do. My eyes meet Venom's and I nod, giving him the go-ahead to intervene.

"Next person who talks catches a bullet!" he shouts. The club quiets down. No one wants to deal with our enforcer and his brand of crazy. We voted him into the position for a reason.

"Alright, now that I got your attention, we need to talk about the Michaelov run. It was a fuckin' shit show from start to finish, and I'm not happy. Between the Hellhounds' interruption and Michaelov insisting we shorted him, it was a mess, plain and simple," I tell them, my eyes moving around the room, looking at each of them.

"Now, there ain't no way around it. We have a rat. If ya got any sense, you'll come clean now so we can shoot ya and be done with it. If not, when we find ya, and I promise we will, it will be a long and slow death."

"How do you know it's not that new piece of ass you shacked up with last night?" Combo calls from his seat in the back.

My temple pulses and my nostrils flare. How fucking dare he bring Ignatius into this. "You keep him fuckin' out of this. You damn well know that the run we did before this one was fucked, too. I didn't even know him yet."

"Sti—" He stops short of finishing the first word of whatever bullshit he was about to spew. Having the cold barrel of a gun pressed against your temple will do that to a man.

"I believe our president told you to keep his new friend out of this, Combo. Now, be a good boy and listen," Venom hisses.

Like the pussy he is, Combo shuts his mouth but huffs as he crosses his arms over his chest. "You'd be wise to heed Venom's warning. Next time you disrespect me, you'll pay for it. I'm still the goddamn president of this club." I wish he'd give me a reason to kick him out. He hasn't agreed with anything I've done since becoming president. Every chance he gets, he disagrees or votes against the rest of us just so we know he's not happy. He hates the male whores. And although he won't say it out loud, he doesn't like anyone who isn't straight.

He's older than most of us in the club and was a member before I was. He was even up for Prez alongside me. But I won the vote in a sweep and he's been a fuck ever since.

"Next order of business is gettin' the RPGs to Michaelov. I'll be choosin' a handful of men to make the drop and you won't know if ya ain't chosen. I'm not havin' another run fucked ten ways to Sunday by the Hellhounds."

"That's not how we do runs. It's club business and we should be able to know when shit happens. It's our money too!" Pepper shouts.

"I don't give a fuck if that's how we do business, usually. We're doin' this my way now 'cause we have a fuckin' rat. Now, unless you wanna confess that it's you, Pepper, sit your ass down and let your officers handle this as we choose. This is a democracy for the most part, but not when it comes to the safety of our club and members. Not when it fucks with our money. Then this becomes a dictatorship and I am your fuckin' king, do you hear me?" I stand from the table, leaning on my hands so I hover over the top.

He looks sheepishly at the floor, not saying a word. "Now, unless anyone else wants to piss me off today, church is adjourned." I bang the gavel on the table before tossing it down roughly and storming toward the door. The fucking disrespect those two think they can show has me about at my limit. It's time they realize I'm done with their shit.

Stopping short at the door, I turn back and whistle loudly, causing the room to go silent. "Pepper and Combo, since you think you can treat me like shit in church, forgetting that I'm president and will always do what is best for this club, you two can be on shit duty for the next month. The whores won't be cleaning the bathrooms. You two will. If ya got anything to say, you can take it up with Venom. I see a prospect cleaning the shitter, you'll be talking to Venom. Are we clear?" I don't let them answer, and instead, leave the room and head down the hall to where I know Iggie is waiting.

I throw open the door to my room and Iggie jumps, squealing as his eyes widen. "Shit, you scared me."

"Sorry, babe." I close the door and lean against it, releasing a sigh.

"Everything okay?"

"Church was rough. Not everyone in this club likes the choices I've made and how I've broadened our horizons. Pisses me off," I tell him.

"Like what?"

"Can't talk to you about club business, baby. But what I can say is that there are a few who aren't open to anything that ain't straight. Ya, feel me?" I tell him that bit, and that's as far as I'm willing to go. I may be the president, but I still have rules, and club business is club business.

"Well, I don't know much about motorcycle clubs, but I do know about not being accepted. I will say I'm kinda surprised that you have guys who are okay with you breaking laws but not liking men? Seems backward." He shrugs and I nod along with him because when you simplify it like that, it is pretty fucking stupid.

"It is what it is. I'm still their president and it was a majority rule so they can deal with it or get out. Now, did Kiki bring you something to eat?"

"Yeah, she did. Brought me pancakes, bacon, and eggs.

We chatted while I ate. I like her a lot. She's fun," he tells me.

"Just what I need, you two becomin' pals." I roll my eyes. "Come on. I should get you home." I hold out my hand and he crosses the room, taking it.

I walk him outside, and once we're inside my cage, I fire up the engine and pull out of the compound. The drive is silent minus the music coming from the radio. We hold hands and just enjoy the ride.

When I pull up in front of his house, I get out and hurry around to his side, opening his door. He gets out and promptly intertwines our hands as I walk him to his door. This is some eighties movie shit, and I kinda like it.

We're standing on his front steps and I'm fighting the urge to not throw him over my shoulder and drag him back to the clubhouse. I'm not ready to part from him yet. It's not healthy and I know that, but I can't help it. I never claimed to be sane.

"I had a good time, Steel. Thank you," he murmurs, turning to look at me.

"I did too. Thanks for agreein' to come with me and for stayin' the night." While this mushy shit ain't me, I know that if I want to keep Iggie, I'm going to have to not be so pushy.

I lean in and wrap my lips delicately around his bottom one.

Iggie pulls me close, his arms encircling me as he leans into my body. Losing the sense I had just two minutes ago, I break our kiss, drop to my knees in front of him, and grab his hands.

"Ignatius, I am utterly obsessed with you. While I'm not usually an askin' man, I'm tryin' to be for you. I want this, us, to be different. It's a little backward after last night, but I want you to be mine. Please, I'm on my knees beggin'. I'll treat you so good." I look up and he's smirking as he watches me through his thick-rimmed glasses.

"What's funny?" I growl, not liking that he's laughing when I'm pouring my soul out to him.

"I can't believe I have a big burly biker on his knees for me in front of my house." He chuckles.

I stand up, pushing him backward till his back hits his front door. "That doesn't answer my question, baby." I kiss his temple, his nose, his lips, and his neck.

"I'm yours," he whispers. "Please, don't hurt me, Steel."

"Oh, I'm goin' to hurt you, baby. But only in ways you'll like," I murmur as I crash my lips to his.

# *sixteen*

## IGNATIUS

THINGS HAVE BEEN GOING WELL with Steel. Better than well, actually. If I wasn't living it myself, I'd probably think it was a dream. He's a perfect gentleman when we're together, minus when we go to bed, but still I have no complaints. I knew I liked being bossed around and degraded in the bedroom, but when Steel does it... it's a whole nother level of sexy.

Christmas is next week, and tonight we're going to the movies. Steel found out I'm a fan of The Hunger Games, so we're going to see the new one. I'm standing in front of my closet, stressing about what to wear. Looking at my watch, I realize he should be here any minute. Shit! It's a movie so I'm leaning toward casual but it's also a date and I want to look good, so maybe jeans. Dammit, why am I acting like a teenage girl going on her first-ever date?

The movie is just shy of three hours, so I should probably dress for comfort. I slide on a pair of gray joggers and a dark green fitted T-shirt before heading to the bathroom. As soon as the light floods the room, the doorbell rings, making me quickly spray some cologne and rush to answer. I fling the door open with a little too much enthusiasm and Steel flashes me a half smile. Grabbing him, I pull him into me and taste the sweetness of his lips.

He wraps a hand around the back of my head, holding me to him as we kiss feverishly. When he pulls away, I fake pout. "Don't be a brat. You just saw me two days ago. We don't wanna be late for the show, do we?"

"We could just stay here and go to my bedroom," I tease, wagging my brows.

He groans, tilting his head back, and looking at the sky. "You're a temptation. But I promised my man a movie and a movie he shall get."

Sighing, I reluctantly join him on the front steps and close the door, ensuring it's locked. We walk toward his truck, and as usual, he opens the door and buckles my seatbelt. Once he knows I'm safely in, he climbs behind the wheel and we're off.

When we walk through the theater door, the smell of popcorn fills the air, causing my stomach to growl. Steel looks at me with a raised brow. "Are you hungry?"

"Yeah. We should get snacks. The movie is long. We'll need sustenance."

"Two tickets to Hunger Games," Steel tells the clerk and sets his card on the counter. After she hands it back, I drag him to the concession counter. "Get whatever you want and I'll just share with you," he tells me.

"Fine, but you'll have to get your own nachos. They're my favorite and I'm greedy."

He erupts into a deep belly laugh, and the concession worker looks at us as though we're completely mad.

"Can I get a large popcorn, a box of Mike and Ikes, a large Cherry Dr Pepper, and nachos?"

"How do you want the nachos?" the worker asks dully.

"Meat, cheese, jalapenos. Give me everything you got."

"Anything else?"

"Yeah, I'll have nachos too, make them the same," Steel tells him. The kid gives us our total, and Steel hands over his card again. We step to the side so others can order while eagerly awaiting our goodies.

Steel shifts his weight from one foot to the other, glancing at me. "Got any big plans for Christmas?"

I smile, considering for a moment. "Not anything extravagant. Probably just spending time with family, you know, the usual." Steel nods, his eyes lighting up with understanding.

"Excuse me, your order is ready!" the teen calls, setting our goodies on the counter.

Arms loaded down, we head to our theater. When we walk through the door, Steel smiles and leads the way to the seats at the very top. "Best view in the house."

I pick the one in the center of the row and he sits down next to me. Right away, he lifts the armrest and pulls me closer. Snuggling into him, I grab my nachos and begin to eat as the lights dim and the opening credits start.

———++++💀++++———

THE MOVIE WAS AMAZING, but long. I had to refill our drinks twice and Steel got more popcorn. Now we have some left in the tub to take home and enjoy later. Even a few days old, movie theater popcorn is the reigning champion.

As he holds the door, I hastily climb into the truck and buckle myself before he can.

"That's my job, Iggie," he growls softly, his low voice sending shivers down my spine as he firmly guides my chin, forcing our eyes to meet.

"Oops. I guess I'm just feeling a bit antsy to get back," I tease, my lip caught between my teeth.

"You're gonna pay for that, baby," he whispers, his warm breath tickling my ear. He shuts my door with a soft click and moves gracefully to the other side of the truck.

"It's Friday, so the clubhouse is gonna be wild. I was thinkin' we'd stay at yours tonight. That work?"

"What's the occasion that they're partying about tonight?" I ask.

"It's one of the brother's birthday. They'll go a little harder than normal."

"Why'd you pick tonight for the movie if you had a birthday party to attend?" I push my glasses up as my nose wrinkles.

"Tonight was the last night it was in theaters and you wanted to see it. Not a big deal. Zero knows the score. He's cool with where I am." He smiles with a dismissive wave of his hand.

He parks the truck on the curb in front of my house. A shiver runs down my spine from the chill in the air as we make the short walk to my door. Despite my shivering, I manage to get the key in the hole and open the door.

Hurrying to shrug off my coat, I throw it over the back of the couch and sprint down the hall to my bedroom. I shed my shoes, socks, and shirt, then eagerly jump onto the bed, savoring the warmth of my blankets. A low chuckle follows a few minutes later as the light flips on.

"A little cold, were we? Don't worry, I locked up." Steel smirks and confidently strips down, leaving him in nothing but his snug-fitting boxer briefs.

"Just get into the bed and warm me up," I playfully snap.

Before I can blink, he lunges onto the bed, landing on top of me. His face hovers just inches above mine. I can't help but study him, anticipating his next move. His mouth lands on mine, his tongue demanding immediate entry, and I open, letting him in. Our kiss becomes a battleground as our tongues intertwine in a fight for dominance. He pulls away, but then bites my lip, making me gasp from the sting.

"Baby, you're addictive," he murmurs against my lips.

"You make me feel like no one else," I admit. I don't think I'm in love... yet, but I do think I could easily get there. Steel makes me feel cherished, sexy, and important. He always listens intently when I talk, no matter the topic or how long I drone on about it. He's always asking about work, what shows I'm watching, or what I listen to in the car. It's like I'm the most fascinating thing to him—that feeling is intoxicating.

"I better be the only one makin' you feel anything," he grumbles. "Especially here." He reaches under the blanket and grabs my cock, squeezing it firmly.

I slap his shoulder playfully. "Not like that, you know what I mean." I laugh.

"I know, baby. You make me feel things too. Not sure what they are, but I can't get enough. I want you with me all the time." He kisses me again as his hand slowly slides under the waistband of my joggers and gives my dick a long, hard stroke.

We remain in that moment; him hovering over me as we

kiss sensually, jerking me tortuously slow. I break the kiss and inhale sharply, feeling my heart race as a wave of desire washes over me.

"More," I whisper.

"You weren't a good boy when we left the movies. Buckled yourself up, not lettin' me do my job. It's time to pay for your sins," he murmurs.

This is what I'm talking about; the sound of him saying "good boy" sends a tingling sensation down my spine, and the thought of punishment has me burning with desire. Whatever the punishment is, I know I'm going to enjoy it. In fact, I'm looking forward to it. I will revel in whatever he dishes out.

+++++💀+++++

## STEEL

"Get up and strip," I command him, his eyes gleaming with excitement. "I want you naked and ready to sit on my face." His body shivers involuntarily, and I grin, loving that I evoke such emotions in him.

We've not done this yet. I've fucked him a few times and we've sucked each other off a lot. But I've yet to eat his ass. The day has come. I want him a quivering fucking mess before he gets his release. Serves him right for taking the right to buckle his belt from me.

He stands from the bed, the sound of fabric rustling as he slowly pushes his pants and briefs down his legs before stepping out of them. Carefully, he places his glasses on the nightstand and eases back onto the bed, taking a deep breath. He's apprehensive and I'm curious as to why. In an attempt to respect his boundaries, I swiftly grab hold of his leg, stopping him from straddling my chest. "What's wrong, Iggie? If you don't wanna do this, we don't have to. It's a big step, more intimate."

I feel his body tense. "I want to. It's just I-I-I've never done this before." His voice shakes as he avoids eye contact.

"You've only ever been with men and no one has ever given you a rim job?"

"No. None of them were willing to do that. They'd fuck me or jerk me off. That's about it. Maybe a few gave oral. I never finished though," he whispers.

My hand lands on his pale ass cheek, the sound echoing throughout the room. "Why didn't you tell me I was the first to swallow your cum?"

"I don't know. It didn't seem like a big deal. Are you mad?"

"No!" I tell him quickly. "Knowin' I'm the only one who knows what your release tastes like is sexy as hell. You can say stop at any time and I will, no questions asked. But baby, I really wanna be the first to fuck you with my tongue, too. Please let me," I plead.

The thought of being the sole recipient of his climax, feeling it slide down my throat and settle in my belly, is pushing me toward the brink of ecstasy. I'm ready to beg him to let me eat his tight little hole. I might explode like a horny teen before I even get to sink inside of him.

"Okay," he breathes. Slowly, he positions his thighs on either side of my broad shoulders. He grabs my legs and braces his weight on his arms.

Not wanting him to second guess this, I move my hands to the top of his ass cheeks, spreading him open and guiding him closer to my face. When he's where I want him, I slide my tongue from his taint to his hole in one firm stroke.

He inhales sharply and I chuckle. "Just wait, baby. I'm gonna make you feel so good."

My tongue glides over his tight hole, tracing circles along the rim, teasing him with every movement. Using his moans as motivation, I take it a step further and push it into his hole a few times. The tight muscle prevents me from entering fully, but I know it's enough that he can feel it and it's good. Continuing my exploration, I lick over his perineum and shove my finger into his tight opening.

"Oh god," he cries.

"No god here, Iggie. We're sinnin' in the most beautiful way."

I fuck him with my finger as my tongue moves along his crack, devouring every inch of flesh. He shivers and I know he's getting close. But I want him teetering on the cliff, ready to dive off after what he did earlier. So I remove my finger and once again attack his star with my tongue.

I move stealthily, seizing his dick with my right hand and expertly pumping his shaft. He's dripping pre-cum like a waterfall and I love that I'm the reason. I'm the one making him feel this good. Me. No one else.

As his body stiffens and his member throbs in my hand, I know he's right where I want him. I stop and sink my teeth into his fleshy thigh. "No! Oh god, please don't stop. I was about to come."

"Bad boys don't get to come. And god couldn't make you feel as good as I can baby. Now be a good boy and wrap your lips around my dick. I don't want to hear ya whinin'."

He whimpers but doesn't say a word, obeying me like I need. His head dips and his lips press against my tip. Slowly, he opens them and glides down my length. When I hit the back of his throat, he swallows.

"Fuck, baby," I groan at the feel of his warm, wet mouth.

Pulling himself back, he moves up and down my shaft at a steady rhythm, sucking me like a hoover. As he places his left hand under my thigh, his fingers begin to explore, creating a sensation of gentle circular motions on my taint. He feels so fucking good. I thrust my hips up, forcing him to take more of me. He gags, which surprises me since he deep-throats me with no problem. I must have caught him off guard.

It doesn't stop him, though, he continues to take everything I give him. His pre-cum drips onto my neck, and I know he's ready for my next surprise.

I wrap an arm around his waist and gently tug him closer, allowing me to tilt my head back and take him into my mouth. I swirl my tongue around his red angry head and he hisses. Dragging my teeth down his tip, I open wide and take him in as far as I can at this angle. I devour him with an unsated hunger, my mouth working relentlessly to pleasure him.

It doesn't take Iggie long to be on the edge of release once more. I take him deep into my mouth and when he touches my throat, instead of backing off, I pull him closer. My gagging has him pulling his hips back, but I slap his ass and growl at him for taking my snack away. I repeat the motion repeatedly, guiding his hips so that he's roughly fucking my face.

His dick pulses against my tongue, and I know he's about to let go. I swirl my tongue around his tip and play with his slit and he explodes. His cum burst from him in thick ropes, filling my mouth with his delicious flavor. I swallow everything minus a little surprise I want to give him. A loud moan echoes through the room—*Jesus, fuck! He's keeping my dick in his mouth as he comes.* The vibration and tender bites on my shaft push me to my breaking point.

I groan as my orgasm hits me in full force. With my thighs tensing and my eyes squeezed shut, I empty myself into his mouth. "Don't swallow all of it," I demand. He takes everything I give him and then rolls off to the side, breathing hard with a dopey grin. "Come here, baby," I call.

He repositions, so he's lying with his head by mine. I prop myself up on one arm and I kiss him dirty. As soon as his lips part, I shove the cum from my mouth into his. He tenses for a minute, then whines and kisses me back eagerly. Swirling my tongue around, I gather the cum and pull it back into my mouth and swallow.

I pull back, breaking the kiss and he's looking at me wide-eyed, pupils blown with desire. "We taste delicious together, baby. Don't you think?"

"Yeah," he whispers.

"You okay?" I ask, checking in on him. If no one ever sucked him off to completion, I know for a fact he's never swapped cum while kissing.

"I'm perfect. You just keep surprising me. You're giving me a lot of firsts. I feel like a virgin with all the dirty shit you do." His cheeks pinken as he laughs.

"Is that a bad thing? I enjoy dirtying you up and I really like knowin' I'm givin' you so many firsts," I reply, my voice low and gravelly.

"No. I haven't found one bad thing about you yet, Steel. You've been just as you promised. I should have believed you sooner when you told me MC Steel and my boyfriend Steel would be separate."

I give him a quick peck and then roll from the bed, heading to the bathroom to get a washcloth to clean us up.

When I get back, Iggie is dozing already, so I softly wipe away the evidence of our fucking, doing the same to myself before throwing the cloth in the hamper and climbing into the bed.

Pulling the blanket over us, I pull him close and chuckle when he snuggles into me, searching for my warmth. I fall asleep like that with my man in my arms and a content smile on my face.

I'm praying the other shoe doesn't drop.

## seventeen

### STEEL

I HATE TO LEAVE IGGIE, but I have to head back to the clubhouse and get some shit done. The order for Michaelov has come in and we're meeting to give him the RPG 18s. I also want to talk with my officers about Pepper and Combo because their defiance and disrespect in church last time was unacceptable. Initially, I let them off with only toilet duty since I was eager to be with my man, but now I'm livid about my decision.

I told the whores to cut them off, and I have Hawk looking into them more. Their comings and goings, spending, and phone records are under investigation. If either is our leak, we'll know, and they'll get exactly what's coming to them.

I gradually ease myself out of bed and gently pull the blanket back up to cover Iggie. Leaning down, I plant a kiss on his temple. I quickly slip back into my clothes and make my way to his kitchen, searching for a pen and paper to leave him a note. It's no surprise that Iggie has a notepad and pen on his island. I grab it and flip to the next empty page.

> Iggie,
> I had to go do some club stuff. I'll text you when I'm back and you can come to the clubhouse if you want. Sorry, I didn't wake you. It was early, and you looked sexy as hell sleeping.
> Steel

I RIP the page from the pad and set it on the counter where he'll see it. Putting everything back how I found it, I see the page in front of the one I just ripped out is the information on the family Iggie had his work adopt. The line for volunteers to help decorate and deliver the tree is empty. He's circled the space a few times and doodled a sad face.

How fucking dare none of the hundreds of employees at Howards sign up to help him for a few hours on two different days. It would take like an hour to decorate the tree and less than that to deliver it. No way is he going to do it on his own. Maybe a few of the brothers and I can show up and help him.

I pull out my phone and search for when and where this tree thing is taking place. Decorating is tomorrow night at seven at the community center. Then Sunday morning is delivery. We can make that work; I quickly jot the club's name down.

Making sure to lock up behind me, I jog to my cage. Not bothering to buckle up, I crank the ignition, and as soon as she starts, I hit the gas. I'm on a roll breaking traffic laws this morning.

I successfully reach the clubhouse without getting a ticket or having an accident. I park by the entrance and make my way inside. Everyone is still passed out from the night before, which is perfect since this is a need-to-know run. Making my way to the office, I lock the door before taking a seat. I need to call my officers. I know I can trust them, so they're the only ones going on this run.

One by one, I let them know to get their asses to my office right now. I may have woken a few of them up, but that's their issue. Remembering I locked the door out of habit, I begin to stand, only to hear a key in the lock.

Pistol's here, and he's the only one I trust with a key to my office. He flings the door open and glares at me. "This better be good, asshole. I was sound asleep. You know it's seven in the mornin', right?"

"You're lucky you've been my best friend since we were in diapers or I'd shoot you for the way you talk to me," I tell him, rolling my eyes at his dramatics. He's always enjoyed his beauty sleep.

"Fuck you. You'd miss me too much. Plus, I wouldn't look good with a bullet hole in my skull." He sits in the seat next to mine and pulls his phone out, typing something before he puts it back in his pocket.

Hawk and Trucker stumble in next, their clothes wrinkled and half-buttoned. My guess is they spent the night together again sharing Gabe. I swear, the three of them are going to press the "no turning whores into old men" rule someday.

"What's up, Prez?" Trucker asks as he shuts the door behind them before bending down to fix his boot.

"When everyone gets here, I'll tell ya. Then I don't have to repeat myself."

Zero bursts into the room, forcefully pushing Viper inside, and slams the door shut with a resounding thud.

"What the hell are you two doin'?" I growl. Zero not only slammed the door, potentially waking everyone up, but he also must have a death wish to be messing with Viper.

"I found this asshole passed out in the hall outside my door. I don't know what the fuck he was doin', but I don't think he slept much." Zero sighs.

Looking at Viper, I raise my eyebrows and cross my arms.

"Don't get your panties in a twist, Zero. I wasn't spyin' on you. Combo is in the room across from yours and is up to no good. I don't know what it is yet, but I'll figure it out." Viper cracks his knuckles, glaring at Zero.

"Alright, but at least warn a guy next time. I about ate shit trippin' over your huge ass in the hall. You'd make a shitty spy, so it's a good thing you're a psycho killer."

"Didn't mean to fall asleep. And fuck you, I'm not a killer. I'm an artist. Do you know how difficult it is to cause maximum pain without immediate death? Or how to hurt them so they scream so pretty? That's art, fucker," Viper says through clenched teeth.

"Alright, knock it off." I stand from my chair so they know I'm fucking serious. "I called you here for a reason. Michaelov's RPGs are in and we're gonna go pick them up and deliver them to him. Just us. No one else knows."

"When do we leave?" Trucker asks.

"Right now. We can stop and get some grub on the way."

Nodding their heads, I reach into a drawer and retrieve walkie-talkies, ensuring each one is in working order.

I round my desk and open the door, holding it for them and handing them one as they pass me.

We make it outside to our cages and onto the road in minutes. Snow covers the ground, taking away the option of having anyone on bikes, which I hope isn't an omen of something bad to come. I can't wait for winter to be over so we can ride our bikes full-time again.

"Listen up," I speak into the walkie-talkie, my voice crackling through the static. "We're about to reach a diner up ahead. Let's pull in for a quick bite."

Static fills the air for a moment before the familiar voice of Trucker comes through. "Copy that, boss."

Pulling into the Farmstand Diner, we head toward a booth in the back. I wanna be able to see everything and everyone who comes and goes from this place. Hell, I wanna be able to see who drives past. I can't wait to get some food in my stomach. Last night, I worked up an appetite.

This place is a ways out of town and we've made good time so far, so I feel comfortable stopping. We should still make it to the pickup point with time to spare.

A sweet and timid server approaches us, carrying a pot of hot coffee. I quickly notice her hand trembling as she pours. My eyes shift across the table to Pistol, and he's arching an eyebrow in her direction. As she fills my cup, I gently place my hand on top of hers, causing her to gasp and lock eyes with me. "You alright there, baby girl? You're shakin' like a washin' machine on the spin cycle."

"Yeah. Ummm, I'm fine," she says with a slight tremor.

"Are you sure?" Pistol interjects, raising a brow at her. "We can help you if you're being hurt or someone is here who shouldn't be."

She tucks a strand of blonde hair behind her ear, gives us a small smile, and heads back to the kitchen.

"That was weird," I tell the guys, dumping some creamer in my coffee.

"Maybe she was just nervous 'cause six scary bikers just walked into a mom-and-pop shop." Trucker shrugs.

"I don't know. This place is on the highway, so you'd think she'd be used to getting all kinds of people in here. Just stay alert," I tell them.

The waitress comes back and this time I look at her nametag; Marni. As she reaches into her apron, she pulls out her pad and gives us a tight-lipped smile. "W-w-what can I g-g-get for you?"

"Marni is it?" She jumps when I say her name, quickly turning to look at the window to the kitchen before turning back to us.

"Yeah," she nods.

"Cut the shit. Somethin' ain't right, and if shit's about to go down, let us at least get these people out of here. What do you know?"

"Nothing. I don't know anything. My foster dad's brother is the cook here. He begged my foster dad to make me work here. He's not a good man. I'll be eighteen in two weeks, and then I'm out of here." She rattles off while pretending to write on her order pad.

"What's that got to do with us?"

"Randy has been trying to get in with the Hellhounds MC and, well, when you guys walked in, he called someone and told them you were here. Then told me to keep you here no matter what it took." She sucks her bottom lip between her teeth.

"Okay, go back to the kitchen and give him that pad with whatever shit you wrote on it as our order. See if you can get an ETA and tell that piece of shit you need to take the garbage out or a smoke break or whatever and meet us in the parkin' lot. Can you do that, girl?"

"Yeah. B-but are you gonna hurt me? I swear I didn't know. I'm just trying to survive until I can leave. My foster parents are shit." She looks like she's on the verge of tears.

"We ain't gonna hurt you, girl. Now get a move on," Pistol growls.

Hurriedly, Marni makes her way through the kitchen door, and we slowly stand and exit the diner. Back in our cages, we hit the gas and I wave my brothers out of the lot back onto the road. We need to get the fuck out of here before the Hellhounds show up. I'm not having a shootout at a diner filled with innocent people. We can come back later to deal with the cook.

I idle by the back door, waiting for her as I promised. Marni bursts into the lot through the diner's back door, her eyes wide and chest heaving.

"Get in," I call to her.

"What?"

"Do you want out? Get your ass in the truck. I promise I ain't gonna hurt you, but we gotta get the hell out of here, girl. Get in or wait another two weeks. This is your out." I have no clue why I'm trying to get this underage girl in my truck, but what's done is done. I know what it's like to have shitty parents. If her uncle is as bad as she made him seem, she'll face consequences when he finds us gone.

She forcefully rips open my passenger door and jumps in, slamming it shut as I press down on the accelerator.

"Where are we going?" she asks.

"How long till the Hellhounds arrive?" I ask, so I know how much of a head start we have.

"Randy told me I only had to keep you occupied for another twenty minutes. He suggested offering to suck one

131

of your dicks to keep you there." I see her staring at me from the corner of my eye.

"You're jailbait, girl. And you ain't my type. I'm a taken man." I pick up the walkie-talkie I left in the cup holder and radio the guys. "It's early, so I gotta assume those bastards were all at their clubhouse, which means we won't be runnin' into them on the road. Marni here says they were still twenty or so minutes out."

"What do you mean, Marni here?" Pistol barks. "Tell me you didn't kidnap a child and bring her with us."

"It's not kidnappin' if she's willin'. I'm not gonna leave some little girl back there to take the fall when they figure out we're not in the booth."

"So you're bringin' a strange girl to our business?" he asks, and I can hear the annoyance in his tone.

"No. We're gonna leave her at the container and circle back for her. Then she can tell us what she wants to do." I give her a half smile as she raises her eyebrows.

"You're a moron," Pistol grunts.

"And you're still my VP. So we do what I say or you can be on shitter duty with the other two cunts who wanted to talk to me like that. You may be my oldest friend, Pistol, but don't mistake that as a free pass for disrespect."

It's radio silent and I know Pistol is aware he stepped out of line. He'll apologize later once he's done being in his feelings.

"What do you mean, drop me off at the container? Just leave me at a bus stop, and I'll be okay." Marni tilts her head and crosses her arms over her chest.

What is with people thinking they can talk to me in any sort of way lately? Fuck me.

"I have some business to tend to and you can't come. I'll leave you there and pick you up when I'm done. Then you can come back to the clubhouse and hide out till you're eighteen and do what you want."

"No. No way. I've never been to a biker house or whatever you call it, but I've heard Randy talk about it enough. I'm not gonna come stay at your club and be some club slut. Fuck that." She bares her teeth at me and I chuckle at such a tiny thing yelling at me. Reminds me of a chihuahua trying to fight a rottweiler.

"It's club whore, first of all, and I have no plans of you becomin' one. You're still underage, so if you stay at the clubhouse for two weeks, you'll be under my protection. When your birthday hits, you can do what you want. You'll be a legal adult. I'll help you any way I can."

"Why? Why help me? You don't even know me," she asks.

"Because I can help and you could have kept your mouth shut back there and let us and the innocent guests get hurt. Instead, you put your ass on the line and told us the truth. So consider this my payback. Now, shut up. I need to make sure this shit stays on plan."

# eighteen

## STEEL

THE RPGS ARE SAFELY STORED AWAY in the back of Viper's cage while Marni is safe and sound inside the shipping container. I gave her some snacks from the glove compartment and a blanket. She's as pissed off as a cat in a bathtub, but she'll get over it. Showing up at Michaelov's drop with a teenage girl would not go over well and we don't need some strange girl knowing our business. I already have enough to deal with trying to find the fucking rat in our club.

We won't have to travel far to reach Michaelov's meet-up location, so we should arrive quickly, provided there are no mishaps. The sudden vibration of my phone on the dash pulls my attention. Swiftly grabbing and unlocking it, anticipation fills me.

> Iggie- Missed you when I woke up.
> Everything okay?

Me- Everything's fine, just had to deal with some club stuff. Did you see my note?

Iggie- Yeah. I also saw you added the club's name to my charity tree paper.

Me- No one from your work signed up. So me and a few brothers will help. You don't need to do it alone.

Iggie- Okay

Me- I'll text you when I'm back

Iggie- I miss you

Me- Same

I SLIDE the phone back onto the dash and scold myself for texting while driving. I need to pay attention to our run. That man has me feeling all tangled up inside. It would be easier if he lived with me, then I wouldn't have to constantly wonder and worry about where he was. Maybe I can get him to wear a tracker, like a necklace or bracelet or something similar. Then I wouldn't worry as much about him and jump as soon as his name lights up my phone.

When we pull into the church's parking lot, it's almost deserted, and Michaelov is already there. With a cigar in hand, he leans against his vehicle, wearing a self-satisfied smirk. Viper parks his truck next to the SUV and immediately jumps out.

Following suit, I slam my gearshift into park and get out, the gravel crunching beneath my boots as I head toward Michaelov.

"No issues this time, I see." Michaelov blows smoke in my direction.

"We're here, ain't we? Now let's get this over with. I got shit to do," I snap.

Michaelov drops his cigar on the ground, rubbing it out with his loafer. "Don't push me, Steel. I've had enough of your fuck ups and attitude."

"If you want to keep gettin' your weapons dirt cheap and my valued discretion, you'll take my shitty attitude and let me handle my club."

"Let's see what you brought today and I'll make my decision." Michaelov sighs. I nod to Viper, giving him the okay to haul them out of his cage.

He moves two wooden crates, shaped like short rectangles, and carefully positions them on the tailgate. With a flick of my knife, I pry the lids off and expose the RPGs inside. "We good?" I look at Michaelov.

"We're good." He pulls his cell from his slacks and my phone dings. I see the confirmation that he has transferred the funds to our club account.

"A real delight, as usual, Michaelov. If you need anything else, speak to me directly. I'll be in touch." I twirl my finger in a circle so my men know we're done here and they're clear to get back in their cages and head home.

I need to make a stop back at the shipping container and pick up my stowaway.

## IGNATIUS

I woke up this morning to an empty bed and cool sheets, meaning Steel had been gone awhile. It's been such a short amount of time, and I already feel myself falling for him. I shouldn't, but I can't stop it from happening. He just makes me feel so alive.

After showering the smell of sex off, I dressed and headed to the kitchen, where I found Steel's note. My belly filled with warm fuzzies. Then my eyes landed on his message scribbled on my work to-do list, assuring me that he and the club would assist me in decorating the tree.

I emailed the entire staff at Howards and got no replies. Frankly, it's disheartening that no one was willing to lend a hand to someone in need, even just for a few hours. It was my idea though, and I was determined to make it happen no matter what, even if I had to do it alone. Steel will never understand how something so small has broken down another barrier I had against him.

Nestling onto the cozy couch, I reach for my phone and launch the grocery delivery app, eager to stock up on essentials. This place looks like Mother Hubbard's cupboard, and I need to fix that. Plus, I think that Steel deserves a home cooked meal as a thank you. I'm going to make him my grandma's Swiss steak recipe with potatoes and green beans. But what should I do for dessert?

*Fuck it, he can have me as dessert. I've never been much of a baker.*

I load up my shopping cart with groceries for the week, as well as the items for tonight's dinner, and proceed to the checkout. Once I'm done, I switch on the TV to pass the time until the delivery arrives.

Engrossed in *Supernatural* reruns, I'm interrupted by the

insistent ringing of the doorbell. I raise a brow as I glance at the time on my phone. It's too early for the grocery delivery, but maybe the driver had someone in front of me cancel. Pausing my show, I reluctantly get off the couch and warily peer out my peephole, curious to see who is at the door. No one.

*What the hell?*

As I cautiously open the door, a musty smell hits my nose, but there's no one to be seen. I step out onto the porch and can't help but shiver at the icy chill in the air. My foot kicks something and when I look down, it's a large manilla envelope.

"Hello?" I call like a crazy person but get no reply.

I bend down and feel the weight of the envelope in my hand before quickly retreating to the warm safety of my house. Steel probably sent me something again. I can't help but smile, appreciating the fact that he never gave up on chasing me and insisted on having a chance with me. Settling back onto the couch, I eagerly tear open the envelope and my eyes are met with a stack of papers that says, 'Do you know the real Ashton Steel?'

Who the hell is Ashton? Is that Steel's legal first name? We never talked about his real name or his past much. I call him Steel. He told me the club members all have road names but his isn't some weird shit like Hambone, so I guess I didn't think much of it.

Grabbing the envelope once more, I carefully flip it over and examine it, searching for any sign of a return address, but find nothing. It's just blank. Returning to the stack in my hands, I flip to the next paper and it's a picture of Steel and me in the alley that night. He's on his knees in front of me, my cock in his mouth, and my head thrown back against the brick wall, a look of pure ecstasy on my face.

*Who the fuck was watching us and taking pictures?*

The more concerning part is that Steel's head has a huge red X over it.

I feel my heart rate quicken as I move on to the next page.

Another picture. This one of us is in his room at the clubhouse, and we're fucking. Again, someone creepily crossed out Steel's face. How the hell was someone able to take this from inside the bedroom?

The next page is a stapled packet of some sort. At the top, it says the Boone County Circuit Clerk Order of Protection. I feel dizzy and my hand trembles as I continue to read. The petitioner is Brielle Deacon, and the respondent is Ashton Steel.

The addresses are all redacted, but it looks like Brielle had to list reasons for needing an OP. She states stalking, threats if she didn't stay with him, and unwanted gifts. Beating up other suitors or males in her life. It went on for a good part of a year before she involved the police.

I feel like I'm going to be sick. My skin is clammy and the hair on the back of my neck is standing on end.

Shakily, I drop the packet on the coffee table, only to be met with another. This one was filed by an Alisha Wilden against Ashton Steel. Her reasons were the same, but there was no violence this time, and she didn't wait as long to file.

What the hell? Tears land on the page, smearing the ink, and I wipe them away. How could I be so blind? Steel is exactly who I initially thought he was. I just fell for his fucking shit because I'm so desperate to be loved. Dropping the papers, watching as they cascade to the floor, I curl up in a ball on the couch and sob.

How could I be so stupid? Why did I have to fall in love

with him? My heart is breaking, and it's my damn fault for being so pathetic.

———•💀•———

I WAKE up and it's dark in my house, the only light from the TV asking if I'm still there. Shit! My groceries are probably sitting outside on the porch for anyone to take. At least it's winter, so I don't have to worry about anything going bad.

There is a deep ache in my heart, and my eyes are puffy and sore from the constant flow of tears. Exhaustion clings to my body, but I force myself to stand up and open the front door. As I expected, my groceries are waiting for me, accompanied by a note from the shopper apologizing for missing me.

Yeah, buddy, I'm sorry I cried myself to sleep while my heart is off in a truck somewhere with a biker man known for his persistent stalking. I carry the bags into the kitchen and start mindlessly putting them away, thinking about how I'll deal with this.

Like his namesake—Steel—breaking up is not something that comes naturally. The papers prove that if I end it, he'll just stalk me. I could get an OP like the girls did, but did it help them or did he simply just move on?

I also want to know who sent that envelope. Who followed me, took those pictures, and left them at my door? Whoever they are, they're about as creepy as the shit they delivered. Maybe it was Brielle or Alisha and they're trying to stay in the shadows so Steel doesn't start following them again.

I hear my phone ringing in the living room, but I ignore it and continue putting my food away. When everything is where it belongs and the savory smell of nuggets and fries fills the kitchen, I make a beeline for my phone.

> Steel- I should be home in thirty minutes. Meet me at the clubhouse?

GUESS IT'S NOW or never. I wanted more time to make a plan, but there's no time like the present. Right? I don't want to talk to him and let him explain himself away and I fall for it again.

> Me- No

> Steel- Okay. Do you want me to come back to yours?

> Me- No

> Steel- Is everything alright Ignatius?

> Me- No. This is over Steel. Don't bother stalking me like Brielle and Alisha either. I know everything.

MY HEART RACES as I close my eyes and blow out a breath. See, that was easy enough, Ignatius. You just had to rip the bandaid off.

141

I practically jump out of my skin when my phone vibrates in my hand while ringing. It's Steel on video chat.

*Fuck. Fuck. Fuck.*

You got this, Ignatius. Answer and tell him it's over and you will get the police involved if needed. I answer and right away see Steel behind the wheel of his truck, driving, but his eyes are on me.

"Dude. He told you it was over in a text message. Video chatting him looks pathetic," a female voice chuckles.

"Marni, I'm not tellin' you again to mind your business," he growls.

Who the hell is Marni? She's not anyone I've met at the club, and he's never mentioned her. Did he leave me this morning to go get a different piece of ass? A piece of female ass?

No. It doesn't matter, because I'm ending this shit with him. I don't get to be jealous because he's not my problem anymore. Just another person who let me down and hurt me in my life. Put him up there with my parents and every other man I've tried to date.

Good thing Draco will be home tomorrow and we have a lunch date that is now going to turn into a drink date.

"Iggie. What the hell's goin' on? I left this mornin' and spoke to you earlier, and everything was fine. Now you're dumpin' me over text? For what?"

"Someone came here and dropped an envelope full of pictures of us together and redacted copies of orders of protection against you. So yeah, I don't want to be serious with a psychopath, nor someone who doesn't take no for an answer." My voice shakes as I speak to him.

"Oh shit," Marni mumbles, and Steel's eyes shoot toward her and then back to me.

"That was a long time ago, Ignatius. I'm different.

Changed. You've not been with me long, but I've never ignored you if you said stop or slow down. I've given you no proof that I'm that same boy. That's what I was: a boy. Yes, I get attached easily and I want what I want and go after it or them. I had no formal charges pressed for Brielle or Alisha and I've been showin' you that I'm good for you. Someone obviously doesn't like us together and wanted to fuck shit up for me. What pictures were in there? I never had no pictures of those girls."

"Pictures of us together, in the alley and your bedroom at the clubhouse," I whisper, heat creeping across my cheeks at talking about this in front of a stranger.

"I'm sendin' someone over to watch your house and to take those pictures to Hawk. He might be able to find out who sent them."

"No! Someone can come for the pictures because I wanna know who left them too, but I don't want anyone sitting outside my house. The one was taken inside your bedroom, so forgive me if I don't trust your brothers. I meant it, Steel, we are done. You want to prove to me you've changed. Leave me alone and let me think." I hang up and crumble to the floor, crying while clutching my phone in my hand.

## *nineteen*

### STEEL

THIS IS BULLSHIT! I storm into the clubhouse, the door slamming shut echoing through the room.

As I walk, Marni's voice suddenly pierces the silence. "Watch it, asshole! You almost hit me with the door."

My eyes burn into hers as I swiftly turn around, an intense stare conveying my emotions. Fuck, I almost slammed the door on her. Dammit. I'm a dick, but I wouldn't hurt a child and that's what she is for a few more weeks. "I'm sorry."

Hawk is at Iggie's now, getting the pictures to see if we can find out who sent them or took them. We can't say for certain if it's two different individuals or not. There's a traitor in this clubhouse who is trying to ruin my relationship with Iggie and betray Hell's Mayhem.

That was a stupid fucking move though, because it just made my suspect pool small as hell. The same two who are on shit patrol. I wouldn't doubt if it's both of them. They're so far up each other's ass.

"Kiki!" She quickly jumps off of Rubble's lap and rushes over to me.

"What's up, Pres?"

"This is Marni." I point to my new guest. "Marni, this is Kiki. She's a club whore and by choice, before you even ask. Anyway. Kiki, take Marni to one of the empty rooms and get her situated with clothes or anything else she needs. She'll be stayin' with us for a while. So I need you to keep an eye on her. Keep her with you at all times. Shit is gettin' ready to go down in here, and she doesn't need to get involved."

"Not complainin' or arguin', Pres, but what about my, umm... other duties?" Kiki asks.

I groan, closing my eyes and rolling them, trying to hide my irritation. What I'm about to say is going to piss off some of the brothers, but they can deal with it.

"You're off duty. If anyone has a problem with it, they can take it up with me. Cody, Gabe, and Daria can handle it until I get to the bottom of the issue." I grab her elbow and pull her to the side so Marni can't hear us. "I want you to keep your eyes and ears open, Kiki. Anything seems out of the ordinary, you come directly to me. Ya feel me?"

"Yes, Steel," she says, rising to her tiptoes and kissing my cheek. "Come on, Marni." She grabs the teen by the hand and drags her from the room.

"Kiki, what the hell, baby? This boner ain't gonna fuck itself!" Rubble hollers after her, laughing.

"Listen up!" I shout, getting the attention of everyone in the room. "Kiki is closed for business. You wanna nut? You call one of the others. She's takin' care of some shit for me for a bit."

"This about that hot little thing you brought back with you? She a new whore?" Pepper asks.

"Her name's Marni and she's underage. She helped us

out and we're returnin' the favor. Touch her and I'll cut your fuckin' cock off." I narrow my eyes at him, so he knows how serious I am. My tolerance for bullshit is pretty high, but I won't have some young girl scared to be in my clubhouse.

Hawk strolls through the door, a smirk playing on his lips, waving an envelope at me.

"Officers, my office now." I head that way, unlock the door, and sink into my chair behind my desk. Leaning forward, I place my elbows on the desktop and press my forehead into my hands, my fingers tangling in my brown locks. This got fucked quickly and I want it resolved even quicker.

Iggie isn't like Bre and Alisha. Did I do what they accused me of? Yes. I learned from it and now harness that obsessive energy in more productive ways. Iggie was hesitant to begin with, so I pulled back and tried to show him I'm different. But someone had to drag my past back into the spotlight and ruin it.

I intended to open up to Iggie about my past and challenges, but the opportunity never presented itself. The plan was set. Help him with the tree thing for work, take him to a nice dinner, and tell him.

Fuck! I slam my fist on the desk, causing a loud thud to reverberate through the room.

Once everyone is in my office, I hear the click of the door as Pistol shuts it firmly, locking it. Hawk drops the envelope to my desk. I grab it, open it, and pull out what Iggie gave him.

First is a picture of us naked in my bedroom. I'm balls deep inside him, and he's biting his bottom lip as he looks at me. A foreboding red X marks my face, impossible to ignore. Who the fuck was in my bedroom and took this shit? Only someone in the club could get access to my room. Even then, I keep it locked, so who snuck in?

The next is that night I sucked him off in the alley after dinner. I'm on my knees, his cock down my throat and his head is against the building behind him, pure bliss on his features. Same as the first, my face has a red X over it.

My pulse quickens at the mere sight of us together. It's only been a few hours, but I already ache with an unbearable longing for Iggie. Not just his body, either. The urge to text him and provide comfort, letting him know that things will work out, is strong. We're gonna figure out who took and sent these pictures. They'll pay for scaring Iggie and invading our privacy.

Placing the pictures on my desk, I carefully examine the faces of each and every one of my officers. My throat burns and a sour taste fills my mouth at what I'm about to say. "Ya'll have seen me naked and I couldn't give a fuck. But you're about to see Ignatius in compromisin' positions. I'm only showing you so you can help me get to the bottom of this. Don't forget it. He is mine."

Since they're my closest brothers, I trust them implicitly, but my attitude shifts when it comes to Iggie. Pistol quickly snatches the pictures and carefully inspects them before handing them over to Viper and so on.

Pistol speaks first. "Nothin' I can see in the pictures themselves, but I definitely think whoever took them and sent them is not happy you and Iggie are together. Seems they have their own obsession."

"I agree, but they have to be workin' with someone in the club to get the pic of us in my room here. No one has been here except brothers and whores. No family, no other clubs, no service workers. So who has ties to Iggie in the club?" Zero asks.

"I ran a background search on Iggie to ensure he wasn't part of a Hellhound family. I didn't find anything. Ignatius Jack Harper, twenty-eight, white male. Born to Patricia and Douglas Harper. Graduated college from Banford with a major in business and minor in communications. Started working at Howards a few years back and never left. Best friend Draco Luther and that's it. His work history and only friend vouch for his cleanliness and loyalty."

"So now what? Is there a way to see where these pictures came from or who sent them?" I ask because while it's nice to know what Iggie told me about himself is true, I knew a good chunk of Hawk's information already.

"I could see if that new bouncer Brian hired could check for prints. He was in the Navy and did Naval Criminal Investigative Service. His name's Zion and he was honorably discharged from the Navy last year. Good guy, but a lot of demons from his time in the service."

I nod my head. "Okay, ask him, but don't give him any information. I don't want to spread this information around. If whoever is involved knows we're on to them, they'll change tactics. Hawk, I want you to tap Pepper and Combo's phones, tablets, laptops, whatever you can."

"That's a slippery slope, Steel. You sure?" Pistol asks.

"Yeah. They've voted and stood against me in every vote and order. You heard them at the last church, blamin' Ignatius for the leak. Now information from my past has come to light and drove a wedge between Iggie and me. They're at the top of my suspect list."

"I agree. They're up to something. I thought it was a coup or some bullshit, but this could've been it. It's why I've been watchin' them," Viper pipes up.

"Alright. I'll back you no matter what, Steel. Just

wouldn't be your VP if I didn't make sure you were sure." Pistol rubs his hands together.

"Then let's get started. I want answers ASAP." I slap a hand on the desk and my brothers all get up and file out of the room.

"First things first, I'm going to sweep your room for bugs. Someone took those photos from inside. I'm going to assume it wasn't a threesome and we know you lock your room and office tighter than Fort Knox." Hawk stands and leaves the room. Shit, I hadn't even thought of that.

━━━┿┿┿┿━💀━┿┿┿┿━━━

I TOSSED and turned all night. In such a short time, I became accustomed to Iggie being beside me. We've only spent a few nights apart since we met and even then, I may or may not have slept in my truck outside his house. But that secret will stay with me.

Tonight, some of the brothers and I were supposed to go to the Community Center and help Iggie decorate the tree for his work's adopted family. There is no chance he will want me to show up and help now since it would involve him being near me. I'd love to go, but I have to prove to him I'm not the creepy stalker I've been portrayed as, so I won't.

Iggie is different. I can't force myself on him and hope he gets over it. No, I need to prove to him I'm listening. Getting out of bed, I make my way to the bathroom and jump into the shower, hoping the hot water will wake me up.

Once I'm done, I quickly change into jeans, a black T-shirt, and my cut. Sitting on the edge of my bed, I roll on a pair of socks and slip my feet into my boots. I get up and make my way to the kitchen for food.

Pistol, Kiki, and Marni sit at the table, the sound of their forks clinking against the plates fills the air. "Mornin'," I greet as I step up to the stove and see they have extras.

"Good morning. It turns out my little bestie here loves to cook and insisted on making breakfast. So we got up at the ass crack of dawn and she cooked while I chugged coffee," Kiki grumbles.

"You're eating good, aren't ya?" Marni sasses, and I can't help but chuckle. The girl may be young and scared shitless of her foster dad and his brother, but she's sassier than hell here.

"Yeah, Little Gremlin. I am. Just next time, can we make food after eight am?" Kiki laughs.

"Fine," Marni agrees around a mouthful of pancake.

I fill my plate with pancakes and sausage, pour myself a cup of black coffee, and sit beside Pistol. "Gremlin, huh?" I look at Marni. "Let me ask you somethin', Gremlin. Why were you shakin' like a leaf back at the diner, but you've had no problem mouthin' off to me or Kiki here?"

Her eyes shift between her plate and me before she carefully places her fork down. "The truth?" I give her a nod. "You're scary as hell, don't get me wrong. But you took me with you when you didn't have to. You could have believed I was helping Randy and left me there to get my punishment. So while you may look terrifying and so do your members, I just have a gut feeling you won't hurt me. Like I know it in my soul."

"Who hurt you? Your foster parents or Randy?" Kiki asks her, gently massaging her back.

"Both in different ways," Marni whispers, her voice barely audible. "I was forced into working at the diner. I was nothing more than a maid to my foster parents, all because Randy pleaded with them and promised them my wages."

"If he had to pay your foster parents to get you to work there, what was in it for him?" Pistol asks.

Marni turns her head and fixates her gaze on the wall to her left. A single tear rolls down her cheek, and she frantically wipes it off her face.

"How long?" Pistol growls.

"From the age of fifteen, when I was legally allowed to have a work permit," she murmurs.

"Never again, Marni. You hear me?" Kiki firmly grasps her face and directs her attention toward her. "For two years, I've been in this club. No one has ever hurt me or forced me to do anything I didn't want to do. If it did happen, I know I could go to one of these two here and the guilty party would cease to exist. As long as you're here, you're safe."

Marni sniffles and uses her sleeve to wipe her nose. "Why do you do it?"

Kiki smiles. "Well, I've always liked sex, and I needed a way to pay for college. I get to live here for free. Not only does the club take care of my every need, but they also cover the cost of my tuition and books. I get to fuck crazy hot bikers and I like the family I've made being here. Even when I move on and ain't a club girl anymore, I know if I needed anything, I could come back here, and they'd have my back."

"Damn straight we would. Kiki is right. We're more family than a club. While a couple of the club whores are here in hopes of snaggin' a husband, we know who is loyal and is here just 'cause they want to be," I tell her, stabbing the last piece of sausage from my plate.

"Okay," is all she says. Her lips twitch with a small smile.

"That leads me to ask y'all a favor. Tonight at seven is the tree decoratin' for the families in the area in need. Iggie is supposed to decorate one for work, but no one signed up to help him. I told him me and a few of the brothers would help, but I'm not wanted anymore. I still don't want him to do it alone, and he deserves to have people support him. So I'm hopin' that you, Pistol." I turn and look at him. "Along with Kiki and maybe Viper can go help him. Please? I don't usually ask, brother, but I am now."

"I'll go help your man. Only because I know you've changed and you're my best friend." Pistol wiggles his brows at me.

"I'm in. I happen to really like Iggie," Kiki says, her smile revealing her genuine fondness for him.

"Can I go?" Marni asks, her voice filled with anticipation.

"Not a smart plan when Randy has to know you're with us. The Hellhounds are already on our asses," I tell her and see the disappointment in her eyes.

"I'll keep an eye on her, but if I say it's time to go, you listen. Got me, little girl?" Pistol stands and takes his plate to the sink.

"Yes, sir." Marni's smile widens as she nods and playfully nibbles on her bottom lip.

"You're going to love Iggie. He is sexy as hell and way too good for our president, but I approve." Kiki gives me the throwback duck lips and raises her brows as she talks to Marni.

"I heard him on the phone in the truck, so I can't wait to meet him in person. Also, I am a huge fan of Christmas, but I haven't been able to celebrate it since I went into foster care at eleven."

"Well, let's get my stuff done around the clubhouse, and then we'll get ready." Kiki stands and grabs her and Marni's plates and dumps them in the sink before they leave the kitchen giggling.

"I have a feelin' you fucked up puttin' Kiki in charge of that girl." Pistol sighs.

"Kiki is just what she needs. A strong woman who knows what she wants, goes after it, and isn't ashamed," I tell him as I move to the sink, wash my plate, and put it away. "I'm headed to my office. Holler if you need me."

I won't be able to go tonight to help Iggie, but I'll send a note to show my support, and my group will be there on Sunday to help deliver the tree, too.

# *twenty*

## IGNATIUS

TONIGHT IS the tree decorating event for work and I feel like shit. I fell for someone I knew I shouldn't have, who broke my heart and now I feel like a complete idiot. My fucking flaw wins again, giving men a chance when I should just keep that door closed.

I'm also dreading tonight because nobody else from Howards is interested in decorating the tree, leaving me to do it alone. But I committed the company to this and no matter how I feel, the family we adopted won't have Christmas without us, so it's time to pull myself up by the bootstraps and head out.

*You know who always wore boots? Steel.*

No! I need to stop going there. I ended things. Time to move on.

Blowing out a breath, I grab the gifts I wrapped earlier and make the first trip to my car to load them up. We don't need them until Sunday, but I want them ready because I've planned a weekend of wallowing in self-pity with Draco, who has just returned home.

During the trips back and forth from the car, I'm overcome by a sudden chill, causing the hair on the back of my neck to stand on end. I toss the last of the packages in the car and spin around, looking for the cause.

No one.

"Steel! If you're watching me, go home. We're through," I call out into the winter air. He could be out there, or maybe it's my mind playing tricks on me. Either way, I'm going to stand my ground.

I hurry back into the house to grab the tote of lights and decorations for the tree. As I'm running out the door, I hook it with my foot to close it behind me. Setting the tote down, I lock it quickly and head to the car.

After placing the tote on the passenger seat, I lock the doors and look around. I can't shake that unsettling feeling, but I still don't see anyone.

*Stop being crazy, Iggie. No one is watching you.*

Shaking my head, I turn the key in the ignition and my car starts. I give it a minute to warm up a little, blowing into my hands. My fingers are like ice. I need to get going if I don't want to be late. Switching the gear into drive, I pull out of my driveway, heading toward the community center.

Trying to calm my nerves, I hit play on my Pentatonix Christmas Album and let the festive music fill the car. The familiar tune of "Little Drummer Boy" fills the air, and I can't resist turning up the volume and belting out the lyrics.

When I pull into the community center's parking lot, it's packed with cars. After driving around for a moment, I find a parking spot near the front. I grab the tote from beside me and get out, walking toward the door. The jingle of ornaments ringing out with every step.

There's a table with two elderly ladies seated, busily taking notes on their clipboards right inside. "Name?" the one on the right asks as I walk up, her glasses perched low on her nose.

"Ignatius Harper for Howards," I tell her with a smile.

"Sign here just saying you showed up and decorated the tree. This is your packet with the address for delivery on Sunday and the family's info if you haven't done the shopping yet. Your tree is number seventeen. Take this door here and keep going until you're in the gym. You'll be in the first row of trees. Should have a notecard pinned to it with the number."

Juggling the tote on my hip, I extend my hand to take the packet from her. "Thank you."

The moment I lean down to sign the paper, the tote slips. A surge of panic hits and my heart about jumps out of my chest. I have decorations inside of it that can break. But it never hits the floor, snatched in mid-air by a pair of hands with perfectly manicured, black-painted nails.

I quickly finish signing my name, then turn my attention to a pair of familiar, dark brown eyes. "What are you doing here?" I ask, my skin tingling as I look around for *him,* but he's nowhere to be seen.

"Prez asked us to come and help since he couldn't make it. He didn't want you to do it alone, so here we are." Kiki shrugs with a huge smile on her face.

"We?" My brows shoot up. I wasn't expecting anyone to show up. I look up and Pistol is behind her, arms crossed and eyes hard as he scans the room. I somehow missed him standing there.

"Hi, I'm Marni. We met on the phone the other day with Mister Cranky Pants. I'm staying at the clubhouse for a bit. Freaking excited to help other people at this time of year." A young blonde with the lightest blue eyes holds a hand out. I didn't see her behind Pistol, she's so small.

"Nice to meet you, Marni. I'm Iggie. Thanks for coming to help. We're tree seventeen." I grab the tote from Kiki and head in the direction the lady said.

I don't even know how to process what is happening. Steel respected my wishes and didn't show up tonight. However, he knew I would be here alone, so he asked some of his friends to help. I know they're not friends in his eyes. Pistol's a brother, Kiki is a whore, and I don't know what Marni is, but in my eyes, they're his friends.

Although we're over, my heart still swoons at the thought he put into tonight. This is the Steel I fell for, not the one I saw in those Orders of Protection.

*No! You're not doing this. It's done.*

We get to the tree and I set the tote down. "I'm going to let you three handle the decoratin' and I'll keep an eye out. No leavin' unless I know, Little Girl." Pistol narrows his eyes at Marni.

*Keeping an eye out for what or who?*

"Sir. Yes. Sir." She salutes and I chuckle.

"Let's get the lights on. While we do that, you can tell me how you ended up in Steel's truck that day and why you're staying at the clubhouse. You can't be more than what, sixteen?"

"Seventeen. Eighteen in under two weeks." She takes the strand of lights and begins to wrap it around the tree. "I was waitressing and my boss was trying to hurt your man and his men. I helped them out and in return, he helped me out of my abusive foster home. But my boss has to know I left with them, so they're being careful in case he's looking for me."

I look at Kiki, who is opening the star for the top of the tree, and she shrugs.

"So, I'm gonna stay at the clubhouse 'til my birthday and then I'm a legal adult so I can do what I want. Steel said he'd help me with whatever I decide." She smiles as she finishes that strand and connects another one.

"But do you have to—" She doesn't let me finish.

"Oh no. No offense to my girl, Kiki, 'cause I love her and she's been good to me, but I couldn't do what she does. Not after what I've been through."

"Thanks, babe. I kinda like you too, Little Gremlin." Kiki laughs.

The night continues, with us chatting endlessly about music, shopping, and books. I like Marni. She's a sweet girl, and I'm glad Steel got her out of her situation. I also find myself feeling grateful that she helped him not get hurt by someone else.

*Did I really give Steel a fair shot?*

I shouldn't care what happens to him, yet a sense of concern tugs at my heart. He hurt me by lying. Not saying anything is lying by omission and no one will change my mind.

We put the last of the multicolored balls on the tree along with the few boxes of Disney character ornaments I could find, and now it's time for the star. The girls aren't tall enough and before I can volunteer, Marni is bounding over to Pistol.

"Pistol, can you put the star on for us? Please?" She pouts her bottom lip and his eyes widen as she stares at him.

"Oh, for fuck's sake," he murmurs, taking the star from her and putting it on the tree with ease.

When he lifts his arm, both girls snicker as they catch a glimpse of his chiseled abs and the ink on his skin. I can't help but shake my head and roll my eyes at their slyness.

"Is that it?" He looks at me when he's done

"Yeah. Thank you so much for helping me. It means a lot."

"Don't thank us. Thank Steel. He asked us to come, so you didn't have to do it alone and because he's a good guy, we came," Pistol drawls.

"Pistol, I'm sor—"

"Nope, I don't want to hear you're sorry. I've known that man my whole life and while he's done some fucked up shit and made mistakes when he was younger, he was different with you. You have to figure it out on your own, Iggie. Now come on, girls, we need to get back. Marni's been out long enough."

Marni rolls her eyes and steps over to me, wrapping her arms around my waist in a tight hug. "Thanks for letting me help, Iggie. Merry Christmas."

"Merry Christmas, Marni. Hey, if you're looking for work after you're eighteen, I could get you a job as a cashier at Howards."

"Thank you!" she exclaims and skips toward Pistol, who looks annoyed with her antics.

"He's right, you know?" Kiki says as she knocks her shoulder against mine. "Prez is a good guy and you can't base your decisions on things he did in the past. I don't know the details and I don't need to. But if I meet someone and fall in love, I hope they don't cast me aside when they find out what I did with the club. You can't make unbiased decisions if you don't hear his side of things."

"Thanks, Kiki," I whisper.

"Anytime, babe." She hugs me and hurries to catch up to Pistol and Marni.

I grab my tote, head out to my car and get in, hurrying to turn it on so I can crank the heat. When I back out of my parking spot and pull onto the road, I don't play music like I normally do. Instead, I find myself replaying Kiki's words over and over again.

Was it fair to judge Steel based solely on the papers, without taking the time to hear his side? I didn't give him a chance to explain or make excuses. Panic washed over me as I took in the papers and pictures, leading me to quickly call off everything.

*Did I make a mistake?*

# twenty-one

### ???

JUST WHEN I think I've gotten rid of that dirty biker scum, he sends his friends to decorate the tree. I should have thought of that, but I was too busy completing my plans. In just a few short days, Iggie will be where he belongs. With me.

The pictures I had my associate take at the clubhouse and the records I got my hands on should have been enough to drive them apart. But while I haven't seen them together since I delivered my package, he's with these other scum-bags now.

Why can't Ignatius see he's too good for these people? That he's meant to be mine? I'm going to show him, though, and prove to him we're in love and meant to be together.

That dirty whore, who I know fucks all the club members, touches him and my blood boils. She needs to learn that he's not for her. She doesn't get to touch him. Not now. Not ever.

Pulling my phone from my pocket as I watch them finish the tree from afar, I text my contact at the clubhouse.

> Me- Your whore with the blonde hair needs to learn not to touch what isn't hers.

> Frank- I'll handle her for a price

> Me- Name it

> Frank- 10k

> Me- Done. I'll have it wired to your account.

> Frank- I hope your scumbag is worth all this

> Me- Don't call him that!

HE DOESN'T RESPOND, but that doesn't surprise me. He's always been an asshole, and his hatred for Steel is what made him too easy to make an ally. A little money and the chance to destroy his president and he was on board and even brought two friends to help with the job.

Which has made it easier for me to get my photos and keep tabs on my soulmate and that trash he thinks he's infatuated with.

Maybe I should have brought him home when I was watching him outside his house, loading his car for tonight. Maybe I should have walked in and offered to help with the tree. Coulda, shoulda, woulda.

Our time is coming and when he sees how good we are together, he won't even remember Steel's name.

# twenty-two

## STEEL

PISTOL TEXTED and said it went well, and they were on the way back. That was like ten minutes ago and I've been impatiently waiting for them to get back so I can get a full report. I'm glad it worked out and my brother and the two girls could help him. The thought of him decorating that tree alone didn't sit right.

This is why I love my club and my brothers. Pistol sacrificed his own time to watch my man and the girls decorate a tree, even though he surely had more fun things to do.

As I lie in bed, my fingers swiping through videos on my phone, a knock on the door interrupts my scrolling.

"Come in!"

The door slowly opens. "Hey, Prez, thought you might like an update on Iggie that didn't come from Pistol," Kiki giggles. She closes the door behind her, approaches the bed, and stands next to it, her eyes fixed on me.

"I didn't know you were back already," I tell her, sitting up and leaning against the headboard.

"Just got back. But it was good. I had fun, actually, and so did Marni. If she decides to stay, Iggie offered her a job once she turns eighteen. You should know Pistol kinda told him off."

I growl, my low rumble echoing through the room. I know my best friend is protective of me, but I didn't ask him to say anything. If he made the situation worse, I will kick his ass.

"Oh, calm down. It wasn't too bad, I promise. But I did kinda agree with him. I told Iggie he shouldn't base his opinions and decisions on your past. He needs to base them on how you are with him now. That he needs to hear you out."

"Why? You don't know what happened or why, Kiki, so why involve yourself?" I ask her, my voice filled with curiosity. I should be mad since she's put her nose where it doesn't belong, but I can't help but think it's shit Ignatius needed to hear.

"You're right, I don't know what happened. But I know you and you're a good man. An asshole, don't get me wrong, but you got good bones. You seemed happy, you both did, and I think you both deserve that."

"Thanks," I tell her. She moves from beside the bed and heads toward the door. "Kiki."

"Yeah, Prez?"

"You know you aren't supposed to talk to me like you do, right? That I should beat your ass in front of the guys so you know your place with me?"

It's true, I let this woman get away with a lot more than the other whores and I know the others notice. I can't seem to care, though. Kiki is one of the best people I know. She's not here to snag her an old man, and she never gives us trouble.

"Yeah, I suppose you should and you can if you need to. I'm not real good at following rules when it comes to my friends. And Steel, while you might be my prez and I respect you in front of the brothers and in public, you're also my friend. I just want to see you happy. You deserve it." She smiles.

With a gentle thud, the door closes behind her, and I lean my head back, thinking about what she said. I suppose she's right. She always acts accordingly in front of the members and when we're in town, but when it's just me and her or even Pistol, she's freer with her mouth. She trusts us and she should. I also guess she's right that somewhere throughout the few years of her being here, she crossed the line for me from club whore to friend.

I don't have time to keep dwelling on her, though. I need to talk to Iggie and tell him I didn't put them up to talking to him about me. I sent them to help, that's it. I need to apologize, even if he doesn't want to hear from me.

Now though comes the hard part, should I call or text? If I call, he could just send it to voicemail and I'll never get to say my peace. But if I text, he can read it and decide not to respond, but at least he knows what I have to say.

Shit! This is hard. Who thought I'd ever be making such stupid but important choices? I'm going to call and if he doesn't answer, I'll text.

Hitting his contact, a sudden rush of air fills my lungs as I expand my chest, trying to contain my nerves.

*It's just a call.*

Holding the phone, my palms become sweaty. Who am I? Or more like, who the hell does Iggie make me?

The phone rings until his voicemail picks up. I hang up and click over to my messages.

. . .

> Me- Hey I called and figured you wouldn't answer but it was worth a try. Just wanted to let ya know I didn't ask anyone to talk to you tonight about us. They were asked only to help with the tree so you weren't alone. So I'm sorry about that other part.

THE BUBBLES POP UP and disappear for fifteen minutes. I watch as my heart beats crazily until finally a message pops up.

> Ignatius- It's fine. Thank you for sending them. They were a lot of help. I wasn't thrilled with their words but what Kiki said does make sense and has me thinking.

MY STOMACH DROPS to my asshole, probably even out of my asshole. He's thinking about what? About us? Christ, at this point, I'm like a lovesick teenage girl. Get me a notebook so I can doodle little Steel *hearts* Iggie all over it.

> Me- Thinking about what?

> Ignatius- This whole thing. Us. I don't even know anymore.

. . .

I'M GOING to kiss Kiki the next time I see her. That beautiful, smart whore. Fuck. I feel like I'm going to be sick.

> Me- Can we talk?

> Me- In person?

Ignatius- Yeah. You should tell Kiki if she ever decides beauty school or sex isn't for her to try a couple's counselor.

> Me- Ha! Where do you wanna meet?

Ignatius- The coffee shop on Main St Monday after I'm off say, 6pm

> Me- I'll be there

Ignatius- Steel I want to know everything and the truth. I'm going out on a limb meeting you so you owe me the truth about it all

> Me- No problem. I planned to tell ya anyway that creep just beat me to it. See you then

HOLY SHIT! He's gonna meet with me and at least hear me out, which is all I can ask at this point. But there's still danger lurking in the shadows, threatening my man's happiness, and that won't stand. I'm gonna need to push harder to find out who our rat is before Monday. All the money in my wallet says it's either Pepper or Combo since they've been against anything involving making the club an ally to the LGBTQ+ community.

I need to call a meeting with my officers and tell them we have forty-eight hours to figure this out.

THE NEXT MORNING, the guys are standing outside my office waiting for me.

"Everything okay, Steel?" Trucker asks, a coffee in one hand as he rubs his brow with the other.

"Yeah. Let's get inside and we'll talk more," I tell him.

I unlock the door and open it. The only sound in the room is shuffling behind me as they follow. Moving to sit at my desk, I kick my boots up onto the top and wait for Pistol to lock the door.

"I talked to Iggie last night." I rub my throat while I speak.

"That's great. I told him a few things last night. Glad I could help," Pistol admits, his face looking proud as a peacock.

"Yeah, we'll talk about that later, dickhead. You're lucky it worked out in my favor so far. It could have gone the other way and then I'd have shot your ass."

"I got too nice of an ass to be shot. It worked out though, huh? Regular ol' cupid." He chuckles, causing me to roll my eyes.

"Enough!" I slam my boot on the desk. "This is serious. The timeline to figure out who took those pictures and who left them for Iggie has moved up."

"When?" Hawk asks.

"Monday morning. It's Saturday, so we have forty-eight hours. He's agreed to meet with me and talk, but I will not risk it if he's being followed or being around me is a danger to him."

"Well, my search revealed nothing on anyone in his close circle. I did tap Pepper and Combo's phones and while they talk a lot of bullshit about all of us, nothing that screamed rat. But I'll keep tabs on them still," Hawk tells the room and I can tell he's upset that he doesn't have better results.

"I want them under a fucking microscope. Nothing is left unchecked," I snap, and he nods.

"Prez, say the word and I'll tail them. They won't even know I'm in the shadows until it's too late." Viper licks his lips and stares at me. He's always hated the two of them for the bullshit they spew, and I've held him off, but now? I want answers. I just have a sinking feeling in my gut they're our leak.

"Hawk, you had our landlines tapped, right? After the *incident*." Zero looks at Viper out of the corner of his eyes.

"That cunt fucked another man the day after we got hitched. He was supposed to be a brother? He deserved to get shot. I should have shot her ass, too." Viper stands, spinning around and punching a hole in the wall.

"Enough! Viper, you'll be repairing my goddamn wall," I tell him and then look at Hawk. "Psychotic ass bastard," I mumble.

"Yes, Prez," Viper growls.

"Yeah, we did have them tapped. I forgot all about that since we haven't had any reason to check them. What's up?" Hawk answers, looking at Zero with a raised brow, not sure what he's getting at.

"I was thinking that if Michaelov said he spoke to

someone about changing his order and it wasn't Prez, then maybe we could go back and see if we recognize the voice on the call."

"They do record so I could, but we'd have to know the date and time of the call. Can we ask Michaelov and see if he remembers?" Hawk asks, turning his gaze to me.

"Yeah. I'll get in touch with him. He won't like it, but tough shit," I tell him. "Adjourned until I hear from Michaelov. Then, Hawk, you can find the call and we'll see if we recognize the voice."

The guys filter out of my office, leaving me alone with my thoughts. I remain seated, wondering how things got so fucked in every aspect of my life so fast.

A knock pulls me from my thoughts. "It's open!"

In walks Cody and I can't help but roll my eyes. He looks like a roided-out John Travolta, but his personality is that of a seagull. His mind is always on one thing and that's whose dick he can ride to get ahead.

"What do you want, Cody? I'm busy."

"You've seemed stressed lately, so I thought I'd come see if I can help you out," he pauses and licks his lips. "In any way?"

I stand up and take the few steps across the room to him. Getting right into his personal space and since he's only five-eleven or so, he has to glance up at me. "I'm good, Cody. Now get out of my office. Don't come in here looking for a quick fuck and act like it's a service to me."

He's either really brave or really dumb, but either way his breath hitches and he runs a hand down my ribs. "Are you sure, Mr. President? I could be a real good boy."

Fuck me. Did he just pull a Marilyn Monroe line on me and think it would work? Who the hell voted for him to be a whore? I'm gonna have to look into that shit cause no means no in this fucking clubhouse.

My arm snaps out and I wrap my hand around his throat, picking him up so he's on his tiptoes. "Don't forget your place, whore. No always means no in this fuckin' club. You hear me? I've never fucked with you before and I sure ain't gonna start now. If I was feeling lonely, I'd be more likely to fuck Gabe or Kiki than you."

His eyes widen and I can feel him swallow hard behind my tight grip. "Yes, Prez," he hisses as I restrict his airway.

Letting him go, he falls back, stumbling, and gasping for air. "Out!" I bark and point at my door. He glares at me, but leaves my office.

# twenty-three

## STEEL

IT'S Sunday morning and Pistol, Marni, and Kiki went to deliver the tree to the family with Iggie. With my head buried in my hands, I sit at my desk, the sound of my sigh echoing in the room as I struggle to come up with a better idea to lure the rat out. My meeting with Iggie is tomorrow, and I can't shake the concern that it might jeopardize his safety.

Someone knocks on the door, pulling my eyes to the black wood. Lately, my office feels like Grand Central Station. This room used to be my sanctuary, where I could sit undisturbed for as long as I pleased. Nowadays, I can't even sit for twenty minutes without someone knocking. Before I can answer, the door swings open, and Combo strides in. This is why I usually lock it, but with time ticking down, I wanted the guys to be able to get in right away if they had information.

"You don't just barge into my office," I bark at him.

"My bad. I swore I heard you say come in," he responds,

but I can tell by the glimmer in his eye he knows I fucking didn't.

"What do you want, Combo?"

"Just wanted to check in, since it seems there's been a lot of secret meetings in this office. Is everything okay?"

"Are you keepin' tabs on my fuckin' office? I can have who I want in here when I want, since it's my goddamn office. This is where I meet with my officers. You ain't one of them, so nothing concerns you that happens in here. Now fuck off." The balls he has all of a sudden. What the fuck is he playing at?

"If something is going on with the club, we have a right to know." He crosses his arms, staring at me and still in my fucking office.

In a split second, I grab the object nearest to me: a stapler. I throw it and it flies through the air straight toward his face, but he ducks at the last second. If he hadn't, it would have probably broken his nose. "Unless you got something to confess, Combo, there ain't shit goin' on you need to know. Now, get the fuck out before you leave here in a body bag."

"Unfit president," he grumbles, but leaves the office, slamming the door behind him.

That was a very strange encounter and I'm sure he had ulterior motives, but what were they? It's odd for him to ask these questions here when he knows he could bring that shit up in church. This just looks even worse for him and his buddy, Pepper. I have no doubt they're our rats, but now we need to gather proof to back it up. Would they stalk Iggie though and drive us apart? While I know they don't like me, what did they have to gain by pushing him away?

My phone beeps and I pick it up.

. . .

Pistol- Tree is delivered. Girls are back and your man is home.

Me- Thanks. Any issues?

Pistol- Nope. I'm supposed to tell you thank you for sending us and he'll see ya tomorrow.

I GUESS that's one less thing I have to worry about. Iggie got his tree delivered and didn't have to do it alone. He's back at home since I had Pistol follow him before he came back with the girls.

Pistol- I'm going to Cockpit

MY BEST FRIEND hates being my errand boy, but he knows he has to right now in order for me to have a chance with Iggie. I appreciate him and when the time comes, and he finds his special someone, I will back him a hundred percent like he has me.

THE MUSIC BLARES from the main room of the clubhouse, vibrating through the walls and into my room. I'm not in the mood to drink or party. The time to figure this shit out is up in twenty-four hours, and we don't know shit.

The new bouncer couldn't lift any prints, so that was a dead end.

I messaged Michaelov but have yet to hear from him. My patience is thinning, so I throw caution to the wind and call him. He answers on the fourth ring.

"Steel."

"I sent you a message and I'm growing tired of waiting, Michaelov," I say, my voice low and serious.

"I was busy. Your issues are not my issues. But now you're calling, so you've made it my problem," he tells me, as if he's bored with this conversation.

"I just need to know the day you called to change your order and the time if you can get it. You were affected by a leak somewhere in our system too, and I'm handling it. If you'd like to keep doing business with us, you'll look at your fucking phone and tell me the day and time. Then we're done here today," I snap.

"Fine. No need to get so hostile, little biker boy. Let me check." The line is silent, minus his breathing. A few minutes later, his voice comes down the line. "It was December fifth. I don't have the time anymore, but the call lasted only a few minutes. I hope this solves your problems, so you stop calling me like we're old friends." I hear the click signifying he hung up.

Wasting no time, I click over to Hawk's name.

> Me- December 5th. No time of call but it lasted a few minutes.

> Hawk- I'm on it. Will have it for you soon.

> Me- Not partying?

> Hawk- This is important to you. I've been searching.

> Me- Thanks.

I DROP my phone onto the bed and close my eyes. Finally, I feel like we have a break and this will be the end of our rat problem.

Hawk slaps me awake sometime later and I blink up at him, a scowl on my face instantly. "What the fuck?"

"I found it," he says.

"Why didn't you start with that? Let's hear it." I bolt up and throw the blanket off of me. "My office."

He follows me out, and I don't even bother locking my bedroom door like normal. I'm too excited and on edge knowing we're on the verge of discovering the truth. Once inside my office, I find my seat behind the desk while he chooses the chair facing me.

"You didn't let me finish." He sighs. "I found it and listened, but they used a voice changer. Can't tell who it is."

The sound of a commotion in the hall grabs my attention, and I fix my eyes on the door. The noise persists for a few more minutes before eventually subsiding.

"Fuckin' drunk bastards. Always fightin' and fuckin' off when they've had too many." I look at Hawk again. "I don't care. Play it. I want to hear it."

He nods and hits play on the tablet. I didn't even notice he had it in his hand.

"Hello."

"It's Michaelov. I'd like to add to my order."

"I can do that for you. What do you want?"

"RPGs. And I want them the same day as the rest."

"They'll be there."

"Send me the invoice."

"See you then."

The call abruptly ends, leaving a silence hanging in the air. Who the fuck was that? I didn't recognize the person, but they also used a voice changer, so I figured I wouldn't. They had to get into my office and take the call, so what were they doing in here? They must have picked the lock since Pistol and I have the only keys. But why? I don't keep anything in here because I'm paranoid, constantly on edge about potential intruders.

The sound of someone knocking on the wall interrupts my thoughts. I glance at Hawk, my brows creasing and my lip curling in annoyance. I am not in the mood for this shit. Whoever is out there causing a scene is going to get their teeth kicked in.

I walk toward the door, Hawk following closely, and open it, but nobody is in the hallway. What the hell? We hear the noise again, but it's not really banging now that we're out here, more like someone knocking repeatedly and it's coming from the closet that we keep the extra blanket and cots in when we go into lockdown.

I remove my knife from my boot and grip it as I place my other hand on the doorknob. I look back at Hawk and he has his gun armed and ready. "One. Two. Three," I whisper and pull the door open.

Kiki comes tumbling out, and she looks like she went ten

rounds with Rocky Balboa. A groan escapes her, and she directs her eyes toward me. "About time you got here. I've been locked in there for a while."

"What the hell happened?" I ask, bending down to get a better look at her. Fuck me. She's got a split lip and for sure a broken nose and a few cuts on her face. That's only what I can see.

"Came down to get a drink since Marni is sleeping," she rasps. "Saw that fucker trying to get into your office. He pulled me into the closet and tried to get me, but I got his ass. I wasn't raised no bitch."

"Who," I growl.

"Cody. Should be in there, knocked out and tied up. Did the best I could before I passed out. Then I woke up and couldn't get out, so I banged on the door. It must have locked behind us in the fight."

Hawk moves past me into the closet further and sure enough, Cody is in there, hands tied behind his back and tied to a sheet that's wrapped around his ankles. I reach into my pocket, grab my phone, and call Pistol.

"Yeah?"

"My office now. Bring the guys. And get Gabe down here too," I bark and hang up.

"What the hell happened?" Gabe gasps as he steps into the hall. He's the first to arrive, and he hurries to Kiki and bends down.

"That cunt, Cody, tried to pull one over on me." She gives him a small smile.

"No," he gasps. "It's okay, babe, you're gonna be alright." He runs a hand down her hair and smiles, then looks at me. "Where is he? I'll kill him myself."

"We got him, don't worry. Well, Kiki here knocked him out and tied him up. We'll handle him, though. Take her up to her room and clean her up. I'll call the doctor to look at her. Also, she's been watching Marni. Can you just keep an eye on her?" I tell Gabe and he looks at me with anger blazing in his eyes.

"Yeah, I got you, Prez. Just do me a favor and make it hurt."

A smile slowly crosses my lips. "Oh, we will."

My officers come crashing into the hall like a row of dominoes. "About time you lot got here," I snap.

"What the fuck?" Viper strides over to us. "Who did that to Kiki?"

"Cody. Hawk has him in the closet. We need to get him to the shed." I nod toward the door in question and Viper steps around us into the closet.

There's some shuffling before the door opens wider and Viper and Hawk come out holding a body-shaped object wrapped in a sheet. "See you there." Viper chuckles.

# twenty-four

## STEEL

CODY, clad only in his tightie whities, hangs precariously from a chain securely bolted into the ceiling. Viper rigged the setup himself, making sure it could hold the largest of men.

The now ex-whore's arms are holding his full weight as his toes just skim the ground. I lean against the back wall next to Pistol and watch Viper get to work.

This is his work area, his specialty, and he's good at it because the guy enjoys bloodshed. Wouldn't hurt a fly for no reason, but give him someone who betrayed or hurt someone he cares about and he loses it.

Viper steps up to Cody and slaps his cheeks a few times. "Rise and shine, shithead."

Cody's eyes flutter open, adjusting to the brightness of his surroundings. Panic washes over him as he begins to wiggle, fighting the chains.

"What the fuck!? Let me down. I don't belong here."

Viper tsks. "Cody, didn't you try to get the jump on Kiki?

Beat her real bad too, didn't ya? But she got one up on your ass. Kinda sad, man. Gettin' ya' ass beat by a woman."

"Fuck you." He spits on the ground at Viper's feet.

Our enforcer is on him in an instant, using his fist to knock the air from Cody's lungs. "Is that how you treat and talk to the people who homed you? You were a guest in our fuckin' house and you disrespect us like that? Disrespect Kiki like that? Why?"

"It'll be worth it in the end," Cody wheezes.

I look at Pistol, shaking my head and rubbing my temple. "What did you say?"

"I said it'll be worth it. You aren't gonna be the Prez soon and then none of this will matter."

Looking around the shed from Viper to Pistol and then behind me where my other officers sit in chairs, watching the show. "Any of you know what he's talkin' about? Something I'm not aware of?"

Their expressions mimic mine, a combination of furrowed brows and mouths slightly parted.

"Continue," I snap in Viper's direction.

He picks up a mallet and swings it, hitting Cody square in his left kneecap. The crunch is loud and there's no doubt it's shattered. "Who are you workin' with?"

"I ain't telling you shit," Cody hisses.

Another powerful blow, this time targeting the other kneecap. Viper doesn't stop there. As the mallet collides with Cody's ribs, his agonized cries fill the air.

"Fuck. Fuck. I was told to take Kiki out. Don't know why, but I got paid ahead of time in cash and a good time."

"Who?" Viper sets the mallet down.

"I'm dead if I tell you. They hate Steel and if I'm lost in the coup, they won't care," Cody whispers.

So for sure someone, or someones, in the club. I knew

we had a rat, but hearing it firsthand validates my thoughts and fuels me to get to the bottom of this. I want them dealt with immediately.

"You're dead no matter what. Cody, my boy, you're not leaving this shed." Viper laughs.

Cody struggles against the chains. "You can't do that. I'm just a whore, not a member. I was obeying member orders. That's my duty as a whore."

"Enough!" I shout. "You also signed a contract stating that you were here on your own free will. That you would uphold the honor and integrity of the club while in its service. We don't hurt women and we don't go behind the back of our president."

Cody whimpers, knowing I'm right. He agreed to be held to the same standards and rules as the members, just without a patch, knowing he was a hole for members to sink into.

"So tell us who turned you against the rest of the club and I'll make sure Viper makes it fast and painless. A nice bullet to the skull. Fuck me around and I'll let him keep you alive for days as you slowly bleed out."

"The only people who ever paid me any attention in this fucking club!" Cody yells. "I wasn't good enough for any of you, but I found who wanted and cared for me. This was my chance to prove to them I was loyal. This was how we'd get to be together!"

My mind begins to race through past parties and times in the main room of the clubhouse. Who was touchin' and flirtin' with Cody? I'm coming up blank. I've never messed with him and know Pistol hasn't since he's straight. But then who?

I look at Viper and shake my head with a shrug. Viper grabs a new tool off his table of treasures and stalks closer to

Cody. "Someone come hold him still, so I can work," Viper calls over his shoulder to the group of us spectating.

I kick off the wall and head to him. "What do you need?"

"Hold his foot still. I'm gonna play a little game my momma played with me."

Leaning down, I grab Cody's left foot as he howls in pain. Yeah, I bet this doesn't feel too good with that damaged kneecap. My grip is firm as I look at Viper. "Now what?"

Viper flashes a cruel smile and holds up a pair of very sharp garden shears. "Well, we know none of us have fucked ya. Right, fellas?"

The air fills with a soft murmuring, as everyone agrees.

"So that leaves just the patched-in members. Not everyone would fuck ya 'cause ya ain't their type. Like Pistol and myself, the dick just doesn't interest us. So it has to be someone who would enjoy dick."

Smart. Viper is often misunderstood as a mindless meathead with a penchant for violence, but in reality, he is quite intelligent. Somewhere along the way, he just went through some shit that made him need a little release now and then. His job as enforcer gives him just that.

"So who could it be? Hmmmm. This little piggy went to the market. This little piggy stayed home. This little piggy had roast beef. This little piggy had none. This little piggy went." Viper laughs as he looks at Cody, the shears positioned by his pinky toe.

Silence. Cody doesn't say a word, just glares at Viper.

"Wee, wee, wee all the way to the floor." And closes the shears, severing the toe from Cody's foot.

Cody screams and I can't believe whoever it is has him so tight-lipped. I'll give it to him. He's holding up better than I thought he would.

"Ready to tell me yet?"

"Fuck." Cody pants. "You."

"Okay, that's fine. My momma always played it more than once."

Viper repeats the rhyme, this time landing on the index toe. He's met by silence again and his rhyme ends the same as before; a long skinny toe falling to the ground.

"Please!" Cody screams.

"Please!" Viper mocks. "Tell me who it is. Minus the men here, those are the only other members who are openly with men. Everyone else is straight. Unless I'm missing someone." He looks around at the guys and they don't say anything.

"Pepper and Combo, but they're straight. Told us very loudly how much they don't approve of LGBTQ anything," Pistol pipes up.

A choking sound comes from Cody, and my eyes flash up to him. Viper notices too, a cruel smile slowly crossing his face. "Is that so? Those bastards are leadin' you on, boy. They've voted against every idea involving this club being open to all sexualities. So if you think one or both of those fucks care about you? You got played."

"Liar!" Cody hisses. "They care about me. Just needed the right man. They told me so themselves."

Viper moves the shears from Cody's foot and trails them slowly up his leg to his crotch. He doesn't hesitate to sink a hand into Cody's underwear, grabbing his soft cock and holding it so he can position it in the middle of the open shears.

I cringe and I hear a few groans behind us, all of us having the same thoughts about losing our cock like this.

"You tellin' me that this little stubby guy was inside one

of those two hateful bastards?" Viper laughs. "No fuckin' way."

Cody's nostrils flare and his eyes narrow. "Combo isn't there yet. He will be, though. Pepper, let me suck him off before I went to your office. A task for a task."

Viper closes the shears a bit, and Cody sucks in a breath. "What task?" Viper asks.

"I got to suck him off to prove they were all in for me. In return, I'd break into Steel's office and see if you guys had found anything about the Hellhounds and Michaelov's weapons. Kiki was the icing on the cake. They gave me two grand to get rid of her. Easy choice. I never liked her."

"Thank you," Viper tells him, snapping the shears shut and an ear-piercing wail leaves Cody as his nubby shaft is cut off. Blood pools in his underwear as they snap back into place, dripping down his legs to the floor.

"Let's go. We have two more friends to bring to the shed, it seems." I turn and head toward the door that leads to the outside.

Viper tosses the shears on the table and follows behind me. "I'll leave him here to bleed. He didn't listen and I don't like to hold up promises to rats."

"You're a sick fucker," Zero tells him as he pats him on the back. "Cutting his dick off, really?"

"Had it coming. You don't touch ladies like that."

# twenty-five

## STEEL

I STEP OUTSIDE into the brisk winter air and wait for the others to join me. By now, darkness has fallen, providing us with cover as we stand by the shed. Not that anyone will be outside this time of night, anyway. Tonight's party is well underway, keeping everyone's attention.

"We need a plan. Storming in there and grabbing ain't gonna work. I have no problem with the club witnessin' their last breath, but I want answers first. Why did they turn on the club and what does that have to do with Iggie?"

I know the two are connected and I'm the tie that binds them together. The only thing I can't figure out is why, and those two bastards are going to tell me.

"I got an idea," Viper announces, his eyes bouncing between us all. "We could go in and announce that Kiki was attacked and didn't make it. Then ask Pepper and Combo to step into the office with us. We wanna talk to them about bein' in charge of findin' new pussy. They'll eat that shit up and when we get em' alone, we drag their asses out here to play."

I nod my head, thinking about what he's proposed. Running through the possibilities that could throw the whole thing out the window. We need this done and over with, so it's worth the risk. "Okay. We need to tell Marni and Gabe to stay with Kiki and not to come out or mention shit to anyone else. Doc should have been here by now, but he knows better than to say shit to anyone other than officers."

"I can do that. I'll go in through the back and let them know to stay put and quiet." Zero raises his hand.

"Go ahead," I tell him, watching as he takes off toward the back door of the clubhouse.

"The rest of you follow my lead and we let them ask questions. Not a doubt in my mind they'll ask about fresh pussy as soon as they hear we lost a whore."

I turn and lead the way to the clubhouse, the sound of fresh, powdered snow crunching under our boots. Tomorrow we'll have to get the prospects out here to shovel.

When we get to the door, I pause to take a deep breath. Inside, the music is blasting, filling the air with a pulsating rhythm. I must remain calm and collected, refraining from losing my temper. Lzzy Hale's voice fills the room as we step inside. Just as the chorus ends, I grab the remote from the bar and pause the music.

"What the hell?" Milking a beer, Rubble sits in one of the recliners and hollers, the sound echoing in the room. He looks to see who cut the music and when his eyes land on mine, he nods once in my direction. "Sorry, Prez."

All eyes turn to me and I will my heart to slow down. "We have an announcement and it's not good. I'm sure you've noticed we've been MIA most of the day. Kiki was attacked, and we have been by her side, offering support and comfort. Unfortunately, she didn't make it."

The room erupts with a cacophony of grunts, growls, and the occasional gasp. Glancing around, I observe that the news has taken its toll on everyone, except for two people who maintain an air of indifference.

"Where's Gabe? He's been gone all day. Was he attacked, too? Same with Cody. Are we under attack, Prez?" Tex questions.

Clearing my throat after shaking my head. "Gabe knows about Kiki and is taking a few days to deal with the news. Kiki asked for him before shit went south. Cody should be here as far as I know."

"Who did it?" Chad asks, his eyes searching for an answer.

While I don't normally like the prospects getting involved in business like this, it's important they know the story we're spinning. After all, when this shit is over, they'll know what happens to rats and how far I'm willing to go to protect this club.

"We don't know yet. She wasn't on Hell's Mayhem's property, so the police are investigating," I tell him. "We will be doin' our own research and will handle whoever fucked with us accordingly."

"Now we're missing three out of four whores. Not that I cared about two of them, but Daria can't keep up with all of us. So when can we expect new pussy?" Combo asks.

"Real fuckin' sympathetic, asshole," Rubble barks.

"Fuck you, Rubble. She was a whore. I'll miss her warm mouth and tight pussy. God rest those." He gestures the sign of the cross. "But we got needs. If you're too busy, Prez, dealing with the investigation and the funeral shit, Pepper and I can recruit new pussy."

*Bingo. Like attracting a bear with honey.*

"Yeah, that sounds good, Combo. Thank you for volunteerin'. Let's go to my office and we'll go over what we're lookin' for." I smile, motioning for them to follow me and head to my office.

Glancing over my shoulder, I see both men trailing behind me, with Pistol and Viper hot on their heels. So far, so good. We just need to get to the office, where Viper and Pistol will incapacitate them before we transport them to the shed.

Slowly, I unlock my office door and step inside. Viper forcefully pushes past the others to stand on the other side of the door.

"Learn some manners, you psycho," Pepper grunts, his voice filled with venom and disdain. He steps into my office and looks around, surveying the place, Combo close behind him. Pistol shuts the door, the click prompting Viper to quickly take action. True to his name, he strikes like a snake, swiftly wrapping an arm around Combo's neck. Combo desperately tries to pry the arm off, but his efforts are in vain.

Pepper barely has time to utter a word before Pistol swiftly brandishes his gun, striking Pepper's skull with a forceful blow that instantly renders him unconscious. With a heavy thud, he collapses to the ground, and Pistol wears a satisfied smirk as he puts away his weapon.

Viper gently lowers Combo to the floor, his body now limp. I think that chokehold would have been powerful enough to render Steve Austin unconscious.

"Alright, let's get them to the shed before anyone sees us and starts askin' questions," I tell them. "Trucker," I call as he rounds the corner in the hall to my office. "Keep watch and signal if anyone is coming. I'll help lug Combo out with Viper. Pistol, get Hawk to help with Pepper."

Trucker nods and stands in the hall, playing on his phone as he leans against the wall. Pistol grabs his phone and holds it to his ear. "It's done. Come help me."

Seconds later, Hawk emerges, his footsteps echoing through the air as we join forces to transport the two slimeballs to the shed. Trucker follows behind as we leave through the backdoor, making sure we're not followed.

Once inside the shed, I help Viper get Combo chained up beside Cody and we put Pepper against a support beam, his arms behind his back and a chain around his waist.

Combo is the older, more seasoned member of the group, so he gets the privilege of having the better seat in the house. We take our spots, preparing to watch the show Viper is about to put on just like he did with Cody.

Speaking of Cody, he stirs ever so slightly, his gasping growing louder as he shudders in the unforgiving restraints. "Please," he whispers.

"Is that what Kiki said when you were smacking her around?" I ask. He's not in good shape; I'm surprised he could even utter the word, please. He'll be dead long before Viper is done playing.

He says nothing in return, knowing that his pleas are falling on deaf ears. "You're not leaving here alive, Cody. You sold your soul to the devil and can burn in hell waiting for salvation." I shrug. "If you stay alive for a while longer, you'll be able to take your buddies with you."

Viper grabs the smelling salts, opens them, and runs them under Combo's nose. As the older Robert Pattinson look-alike wakes up, he groans. The realization of his location dawns on him, and his movements immediately become frantic.

"Welcome to the shed, Combo. Is this your first time visiting? I hope the accommodations are to your liking and you'll consider leaving us a five-star review." Viper cackles, grabbing a hammer and flipping it in his hand.

"Fuck you. You crazy son of a bitch!" Combo shouts.

"That's not very nice. You didn't even know my mother. She was a nice lady, a little rough around the edges, and had a mean left hook, but a nice lady nonetheless."

This is why everyone thinks Viper is batshit crazy. He makes light of the fucked up shit that happens in the shed and has no issues taking a life. He likes to play and tease before he ends his prey like a cat with a mouse.

"Now the reason you've found yourself here is that your boy Cody here roughed up Kiki, and after a few nursery rhymes, he sang like a birdie, telling us all about your guys' deal." Viper jerks his head in Cody's direction.

Combo turns and gags when he sees Cody's almost life-less body hanging next to him. "God dammit! I'm a long-time member of this club. You can't do this." He twists and swings his body, trying to get free, but it's useless.

"I can and I did. I am the fucking president of Hell's Mayhem and you seem to have forgotten that. You betrayed me and this club, and we caught you. Time to come clean, so maybe the devil will spare you." I step forward, informing him his fate's been signed, sealed, and delivered the moment he ended up here.

Viper chuckles. "You've made Daddy President angry. It's time for a spankin'." He draws back and swings, the hammer landing square on Combo's kneecap. He screams as the audible crack echoes off the walls.

"What the hell's goin' on?" Pepper murmurs, looking around disoriented. He tries to move his hands, but they're locked behind his back. "The fuck are you playin' at?"

Viper turns around. "Pepper! I'm so glad you joined us. We are playin' a game called Mousetrap. You played before, right? It seems you three fell into our trap."

The accused struggles against his chains once more. "I ain't done nothin'! I've only been in the club for a few years. Combo vouched for me. I have to do what he says!"

"Shut up, Arthur!" Combo yells at his buddy.

"Oh, no, Arthur, tell us more. We wanna know why you've been telling the Hellhounds our business. Why fuck with the shipment?" Viper asks.

Pepper looks over at Combo and then back at Viper before shaking his head. "I'm not saying anything."

"Well then, let's get back to our game." Viper turns to Combo. "Let's try again. Why did you rat us out to the Hounds?"

"Fuck you," he spits.

Viper winds up and cracks the hammer against the other kneecap. Shit, the sound gives me shivers and I know it has to hurt like a motherfucker.

"Fuuuck!" Combo screams.

"I'm asking one more time before I bring out the stabby toys. Why did you do it?"

Combo hocks a loogie and spits, it landing on the toe of Viper's boot.

"Wrong." Viper grabs a hunting knife and waves it in Combo's direction. "Why did you do it?"

Combo turns his head to the side, meeting Pepper's gaze without speaking. Viper plunges the knife into his abdomen, Combo's body tensing instinctively in response. His agonized screams fill the room as Viper mercilessly stabs him, until eventually, he leaves the knife embedded in his shoulder.

"Okay! Okay! I joined this club 'cause it was powerful.

'Cause the people were my people. Then Steel got voted as Prez and shit went south. I won't be part of a club like that. I'll be damned if some dick sucker is going to strip me of my patch. So I was sinking the ship from the inside so I could step in as the new president to fix it," he tells us, breathing heavily from the pain.

"What is your deal with gay men?" Viper asks. "I know you've enjoyed a two-girl show; it's just men. Why? They ain't tryin' to fuck you, so what's it matter?"

"They ain't real men and shouldn't be in power! It's disgusting."

Viper grabs the knife and twists it as Combo howls in agony. "I don't much like how you're talkin' about people I like. Fuck you and your close-minded ass. You're in timeout while I go talk to your boyfriend here."

Viper steps over to Pepper, grabbing a croquet mallet as he passes his area of goodies. "Arthur, can I call you that? Actually, I don't care. Why did you go along with him?"

Silence.

"Have you ever played croquet? I used to be pretty good at it, but sometimes my sister would get pissed and crack me with her mallet. Savage little thing, she was. Let me demonstrate." He winds up. "Four!" he shouts, and the mallet sinks into the soft flesh of Pepper's cock.

Tears stream down Pepper's face, accompanied by fits of coughing and dry heaving.

"Now tell me, why did you follow this asshole's plan?"

"I told you. He vouched for me, I owed him my loyalty," Pepper wheezes.

I kick off the wall I'm leaning against. "No! You owed this fuckin' club your loyalty!"

Viper walks behind the beam he's secured to, gripping the mallet. A series of cracks reverberates in the room and when I peek around to the back of the man in question, his fingers are all at odd angles.

"I had to! I didn't have nothin' to do with the Hounds, though. That was all him. I only helped with Kiki and the papers. I couldn't turn down the money."

"I'll fuckin' kill you, Pepper!" Combo screams.

"Shut it, asshole. You're both dyin' anyway, so might as well tell the truth. I might make it fast and easy then," Viper scolds.

Papers? Is he talking about the ones that were dropped off to Iggie? If that's the case, then why? I know he wanted to ruin the club and me, but where does Iggie fit into all of it? I could fail as president and still be with Iggie. He'd just go with me wherever I went. It makes no sense to add that layer to their club takeover goals.

"What money?" I ask.

"I don't know who it's from, but Combo had someone who didn't want you near Iggie. They'd communicate. I wasn't allowed to be part of it. But I was paid to get those papers and pick the lock to your room to get the pictures of you and him together. I gave them to Combo, and he dealt with them from there. I got ten grand for it. And I was gettin' paid to handle Kiki, but had to split it with Cody." He looks over at the dead whore. "Not that it matters now."

My body is shaking with pure white hot rage. Who the fuck would pay them to keep me from Iggie? So, the thing with Iggie isn't about me? It's him, and I just happened to fall for a man with a stalker. He didn't have any exes that he was on bad terms with, as far as I know. Iggie also only has one friend, and I doubt he's paying people to keep me away. He's straight and, according to Iggie, is the one who sent me that first text from the bar all those nights ago.

"Take him outside." I look at Hawk and Zero. "Tie him

up to a tree for a bit before it's time. We need to talk in private to Combo here."

Hawk and Zero move toward Pepper, undoing his bindings and dragging him out the shed door.

I cross the room to Combo. "Who was paying you, Frank, and why?"

"Blood ain't always thicker than water, is it, Ashton? Your little cock boy is gonna find that out the hard way."

"This mouth sure talks a lot of shit." I look at Viper. "Why don't you spruce it up a bit?"

Viper rubs his hands together. "Oh, Steel, you naughty little thing." He heads to his table of items, grabbing what he needs. "Hold his head still."

I step behind Combo, feeling the warmth of his head in my hands. Viper forcefully inserts a dental mouth gag into Combo's mouth, spreading it open by pulling the handles apart.

"When I was little, I thought bein' a dentist would be cool. Now it looks like I can practice." He wags his eyebrows at Combo before he inserts the dental forceps into his mouth and chooses a tooth.

With controlled movements and intermittent grunts, he focuses on his task. When he jerks his hand back forcefully, he holds up the forceps, revealing one of Combo's teeth. "I did it! Now, did you wanna tell us who's paying you to fuck with Ignatius?"

He tries to talk, but it's unintelligible with the gag in. Viper pulls it from his mouth. "Okay, go ahead."

"I don't know who it is. She got my number from someone and refers to herself as The Manager. We only text and she electronically sends my money. I only know she's a lady cause she paid me three hundred bucks to do a video sex session with her. Wrinkly ol' pussy with a huge gray bush, but whatever, it was just some videos, and I got paid."

"You're fuckin' sick. You know that, right?" Viper questions.

"I've heard enough. Take him outside with his buddy. Trucker, get the rest of the club. I want everyone out back. Prospects, whores, all of them!" I shout to my road captain and he winks before quickly making his exit.

Thirty minutes later, everyone is outside minus Marni and Kiki, who Trucker gave a pass to, but Gabe is here in the front row. "Where's Cody?" he asks.

"Gone," I tell him and he smiles at me.

"Thank you."

"No need to thank me. Kiki is Hell's Mayhem family and we protect our own." It's time to end this and figure out who the fuck this Manager is that was texting Combo. I need to talk to Iggie about this when I see him. He might know who it is.

"Everyone!" I shout before putting my fingers in my mouth and blowing, the shrill whistle shutting everyone up. "It's cold out here, so let's make this fast. Earlier I told you a lie and for that, I apologize, but it was a means to an end. Today, someone attacked Kiki, and she is in rough shape. But she's alive and inside. I'm sure when she's recovered she'll be back givin' us all hell."

"Who did it?" someone calls from the group but I can't see who.

"Cody. And before you ask, we handled Cody. We will be looking for a new male whore, but that's not why you were called here. As you know, we've had a rat in the club. Someone has been feeding information to the Hellhounds about our comings and goings. It was Pepper and Combo. They're also the ones who paid Cody to attack Kiki. It seems they didn't like how progressive Mayhem has become. So let this be a fuckin' lesson to the rest of you. We won't tolerate hatred and close-mindedness. You don't have to like it, but we will not be hateful to our members based on their sexuality, gender, hell, their fucking skin color. Are we clear?"

"Yes, Prez," rings out in the chilly night air, causing a grin to form on my face.

"Alright then, we need to take out the trash and then I have more work to do. Viper if you would do the honors."

"With pleasure, Prez," he replies, stepping up between the two trees where Pepper and Combo are tied. He pulls his gun, putting the barrel against Pepper's temple. "May the devil have mercy on your asshole." He pulls the trigger, the sound of the gunshot pierces the air and just like that, we are down to one rat.

He looks over at Combo. "You won't get it so easy, you fucking hateful cunt. May the devil fuck your asshole every night." He holsters his weapon, exchanging it for a blade, and slowly slides it across Combo's throat.

Combo's eyes widen in horror as blood spurts from his throat. As life slowly drains from him, he coughs and gurgles, each breath becoming more labored.

"You can return to the clubhouse. Let this be a lesson to you all. I will not tolerate rats in my fuckin' club!"

A round of cheers goes up before the group turns and heads back to the clubhouse.

I look at my officers. "You guys got this?" I motion to the two shitbags. "It's almost dawn and I want to get cleaned up before I see Iggie. Hopin' he can shine some light on this Manager situation."

"We got you, Steel. Go talk to Iggie." Pistol waves me away.

## twenty-six

### IGNATIUS

I'M RUNNING LATE to work this morning and Barron is going to have my ass. While he will likely be okay with it, I absolutely despise being late. I slept through my alarm, which rarely happens, but with everything going on lately, I've been exhausted.

The red light down the block from Howards seemed to stretch on for an eternity, making me more frustrated by the second. It's a strange phenomenon—whenever you're in a hurry, stoplights seem to stretch out their red phase just to test your patience. As my phone rings and a message comes through simultaneously, the traffic light turns green and I swiftly accelerate through the intersection.

In my morning haste, I neglected to enable Bluetooth on my phone, leaving the caller to wait. I refuse to drive and text. My cousin's death in high school left a lasting impact, leading me to adopt a strict mindset regarding the matter. I'll check it when I get in the building; it's either Steel or Draco and both can hold their horses.

Pulling into a parking spot, I hastily retrieve my phone and bag, step out of the car, and hurriedly enter the building. Howards opens in twenty and I was supposed to be here forty minutes ago. The associates are all counting their drawers as I hurry by to the elevator. The doors slide open instantly after I press the button to go up, surprising me.

Thank God for small miracles.

I step in and hit the floor number the offices are on. The doors start to slide shut, but right at the last second, a hand sticks between them, stopping them.

"Ignatius. Hi. I haven't seen you in a while. How are you?"

This day couldn't get any worse. "Hi, Nancy. I'm good." I don't ask how she is because I want this conversation to end or the doors to open and let me off on my floor.

"I miss you downstairs," she says, her voice filled with longing as she steps closer. I take a step back, feeling a sudden unease. "Do you miss me? We always had such a good time together."

"I have been so busy with everything I haven't had time to even think about downstairs."

For the first time today, the world smiles down on me. The doors slide open and I move past Nancy out of the elevator and hurry to my office. As her heels click behind me, the sound reverberates, making my skin crawl. I have no idea why she's following me, but I know I need to reach my door quickly.

Once inside, I quickly turn and lock it. I then reach out and close the blinds to the wall of windows. The door knob jingles for a few seconds but then stops and there's silence. I wonder if Nancy knows her behavior gives off the impression of a complete psycho, resembling an obsessed stalker from a Lifetime movie?

Sighing, I move over to my desk and settle into my soft chair, ready to begin my daily tasks. My goal for Christmas is done since I got the tree and gifts delivered, but I'd like to start on next year's ideas and brainstorm how to get more of the employees involved. While it was amazing for Hell's Mayhem to help, they didn't have to, and they really saved my ass.

I also just learned last week that Howards gives a scholarship each year to a local high school student who plans to pursue a business degree. I'm in charge of going over the applications, pulling the top ten candidates, and presenting them to the Howards so they can pick a winner.

Since it's December, and school ends in May, I need to start working on it. An email I received mentioned a scholarship ceremony in April, where we'll announce the winner in front of a big audience.

I haven't mentioned it to Barron yet, but I'm considering planning some public events to raise funds for another scholarship. Given that business remains predominantly male-oriented, I aim to award two scholarships in April—one for a male and one for a female—to promote gender diversity in the field. I'm thinking of a bowling event and a dance.

The unexpected knock on my door makes me jump, my heart racing. I get up nervously and part the blinds, holding my breath. It's not Nancy. Sighing in relief, I unlock the door and swing it open with a smile. "What can I do for you, Barron?"

"I was hoping to talk to you about an idea I had. You did an impressive job in a short time for the holidays, single-handedly. My idea might help raise spirits around here so more people help in future signups."

"Perfect. Come in." I step to the side, holding the door

open as he moves past me into my office. With it closed, I settle back into my chair, feeling its comforting embrace as I lean back and cross my legs.

"Hit me with it." I chuckle.

Barron's smirk grows wider as he casually leans against the door, exuding confidence. "So when I was little, my grandpa used to throw an employee dance. I remember it was fancy—a black-tie affair—and I used to beg to go with my parents. We served dinner and danced. It was just one night when everyone came together and had fun. No bosses or guidelines, just fun."

"So like a company Christmas party, but not at Christmas. I like it." I nod, my brain already running wild with ideas.

"You would bring it back to Christmas. It really is your favorite day, huh?" He laughs while shaking his head.

"Leave me be," I joke. "Okay, so when are you thinking you want to do this and any ideas on the venue or anything else? Or do I have free rein? Oh, and I'll need a budget."

"I was thinking, June, so the weather is nice and we don't have to worry about roads, and that gives you almost six months of planning. Is that enough time?"

"It'll be tight, but I can make it happen. Let me get to work. First, we'll need a venue and date so I'll look up a few places and see what they have open for this summer." I turn to my computer, wake up the screen, and begin to type.

"Well, alright then. I'll leave you to it. Try to keep it under seventy-five," Barron says, knocking on my door once as he leaves.

Searching for places large enough for our employees and a plus one is the first goal, then I'll narrow it down to dates and prices.

I'm clicking and writing down numbers and places to

call like a madman. Now it's time to actually start calling and seeing what everyone can offer me. Dialing the first place, I speak to a man who has no dates until September, so that won't work. The next is a snobbish-sounding woman who has June dates but wants the entire rental fee in full since it's 'last minute'. So that's going to be a no as well.

The next name on my list is in a huge barn that someone has turned into a winery and venue.

"Hello," an older lady answers on the second ring.

"Hi. My name is Ignatius, and I work at Howards. We are looking for a place to host our first annual employee ball. Can you tell me about your price packages?"

"Of course. Of course, we have the upstairs for a more formal dinner party setting, while the downstairs serves as a bar and party area. We can hold up to five hundred guests with the fire code, so that's tight. For a full night's rental, you're looking at ten thousand."

"Okay, and can we come in the night before and set up? Do you have an approved catering and bartending list, or can we use our own found services?" I ask, hoping there aren't a lot of hoops to jump through because that's an amazing price for what I'm looking for.

"We have an approved catering list, but it's pretty long. We've worked with almost everyone in the area. As for bartenders, we have a bartender who comes in and works our events, which just makes it safer for our liquor license. Usually, she's twenty an hour, but I used to work at Howards as a teenager, so I'll cover her night's wages."

"Oh, my gosh! That's so kind of you! Tell me you have June weekend dates available or I might cry," I joke.

"I do. A bride just called and canceled, so I have June twenty-ninth open."

"Perfect! I'll take it. Can you send me the invoice? My

email is IgnatiusHarper@howards.com and I'll get that paid immediately. If you could send the approved catering list too, that would be amazing."

"Sure thing. Thank you, Ignatius. I'll have my grand-daughter send that invoice now. I'm not too tech savvy."

"Sounds good." I chuckle and hang up.

I SUDDENLY HEAR my phone beeping, signaling it's time to clock out. *Where did today go?* The moment I finished the conversation with the barn, I hurried down the hall to Barron's office, eager to let him know we had secured a date and place. To say he was excited that it's a sure thing is an understatement—he practically jumped for joy when he heard the news.

In a rush, I reach for my phone in the desk drawer. With a swipe, I turn off the alarm and immediately notice a text and a series of missed calls. All from Steel. It was him calling this morning, and I completely forgot to check my phone after I got here. Nancy's stalking took me by surprise, causing me to completely space out.

I'm not worried though because I'm meeting him in under an hour at Brew Me, just a few blocks over. I pack my bag, carefully placing my lunch container inside and tucking in the folder with the information Tammy from the barn sent. I regret not asking her name when we were on the phone, and now I can't help but feel guilty. Her signa-ture on the contract made me realize it just now. I was just so excited when I found out they were affordable and could host us.

Next time we speak, I'll make sure to apologize.

As I open my office door, I glance down the hall, ensuring that Nancy is not lurking nearby. Given her tendency to leave early, I highly doubt she's still here, but her behavior this morning has made me nervous.

When I don't see anyone, I close my door and walk toward the elevator. Pressing the button to go down, I listen for the mechanical hum—the anticipation building the longer I wait. Finally, with a soft whoosh, the doors slide open, and I step inside, hitting the button for the main floor. I swiftly retrieve my phone from my pocket and text Steel.

ME- HEY SORRY I missed you this morning. I got busy and forgot I had a missed call. I'll tell you about it when I see you.

Me- I'm on my way

THE DOORS OPEN AGAIN, and I quickly put my phone away before stepping out of the elevator. As much as I adore winter, I'm looking forward to nicer weather. I miss the sensation of walking outside without fear of freezing to death, and the idea of sipping a cocktail on the patio only intensifies that longing.

With the sun already set, the temperature has dropped significantly from this morning, leaving me shivering as I make my way to the parking lot. "Have a good night!" I call to Bernie, the night security guard.

"Have a good one, Ignatius." I watch as he locks the door behind me and starts another patrol lap of the lower level.

The biting cold makes me shiver involuntarily, and I quickly tuck my hands into my pockets. The parking lot only has my sedan left, and I'm disappointed that I didn't park in the better lot at the back of the building. The one that has cameras and working lights. Unfortunately, I was running late and settled for the first available spot.

Walking quickly to my car, I begin digging through my belongings, looking for my keys, but they seem to have vanished. "What the hell?" I mumble aloud. If I left them in my office and have to call Bernie to go up and get them, I'm going to be absolutely furious. I thought I grabbed them this morning, but now I'm not so sure.

Before I bother Bernie, I cautiously reach for the door handle, hoping it's unlocked and the keys are in the car. Sure enough, the door opens with ease and I shake my head, sending up a prayer that I just had a moment of idiocy and left them in the ignition.

I toss my bag into the empty passenger seat and slide into the driver's seat, my eyes immediately searching.

Nothing.

*Fuck.*

I sigh deeply, feeling the exhaustion weighing on me, and sink back into my seat, resting my head against the headrest. Closing my eyes, I blow out a breath.

When I open them, I am startled by a fleeting figure reflected in the rearview mirror. The adrenaline rushes through my veins, causing my heart to speed up and my breath to quicken. Doubting my senses, I start to glance behind me to examine the backseat, but before I can fully turn, a figure suddenly springs up from the floor and tightens a slender, unknown object around my throat.

205

Panic consumes me as I kick at the floorboards, my hands pulling at whatever this rope-like thing is so I can breathe. The gap between them is so narrow that I can't even slip my fingers through, causing my lungs to ache.

Everything around me darkens, and I can't wrap my head around the fact that this is really happening. I should have known better—should have gone and got Bernie and had him look for my keys and made sure all was good with my car.

Right before the world disappears, the person choking me loosens their hold, and I strain to make out the faint sound of a whisper. "Don't worry, baby. We're together now."

# *twenty-seven*

## STEEL

SITTING INSIDE BREW ME, I patiently wait for Iggie, savoring each sip of my black coffee. I ordered his favorite iced caramel macchiato with white mocha for him, but the ice is almost melted. Meeting with him was already going to be difficult, but I never imagined he would flake.

He texted and said he was on his way and wanted to know the truth about everything, so would he really tell me he was coming to not show up? We haven't known each other that long, but I know well enough this isn't him. Gulping down the remainder of my coffee, I quickly grab his drink and exit the coffee shop. A strange unease lingers, a sensation that I can't ignore, seeping into my bones.

When I reach my cage, I carefully place his drink in the cupholder and turn the key in the ignition. Pulling out of the street parking spot, I head in the direction of Howards.

As I get closer, my stomach churns and my heart starts racing. The building appears deserted with all the lights turned off, except for the faint glow of the security lights. So he's not still inside... willingly, that is. I circle the block and turn into the back parking lot I know Iggie prefers. No sign of him or his car.

*Fuck. Where is he?*

I decide to check the side lot and as I pull in, it appears empty at first until I spot Iggie's car alone in the distant corner. Of course, he would park where there are no lights. I'm going to spank his ass when I see him after I make sure he's okay. When I pull up next to his car, a sense of dread fills me from what I see.

The driver's door is slightly ajar, and I know he wouldn't leave it like that. Jumping out of my cage, I round the hood and look his car over. Nothing else is out of place, but with the door slightly open and his bag occupying the passenger seat, it is evident that he was recently here.

I open the driver's door and give the car a thorough once-over, but there's nothing else unusual to note. Then my eye catches something black and gleaming, wedged between the seat and the door, almost hidden underneath. It's his phone.

Something is wrong. This screams of foul play. I need to get the guys over here. No, wait, scratch that. I need to get Viper and Pistol, and then we'll get the rest of the club in on it. I don't want a bunch of people contaminating the scene of the crime.

"Hey! What are you doing here?" The blinding beam of a flashlight catches me off guard and I whip my head around, squinting to see who it is. The night guard from Howards is cautiously approaching, his hand resting on his belt.

I shield my eyes until he gets closer and drops it from my face. His name tag says Bernard. "Had plans with someone tonight and they didn't show. I came to check on him. This is his car, but there's no sign of him inside. Do you know Ignatius? Did he leave tonight or is he inside working still? I just wanna make sure he's okay."

The guard's eyebrows shoot up, and his eyes widen. "Iggie left a while ago. I locked up after him. Shit, let me call for backup. We'll need the Boone County Sheriff." He reaches for his radio.

"No!" I bark, and he jumps back. "No cops. Iggie is mine and I'll handle it," I tell him a little more calmly.

"I'm sorry, but I can't do that," he replies. "If this was foul play, the cops need to handle it."

Turning, I let him see my cut, looking at him over my shoulder. "There's no need. I said we'll handle it."

"O-okay. Well, if I can help, let me know. Iggie's a friend, a good person, that one."

"I will. But for now, head back inside and keep your mouth shut. I don't need anyone knowin' shit yet."

"If it helps Iggie, I won't say anything." He turns and heads back toward the door.

Fury courses through me, causing spots to dance across my field of vision and my lungs to gasp for air. I pull my cell phone out of my jeans pocket and quickly dial Pistol's number.

"Hello."

"I need you and Viper to get to Howards right fuckin' now."

"Everything okay?"

"Nope. It's really fuckin' not. Just get here." I hang up and get in my truck, waiting for my vice president and enforcer to arrive.

It doesn't take long before Pistol's truck screeches into the parking lot, coming to an abrupt stop beside mine. Both of them are out and in front of my truck door in seconds.

"What the hell is going on?" Pistol's voice is filled with confusion and frustration.

"Iggie didn't show up to our meeting. I came to check on him since that's not like him. He texted me and said he was on his way. I get here and find his car door open, and his phone on the floor. Something ain't right."

"Are you sure he's not just inside, Prez?" Viper's voice falters, a hint of doubt creeping into his tone.

"Yeah. Security came out to see what I was doin' and he said he locked up after Iggie walked out to leave. I'm tellin' ya somethin' happened. Somethin' bad"

We search the car from top to bottom, but there is nothing unusual and the surrounding area is completely clear.

"Nothing else seems off. What do you wanna do with the car, Steel?" Viper asks.

I didn't even think about that. It's not safe to leave it here, exposed and accessible to anyone passing by. The keys are gone, but that's nothing to Pistol. Shit! What do I do?

*Fuck it.*

"Pistol, wire it and drive it back to the clubhouse. No one else needs to be involved, and if we leave it here, someone will surely report it and the authorities will be notified. We're handlin' this. Whoever took him is going to pay for touching him."

"I'm on it," he replies, determination in his voice. "Just give me a sec." Pistol grabs something from his truck before climbing behind the wheel.

With a steady hand, he pushes the screwdriver into the ignition, forcefully hammering it in. As he turns the tool, a wide smile spreads across his face, accompanied by the hum of the engine coming to life. He looks at us, grinning. "Haven't done that in a while. Viper, drive this back to the clubhouse and we'll be behind you." He gets out and lets Viper slide behind the wheel.

Viper backs up and takes off, leading the way, with us riding his ass the entire time.

As we pull up to the shop, the familiar scene of our bikes and vehicles awaiting maintenance greets us, interspersed with the occasional client's car in line for a custom build. Viper leans on the horn, signaling for the overhead door to lift, allowing him to drive Iggie's car inside.

My truck rolls to a stop and I hop out, striding toward the garage where the rest of my officers are. "What the hell is this?" I ask.

"Pistol called. Said we should meet out here and something happened to Iggie." Trucker pipes up. "The rest of the club is on standby. What happened?"

I start from the beginning, recounting every detail I shared with Viper and Pistol. Anger flickers across their faces the more I reveal. When I finish, I observe in silence as they conduct their own investigation.

"What about CCTV footage?" Zero asks.

"Howards has cameras, I think, but not in that lot. It's why Iggie didn't usually park there and because the lighting sucks."

"What about any of the surrounding businesses?"

Checking the other businesses for surveillance cameras didn't cross my mind.

*Fuck, Ashton, what a fuckin' rookie move.*

"Fuck!" I roar, kicking the trash can beside me across the garage and the contents fly everywhere. I turn around, slamming my fist against the brick wall of the garage.

Pistol's arms wrap around me, effectively restraining me from causing any more harm. "Relax, man. We got this.

Hawk can do a thorough search of the surrounding areas, making sure to check for any surveillance cameras, right?"

"Yeah. Easy as pie. I'll go get my laptop now."

"You need to cool off, Steel." He releases me. "Don't let your rage control you. We're going to find out who did this and make them wish they never touched your man. Until then, why don't you check on Kiki? She's been askin' for ya." Pistol tilts his head as I spin to glare at him.

He's right. I need to stay calm, cool, and collected in order to do this the right way. Rushing and getting worked up won't help Ignatius. He needs me at my best so I can bring him back faster.

"Alright," I breathe. "You're right. I'll go check on her now. But I wanna know the minute you find something."

"I swear." Pistol holds a hand out for me to shake, and I take it in mine, squeezing tightly.

"YOU LOOK like something the cat drug in," Kiki groans, lying in her bed with Marni next to her.

"Not like you look much better," I snap at her.

She throws her head back, her laughter echoing through the room. "Fuck, don't make me laugh. It hurts."

"Sorry babe. How are you feeling? You really do look like hell." I roam my eyes over her face and what I can see of her upper body.

Her face is a canvas of bruises, with her left eye swollen shut and stitches holding together the skin on her right temple and bottom lip.

"Feel like I went a couple rounds with Tony Stark, but

I'll live. Nothing's broken, but I got a few cracked ribs and bruised to hell. What about Cody? You better have cut his dick off."

I settle myself at the foot of the bed, sinking into the soft mattress. "I did better than cut off his dick. Although Viper did do that. We killed him. He was working with Combo and Pepper. They turned their backs on the club."

"That's why you called everyone outside? Public execution?"

"Yup."

Marni lets out a sudden gasp, causing Kiki to turn her head. "They don't kill unless someone truly deserves it," she explains. "Promise. Don't worry, there are no serial killers lurking around your place of stay. But damn, that would make my little dark romance heart happy," she murmurs with a wistful smile.

"I don't care about the killing. I've seen death before. Think you could kill my uncle?" she asks.

"S'not how it works, Marni. If your uncle hurts the club, yes. If you were part of the club and he hurt you, yes. But we can't just turn into assassins. I'm tryin' to make the club as legit as possible," I tell her honestly.

I know we won't ever be totally legit. We're a fuckin' MC, but I'd like our money to come from legal means. That's why I've been advocating for a complete remodel of the strip club and brainstorming fresh ideas to attract and retain customers. It's also why we are building the new club. And we've batted around the idea of opening the shop to more than just custom builds—a full-blown auto and bike shop. Hell, with some of the guys we got here, it could be anything with a motor.

"I see," Marni whispers, her fingers nervously tugging at the threads of the soft comforter.

"You're here now, Marni. If your uncle comes lookin' and causin' trouble, we'll take care of it, but that's as far as it goes. And if you leave here when you're eighteen, we can't protect you wherever you run off to."

She nods but remains silent, wiping her eyes with her sleeve.

"You didn't come up here to check on me just 'cause, Prez, and now you've made my nurse cry. Why are you here?" Kiki asks.

Smart, this one is. She's perceptive as hell, catching onto things others often overlook, and never afraid to voice her opinions. The reason she gets away with talking to me like she does is because she's smart enough to do it privately and, well, if it wasn't for Pistol, I'd say Kiki is my best friend.

A whore as my other best friend. Christ, I might be gettin' soft, but Kiki is a tough bitch, and she's unapologetically herself. She'd be a great member of the club if she had a cock.

"Iggie agreed to meet and talk to me. I went to the meeting place, and he never showed up. Not like him, so I went to his work to check on him."

"Steel..." she warns.

"No. I'm serious. I had a gut feeling something was wrong, and I was right. His car was in the parking lot, but he wasn't. Without goin' into detail, someone kidnapped him. I know it. Hawk is pulling CCTV footage from the area to see if we can see anything."

"Oh, Steel. I'm so sorry," she apologizes, her eyes filled with tears.

"I don't need your apologies. That's what people say when you lose a loved one. And while Iggie might be lost right now, he won't be for long. We're going to find who did this and I'm going to rip their fuckin' throat out."

Kiki opens her mouth to say something, but before she can utter a word, Viper swings open the door, instantly filling the room with his presence. "Hawk has something, Prez."

I spring off the bed and rush toward the door, my heart pounding. "Thanks, Kiki. Holler if you need anything. Marni, keep your eye on her."

I rush down to my office, where I know Hawk will be waiting, and pause to inhale deeply before entering.

"Have something good for me, Hawk," I tell him as I move behind my desk and sit down.

"The building across the parking lot has cameras and one catches the corner of the lot Iggie's car was in. I know what happened now, we just have to find the who."

"Show me," I force out through clenched teeth. At the same time, Hawk sets the laptop in front of me and hits play.

"About thirty minutes before Iggie got out of work, this masked person unlocks his car and gets in the backseat. They don't do anything but crouch down and wait for him. And they came from inside Howards. I don't know if they work there or were shopping, but it's a clue." Hawk plays the footage and it's as exactly as he says.

Dread pools in my stomach and my blood feels like it's boiling. "Fast forward to when Iggie comes out."

"Here we go," Hawk whispers.

The footage is black and white, slightly grainy, but I can make Iggie out as he walks to his car. He stops next to the door and digs in his bag briefly before his head turns to look toward the building and then back to his car.

He throws his bag inside and slips behind the wheel. He sits there for a minute looking around, like he's looking for something. Then he leans back in his seat and that's when the person in the backseat slithers from the floor like a demon in a movie. Judging from their arm position and the way Iggie thrashes in the seat, it looks like they wrap something around his neck.

His fight is in vain, though, since he stills and my heart shatters. The slim figure gets out of the car and puts a hand to their ear. I'm assuming they're calling someone, and I'm proven correct when a white box van reverses up next to the sedan. The rear door is even with Iggie's driver's side back door.

Together, clad in all black attire, they forcibly remove Iggie from his car and load him into the back of the van. With a slam of the doors, they speed out of the parking lot, heading westward.

I rocket from my chair, sending it careening back against the wall. "I want to know where they went with him. Use traffic cams or other footage from businesses on the street."

"On it, Prez." Hawk grabs his computer and begins to type furiously.

We need a plan, and I want eyes everywhere. This is my fuckin' town and someone stole what is mine right out from under my nose. I'm going to find whoever they are and rip them to fuckin' shreds.

Storming from my office, I enter the main part of the clubhouse. "Listen up!" I shout, getting everyone's attention. "You all know we're on alert. I want boots on the ground and everyone lookin' for Ignatius. If you see him, you call me. Are we clear?"

*Yes, Prez* fills the room and pride washes over me. This is why I joined this club and became the president. I wanted brotherhood, family, and something we'd all be proud to be a part of.

"Prospects! I want you to go to Iggie's house. No one goes

in unless it's me. I want to know everyone who even drives past."

Chad nods and leaves behind the bar, headed toward the door with Nate on his heels.

"Rubble, Tex, take Zombie and stake out Howards. When they open, I want Zombie to go inside and see if he can find anything out. I have a feeling whoever took him is either a frequent guest or works there. See if you hear anyone missing work or a guest that they're surprised doesn't come in."

The men in question stand up. Tex slaps Zombie on the shoulder, motioning for him to follow. The three of them leave, with Rubble leading the way and Zombie not far behind. He's the best one to send inside since he doesn't speak. Mute that one. No idea why, but he's a good man with a pristine record in the Navy and no medical reasoning behind his lack of words. Suits me fine. We get on without him talking and he hears more than the rest of us.

Finally, I turn to my road captain. "Trucker, I need you to find and bring Iggie's friend Draco here."

"No problem. Do you want me to tell him what's going on so he comes willingly or just drag him along?"

If we hurt Draco, Iggie will have my ass and that's not on my list of things to do. I need his friend to come here and tell us everything he knows about Iggie's life. I know a good chunk given my obsessive, borderline stalking tendencies, but he's known him longer.

Fuck! I should have put the tracker in Iggie himself and not his car. Not a mistake I'll let happen twice.

"Tell him Iggie's in trouble and we need his help. If he doesn't come willingly, do whatever needs to be done to get him here."

"Consider it done. I'll go grab his address and other

information from Hawk and be back." Trucker moves past me, heading to my office where Hawk still is.

"The rest of you cruise the town. We're looking for a white box van. The plate number was covered up, but you all know the deal. You see something suspicious, follow your gut. If you see Ignatius, I want to know. Also, the person who took him goes by The Manager, so if you hear anything of the sort, I want to know."

I watch as the rest of the club gets up and exits through the door, ready to start scouting the town for my man.

*Hold on, Iggie. We're coming for you. And when I find you, I'm going to bathe in the blood of those who dared take you from me.*

# twenty-eight

## IGNATIUS

STEEL HOLDS my hand as we walk downtown, checking out all the shops and reveling in the slightly warmer spring air. Since this is the Midwest, winter isn't always freezing; with the thermometer reading in the forties, it feels almost like summer to us Illinoisans.

We're headed to lunch and then Steel has promised me a ride on his bike since the roads are finally clear.

The thought of being nestled behind him on his motorcycle brings a smile to my face, one that I can't get rid of. There also might be a slight bit of nerves since this will be my first time on a bike.

But I can worry about that later. Right now, it's time to eat and I'm starving.

Steel opens the door to the Machine Barn and holds it open, allowing me to enter. He graciously holds it open for the elderly couple behind us, and my heart flutters at his chivalry.

I can't believe I was ever hesitant about being with him

or believed he wouldn't treat me with the utmost respect... unless we're in the bedroom, that is.

I sense his presence as he steps up behind me, his finger effortlessly sliding through my back belt loop. "You like seeing me be all chivalrous, don't you?"

"Yeah," I whisper, my attention shifting from him to the hostess making her way toward the podium.

"Who knew being mannerly toward grandparents did it for you, baby," he teases, his hot breath against my ear.

"Stop." I smile.

"Just the two of you?" the hostess asks, bending down and grabbing the silverware and menus.

"Yes ma'am," I reply.

"Perfect. Follow me." She heads toward the main dining room. "Our specials today are the Farmer's Daughter Breakfast and the Cattlemen's Meatloaf. Depends on what you're in the mood for since one is breakfast and the other is lunch."

We stop next to a small square table, and she motions us to take a seat with a subtle hand gesture. "My name is Kira and I'll be your server today."

"Thanks, Kira. Can we get two coffees and some water?" Steel requests and she nods.

"I'll be right back with those."

Steel and I sit at the quaint table, we browse through the menu, our stomachs growling in anticipation.

Kira returns with our drinks and after a moment of deliberation, we both settle on the Cattlemen's Breakfast. Our food comes out in no time and we get lost in conversation as we eat, sharing our aspirations and dreams for our future together.

Time seems to warp as we lose ourselves in each other's company. Before we know it, our plates are nearly empty, and the waitress returns to whisk away the remnants of our meal.

I'M SO full that even though the Apple Dumpling looks tempting, I can't possibly eat another bite.

"You ready, babe? Gonna be able to ride now that you ate so much." Steel chuckles.

"I'll be fine. Wouldn't miss this chance for the world. I'm ready to pop my bike cherry." I wiggle my eyebrows.

A low growl rumbles in his chest. "I can pop another bike cherry too. I know a place."

My belly warms at his words. Now is not the time. We're in a restaurant, for crying out loud. I can't help but roll my eyes and shake my head. "Come on, you dog. Let's go."

Steel grabs the bill and we head up front to pay. I met Steel here since I ran into the office to get some work done, but now it's time for him to take me out on his Harley.

Getting to his bike, Steel grabs a helmet from his seat and hands it to me. "Safety first."

"Where's yours?" I ask, looking around but not seeing another helmet.

"I don't wear one, but you do. Now, put it on, Iggie."

"Yes, sir," I whisper, securing the black helmet tightly over my dark golden hair and fastening the chin strap.

Steel throws a leg over the bike and looks at me, holding a hand out for me. Grabbing it, I climb behind him and put my feet on the peg-looking things on either side.

"A natural already." Steel smiles, his eyes twinkling with pride. "You got your feet on the pegs. Now, wrap your arms around me, but not too tight like you're scared. Just a natural firm hold, ya feel me? When we turn, just lean with me. I won't let nothin' happen to you, Iggie."

I know he won't. But despite wholeheartedly trusting this man, my heart races in my chest as my mind fills with anxious what-ifs.

Shaking it off, I blow out a breath and wrap my arms around him. "Alright Steel, show me what ya got."

Steel lets out a seductive chuckle, sending a shiver down my spine. He turns the key to the ignition, and the bike roars to life. I've never felt anything like the intense vibration and raw power coursing underneath me. We pull away from the curb and fly down the street. The wind beats at my face but I can't seem to care.

A smile creeps over me and I lose all sense, putting my arms out like Rose in the Titanic. Free. I feel free.

"I love you, Steel!" I shout over the purr of the engine.

He reaches behind him, squeezing my thigh. "I love you too, Iggie. Have since that first day I saw you," he shouts back.

"ARE YOU OKAY? Baby, are you okay?" Nancy's voice cuts Steel off.

*Why am I at work? And why is Nancy in my office?*

The memory of leaving Howards is hazy, but I can still feel the smooth leather of the car seat against my back as I got in. Maybe I fell asleep in my car. It was all a concoction of my mind, none of it was real. Can you dream that you're dreaming? Because I know Steel and I have never taken his bike out together.

And Nancy has never been in my office as far I know. So what's going on?

In an instant, it all comes crashing back like a tidal wave. I indeed left work except I got in my car and couldn't find my keys. Someone was in my backseat and they choked me out.

*Fuck.* Please, when I open my eyes, let me be safe and not kidnapped. Actually, let me open my eyes, period. It will mean I'm alive, at least.

Blinking them open, I take in the space I'm in. It resembles a garage, but someone has transformed it into a makeshift bedroom, complete with a bed and a small desk. One look at the overhead door mechanism and the track on the ceiling is all it takes to confirm that it's still a garage.

"You're awake! Good, I was worried, babe. Mom told me not to panic, but I couldn't stand it if I lost you."

"Nancy, what did you do?" I croak, my throat dry and sore.

My coworker stares at me, her eyes vacant and devoid of understanding. "Iggie. I've asked and chased long enough. This playing hard to get needed to end."

"I'm not playing hard to get, Nancy. You're a nice woman and all, but I'm not interested," I tell her, hoping that this delusion ends, and she frees me.

"Don't say that!" she screams, the sound echoing through the room as her hand slaps me hard across the face. The force of the impact makes my head snap to the right, eliciting a sharp gasp from me. "I've put up with you touching that filthy biker and playing house with him. Then you leave the department so I can't see you anymore. I won't stand for it any longer!" She stomps her foot and stares at me.

I knew this woman was weird and slightly obsessed with me, but never did I think she'd knock me out and tie me up in some sketchy garage.

Nancy flips a piece of strawberry blonde hair from her face and pushes her glasses up her nose. "Mom and I converted the garage into your bedroom. I've been planning this for a while. Do you like it?"

This can't be happening. My chest feels tight as my heart races and a throbbing pain pulses through my head. Are there long-lasting side effects of being choked unconscious?

I feel like I'm floating in a hazy dream, but it's not a pleasant one. It's an unsettling sensation. Where's my phone? I was supposed to meet Steel at Brew Me and now I obviously won't be there.

He'll probably think I just stood him up since I broke it off with him. Instead, I'm a prisoner in this crazy bitch's garage and no one will look for me.

"Where's my stuff? My car?"

"You won't need a phone, and I didn't need that trashy biker following us. I'm sure he has GPS or something on your car. It's what he did to those women."

"He's not trashy," I spit. She fails to realize that while Steel may have been a slight stalker, he didn't kidnap and tie someone up in his garage. She's a lot more off the rails than I ever imagined.

Steel may be a biker in an MC, but he never once treated me like less than. He would have never tied me up and taken me hostage. I broke up with him and he respected my wishes. Nancy, though, can't even take the hint that I'm not into women and now look where I am.

"Don't be stupid, Iggie. He was beneath you. I know you were slumming it to get back at me, but that wasn't the way. I had to show you. Do you know how hard it was for me to get those pictures I sent you? What I had to do to get them and those files? What I begged Mom to do?"

"You sent the pictures and the reports?"

"Of course I did. You needed to know who Ashton Steel is. He forced those poor women to get protection against him by stalking them. It was only a matter of time before the same thing happened to you."

"How did you get those pictures?" I ask, not sure if I want to know the answer, but apparently, even in this situation, I'm a glutton for punishment.

"I've been watching you, following you. Then I had Mom make a contact in his little club. They're not as closely knit as he thought. Some money and sexy video calls with Mom and they had the pictures. Hell, they even beat that little bitch who touched you. Kiki was it?"

"Is she okay?"

"Don't know, don't care. She should have kept her nose out of our business and not touched what's mine."

"Nancy, listen to me. I am not yours. I am gay. It's nothing against you. I'm just not attracted to females. Do you understand? Now, let me go and we can forget all about this." I'm trying to reason with her so she lets me go. I've never led her to believe anything other than I'm attracted to men, so how did she get this delusional?

"He said you'd be stubborn."

He? Who is he and why does Nancy think he knows anything about me? There are only two men who know me well, Draco and my dad. Draco would never give this woman false hope and Nancy doesn't know my dad. So who could she be talking about?

"He said what? And who is he?"

As she approaches me, she gracefully climbs into my lap, positioning herself so she is straddling me, rubbing a hand down the right side of my face where she slapped me. "He said you'd swear women just didn't call to you. But you were born a man and men are attracted to women. You just have to be shown. How can you not appreciate something you've never experienced?"

Nancy grinds against me and my stomach flips. Trying to ignore the assault I'm enduring, I push again for more information. "Who is he?"

"He as in y–"

"Nancy!" Susan barks, and I snap my eyes to her. She's standing right inside the door, hands on her hips and a scowl on her face. "You will not bring him into this. He helped as much as he could. You know he has too much to lose."

Nancy rolls her eyes, sighing. "Yes, Mother."

"Glad to see you're up, Ignatius. I see you and my daughter are getting on already."

"Nancy, you don't want to do this. You'll lose your job and go to jail; you both will."

She heads our way and leans against the wall to my left. "Worth it to see my baby happy." Susan smiles at Nancy. "My contact in that silly biker club has promised that once he's the leader he'll make sure I'm taken care of. A return on my investment you could say."

"Susan, please."

She ignores me. "I came out here to let you know dinner will be ready in an hour and I'll bring two bowls out."

"Thanks, Mom. We'll be done by then."

Susan turns and heads toward the door, turning to look at us one more time before exiting.

"Now," Nancy purrs, rocking her hips against me again. "Where were we?" She humps me slowly repeatedly and I'm on the verge of blowing chunks. She smells like a vinegar salad and this isn't what I want.

"Nancy. You need to stop. This is sexual abuse. Did you know that?"

"No, it's not. A woman can't abuse a man. Plus, you want it. Deep down I know you do."

"I don't," I snap.

I attempt to untie the rope while she ignores me, desperate to push her away.

"Why aren't you getting hard?" she whines.

I give her a look, as if she's a complete idiot, because, well; *Why would that happen?* "Because I don't like women, Nancy. You don't do it for me."

She blows out a breath and gets off of me. "Well, it's almost dinnertime, but I have one more trick to try later before moving on to my last resort."

With that, she leaves the garage and I'm left alone tied to this fucking chair.

My mind races with questions, each unanswered one like a knife digging deeper into my flesh. What could I have possibly done to deserve this torment?

# twenty-nine

## STEEL

> Trucker: On our way back. No issues. He's pissed about his buddy though

> Me: I'll tell him everything once he's here

> Trucker: Okay. I don't like it, but you're the boss

Trucker must be gettin' soft on me. He's never cared if someone is mad or upset before. He's analytical. It's why he's my road captain, it's the perfect position for him. He goes over every possible route for runs, whether fun or work, and picks the safest, best one.

I'm hoping Draco can shed some light on who this Manager person might be. They have to be someone Iggie works with. It's the only way they'd be able to get in his car and know when he'd be off. Someone who knew his schedule, but who?

He never talked about anyone at work that he was close to. Hell, he only ever mentioned Barron and I doubt the Howards' CEO, who's known as this town's most eligible bachelor, kidnapped my man. But that also might be the perfect cover.

"Hawk!" I shout. Rushing into my office, my secretary looks exhausted, his hair tousled and his clothes wrinkled. We've been awake for what feels like an eternity, and he has spent the majority of that time fixated on a screen. Dilated and glazed over pupils, he looks as though he could use a quadruple espresso to wake up.

"Yeah, Steel?"

"Zombie didn't find out anything when he went to Howards. If you haven't already, look into Barron Howard. He's the CEO, but also Iggie's boss. I want to rule him out as The Manager."

"Already done. He and everyone on the upper management floor since I know Iggie just got that promotion. They're all clean."

"Fuck! Okay, then we wait till Trucker is back."

I'm losing my goddamn mind thinking about what Iggie could be going through. If one hair on his sexy little head is out of place, I'm going to flip my shit. Who and why would someone want to kidnap him?

He won't leave my sight again. I don't care if he hates me for the rest of his life or mine. I'll chain his ass to my side so I can make sure he's safe. If I could bring those bastards back from the dead, I'd kill them myself and demand to know who this Manager is.

While I wait for Trucker and Draco to get here, I'll message Michaelov and ask if he knows anything about this

Manager. I will also let him know we have dealt with the problem. I doubt this is the last time we'll have to deal with the Hellhounds, though. Far from it.

I need a drink.

Exiting my office, I make my way to the main area of the clubhouse. Placing my phone on the bar with a thud, I slide onto a stool and settle in. Fingers tapping, I navigate to his contact and open our message thread.

> Me: Rats exterminated. Do you know anything about someone who calls themselves the manager?

> Michaelov: Glad to hear it. And no. Stupid name who are they?

> Me: Not sure yet. Thanks. Let me know if you need anything

> Michaelov: Soon

A SIGH ESCAPES me as I rest my head in my hands, feeling the exhaustion wash over me. How did shit get so fucked?

The door to the clubhouse swings open and Trucker comes in with Draco following. I've never seen him except in pictures that Hawk found. He looks exactly the same; dark, messily styled hair with honey eyes that are full of fury and locked on me. He storms over and shoves the stool beside me, causing it to topple over.

"Where is he?"

"I don't know. I'm hoping you can help me with that." I turn so my whole body is facing him.

"What do you mean, you don't know? What happened?"

Grabbing my phone, I stand up and acknowledge Trucker with a nod. "Let's go to my office. I'll tell you everything I know."

We get to my office and I motion for him to sit behind my desk. I shut the door, leaning against it. "First, you met Trucker since he brought you here. This is Hawk. He's trying to track Iggie down via stoplight cams and other public cameras."

"Is that legal?" Draco asks.

"Look around, man. You're in a motorcycle club's headquarters. Do we look like we mind the law?" Trucker mumbles.

"I had Trucker get you because last night Iggie was supposed to meet me at Brew Me so we could talk and he never showed up."

"He told me he ended things with you, so are you sure he didn't just stand you up?" Draco narrows his eyes at me, his head tilted slightly.

I like that he's not scared, knowing he's in my office and outnumbered, yet he still defends Iggie. Once we settle this, I guess Iggie and he can remain friends. He'll have to come here to see him though because, as I said, Ignatius is never leaving my side again.

"He's the one who initiated the meeting. I went to check to see what held him up and his car was in the parking lot still, but he wasn't. His phone was on the floor and the door was open. Didn't sit right with me, so Hawk here pulled up the next-door building's camera and it shows that he was kidnapped."

"What!" With a sudden burst of energy, he launches

himself out of the chair, causing it to collide forcefully with the wall. "Did you call the cops?"

"No. We'll be faster than the cops and the right kind of justice will be served to someone daring to touch what's mine. Not all the cops are exactly on the right side of the law either, so we're handling this in-house."

"So, what do you want or need from me? I'll help however I can."

Interesting that he accepted no cops that fast. Either he's anti-police or he's had a run-in with a crooked cop and knows how some of them operate. We'll address that later because my curiosity has been piqued.

"We had some members who didn't agree with Hell's Mayhem being open to all sexual orientations. They've been dealt with but before they... left, they told us a woman who calls herself 'The Manager' was having them target Iggie. She's the one who sent some papers and pictures to Iggie, real creepy-like, and what forced him to end things with me."

Draco paces the floor behind my desk, one hand on his hip and the other covering his mouth. "I don't know. The Manager? What kind of name is that?"

"Hoping you could help us with that."

"Do you know anything like ethnicity, tall, short?"

"It was two people who took him. Short, stout, like two teapots." Hawk laughs and I glare at him.

This is not the time for fucking jokes.

"Sorry, Prez. Blame it on the lack of sleep."

"Just find something we can use," I tell him.

"I've tracked the van from Howards to Highway 20 and then nothing. There are no businesses or cameras since it's a highway. But they went East on twenty."

What is east of town that they'd take Iggie that way? It's a long stretch of farmland and a few houses in a no-name town.

"Have you contacted his parents?" Draco asks, startling me from my thoughts.

"No. Hawk has their house phone, but I didn't call. Iggie said their relationship was rocky at best, especially with his dad." The thought of calling them crossed my mind, but then I remembered Iggie telling me about his dad not accepting him when he came out. His dad always had mistresses and his mom lived in denial. They didn't even bother to inform him they were going on vacation; he found out through a text message just as they were leaving.

"Good. They'll cause more headaches than what they're worth and his dad is someone you should check up on. He's always been hard on Iggie, but it got bad when he told them he was gay. The snide comments and thrown insults were nonstop."

"Once everything is settled, I will visit them and show them what it means to be a decent human."

"Draco, do you have his dad's cell phone? I couldn't find one registered to his name with any service provider. His mom was easy, but his dad... not so much. No way does he not have a phone." Hawk leans back in his chair, crossing his arms.

"Douglas doesn't have a phone connected to a service like a normal person. The government might be listening to his calls, so he has a pre-paid that he puts minutes on every month. Hold on. The number is 814-518-4151," Draco tells Hawk as he looks at his phone to retrieve it.

Hawk hits a few buttons before groaning. "Not even a smart prepaid phone. Not impossible, but not easy. You can pull call records, but not always. I'll work some magic and see what I can do."

"Do it."

"Anything else I can help with?" Draco asks.

"No. But don't go too far. Trucker, why don't you two go out to the bar and have a drink and some food? I'll let you know as soon as we know something."

"Sure. Come on, man." Trucker motions for Draco to follow him, and I move away from the door so they can leave.

"Thanks, Draco. Sorry, we had to meet like this." I offer him my hand and he takes it in a firm shake.

"Get my best friend back and we're good."

# *thirty*

## IGNATIUS

I NEVER KNEW how alone or small I was until I found myself in this situation. Being tied up and at the whim of my crazy ex-manager and her daughter, I have never felt so powerless and insignificant. From the sliver of the outside world I can see through the window, it's been two days, and no one has come to get me.

Nancy hasn't left me alone for long... and I mean at all. When I have to use the bathroom, she does one of two things and neither has helped my self-worth. She had her mother give me a pee bag and Susan attached it herself. Tears welled up in my eyes as she gently tugged at my pants, placing the oxygen mask-like device over my penis. It's connected to a tube and then there's a bag taped to my leg to collect my urine.

I did make a break for it, but Nancy shot me with a stun gun. Needless to say, I hit the ground hard, the sensation of fifty thousand volts coursing through my limbs. When I woke up, she was ranting and raving while smacking the hell out of me. I'd try again because I want the hell out of here, but now, when she lets me use the toilet once a day, Susan comes and assists. What's worse than one kidnapper watching you shit, her uptight fucking mom doing the same.

"Today, baby, I have a special surprise for you. We are having a guest and you're going to be over the moon," Nancy coos before turning the blender on and pureeing some magenta concoction.

A visitor? She has to be the most out of her mind kidnapper. Like, I've seen every episode of Criminal Minds and S.W.A.T and never once did any assailant in those shows let their victim have visitors. Who the fuck could she have come to visit that I'd be excited to see?

"Unless it's the cops, I doubt I'll be that excited," I tell her.

"Don't be silly. It's not the cops. They'd take you from me and I can't have that. But it is someone you know and love. I'm hoping after your visit you'll understand why we are meant to be. Why, deep down, I know you love and want me like I do you."

"Nancy, you cannot dictate who I'm attracted to and have feelings for. I'm gay." I cannot believe I'm telling this psychopath the same shit again.

"Don't downplay my love for you. You belong to me, and no one else." She slams a cup on the counter and pours her blender mix into it.

There was a moment when I was also claimed by someone else, if only temporarily. But my relentless self-doubt and refusal to listen to others destroyed that opportunity. Steel pleaded with me to let him explain, but I turned a deaf ear. Perhaps the only person who could locate me and free me from this garage is under the impression that I ghosted him.

"Now, I made you breakfast. Are you going to eat your meal obediently, or will I have to resort to tube feeding you?"

Tube feed me? Surely she can't mean that.

"Do you know how to do that?" I ask.

"No, but I'm confident someone has made a YouTube video about it."

"What's in that?" I ask, eyeing the glass as she directs the straw to my mouth.

"Yogurt, berries, pineapple, and dragon fruit. It's a breakfast smoothie, Ignatius, not rat poison." She shakes her head, rolling her eyes like I'm the crazy one here.

Parting my lips, I let her stick the straw between them and suck. I won't lie, the smoothie isn't bad, but considering it's the only thing I've had since I arrived here, I can't really be picky.

I finish the smoothie, hearing the satisfying slurping sound as I take the last sip. Nancy places the empty glass in the sink before returning to me, carrying a bowl and a sponge. "Alright, let's make sure you're presentable before your guest arrives."

No way is she about to give me a sponge bath like some retail Nurse Ratched. I lean back as far as I can in this damn chair and thrash from side to side.

She is not undressing me and touching me any more than she already has.

"Don't fight me, Ignatius. You have to be presentable when he gets here. You don't want more problems than you already have, right?"

What could possibly be a bigger problem than this?

Once again, she positions herself on my lap, and a small, desperate sound escapes my lips.

"Shh... it's okay, babe. I'm just gonna wipe you up a bit." She uses the rag to wipe my face and hair, scrubbing my scalp. Then she washes my neck before dipping and wringing out the rag. Next, she swiftly slides her hand under my shirt, giving each armpit a brisk swipe.

Dipping the rag once more, she drops to her knees at my feet and puts her hands on the button of my pants.

"Please," I whisper.

Nancy's sympathetic gaze meets mine before she lets out a heavy sigh. "Fine. But you can't stay filthy forever. Plus, if we're going to be together, I'll see your cock regularly. No need to be shy."

She stands, snatches her bowl, and makes her way back to the sink, discarding the dirty water. "You don't have to be embarrassed about your size, honey. I'll love you no matter what."

I close my eyes and drop my head back. Because that's what I was fucking worried about.

━━━┿┿┿┿✦💀✦┿┿┿┿━━━

I'M SUDDENLY WOKEN up by Nancy shaking my shoulder and whispering in my ear. "They're here. Wake up. They're here."

With a groggy haze, I blink my eyes open and glance at her from the corner of my eye, only to be startled by the rattling doorknob. My gaze snaps that way and I watch as the door slowly opens, revealing Susan, and behind her is... "What the fuck?"

My dad steps into the garage, his hand-woven with Susan's. The moment he sees me, he immediately drops her hand and his eyes widen. "Ignatius. Son. What's going on?"

"Dad. You need to get me out of here. These two kidnapped me and think I'm going to be with Nancy and that's not happening. Go call the cops. Call Mom!" I shout at him, my voice shaking with anger and fear. He remains frozen, his eyes locked onto me, resembling a deer caught in the glare of headlights.

"Nancy. Susan, why is my son tied to a chair? Let him go right now." My dad steps toward me, but Susan grabs his arm.

"Douggie, baby, that's enough. Now, Ignatius can get himself out of here. Nancy is waiting for him, all he has to do is agree to be with her. Stop this silly rebellion of liking men and come to his senses."

I never expected that when Nancy said I had a visitor, it would be my dad. As soon as he walked into the garage and laid eyes on me, his surprise was evident. I don't know if I could have handled the situation if he had been aware of what was happening.

"How do you guys know each other?" I ask, my words barely audible. I don't know why I ask, it's like word vomit, but I can't help but wonder how on earth my old boss and my father crossed paths.

"I met Doug a year or so ago. We met at Howards, actually. He came to see if you wanted to go to lunch, but I told him you couldn't take a long lunch. When he asked where he could find you, I explained that you were occupied with an important meeting. Instead, I suggested going to lunch together, and he agreed. We've been together since." She bats her lashes at him and he raises a brow at her.

"We've been dating. According to Nancy, you've been

socializing with bikers and developing a romantic relationship with one of them. She said this was an intervention." He turns to Susan. "You never said my son would be here against his will. Kidnapping, really? And trying to get him to be with Nancy? He's not straight, Susan, I told you this."

"He's confused. We read about it and he just needs to be shown. He can't dislike something he's never had," Nancy pipes up, her voice filled with conviction.

"You were sleeping with a psychopath, Dad. Are you happy? Fucking that bitch has led us here!" I scream.

A hard slap across my face knocks my head to the side, and I look over at Nancy.

"Don't talk about my mom like that. I love you, Ignatius," she whispers, her words tinged with a hint of sadness, "but I can't allow you to disrespect her like that."

Susan steps away from my dad, her head cocked to the side as she locks her gaze on me. "I brought your father here because I think it's important if we're going to be a family to air out all our secrets. So do you have anything you'd like to get out in the open, Ignatius?"

"Go to hell," I spit at her, venom dripping from my words.

Susan casually places her purse on the table and rummages through its contents until she finally withdraws her hand and reveals a gun. Instead of aiming it at me, she points it at my dad.

"Susie. Darling, what are you doing?" He stands there, his eyes wide as his body trembles, clearly shaken.

"Shut up, Doug. God, you're so annoying and self-righteous. Playing this game with you has felt like a never-ending chore."

I have no clue what is happening right now, but it seems

like the mother-daughter psycho duo might have also caught my dad in their web.

"Put the gun down," he pleads, his voice trembling with fear and desperation. "We're happy. I'm leaving Patricia for you. Don't ruin that."

Real nice, Dad. His son is tied to a chair and now his mistress brandishes a gun, but he's still not the problem. Typical fucking Doug Harper; an asshole.

"There is no us. You were a tool, a desperate attempt to make your son see reason." Susan's lip curls with disdain as she steps closer to him, her voice dripping with disapproval. "You're not doing a good job." She flicks the safety off and steadies the barrel at my dad's head.

My heart is pounding so fast it feels like it's sprinting a million miles a minute. What the hell is happening? How did no one know these two were this fucking insane? Susan turns around, her eyes locking with mine.

"So what's it going to be, Ignatius? Will you finally surrender to destiny and become the man my daughter truly deserves?"

Is she asking me to choose between betraying myself or my dad? For years, our relationship has been marked by tension and distance. I never wished for this, though. I don't want to have to choose.

I look at my dad, his face drained of color. Tears are welled up in his eyes, mirroring my own. I plead desperately with Susan, "I can't choose." My voice is barely above a whisper as the tears break free, cascading down my cheeks.

"You can and you will!" The sound of Susan's scream fills the room, her hand trembling uncontrollably as she clutches the weapon.

"Please. I can't. Please!"

With a tight squeeze of his eyes, my dad opens them,

causing a solitary tear to trickle down his face. "Yes, you can, son. Choose you. I may not understand nor agree with your life, but I love you. I haven't been a good dad. Let me do this. Choose you."

"No," I sob.

"Yes, Ignatius. Choose yourself and when you get out of here—'cause I know you will—live your life to the fullest, embracing every opportunity that comes your way. Make better choices than I did. Look where they got me."

"Dad," I manage to choke out between sobs, my whole body shaking.

"Enough!" Susan bellows. "What's it gonna be?"

I look at my dad, and with a single nod of his head, he reassures me. I shift my gaze towards the ceiling, gathering my thoughts, and finally, I take a deep breath. "No."

My dad is staring at me with love in his eyes for the first time in a long time, and I cry harder. When she pulls the trigger, blood splatters everywhere. A hole in my dad's face as his body slams to the ground is the last memory I'll have of him.

"Noooooo! Pleeeease," I scream, my voice echoing through the empty room.

"You'll see. This is what's best for you. All the online forums said so. We're doing this for you," Nancy says, setting a hand on my shoulder and squeezing.

"Don't fucking touch me," I hiss.

"Ignatius, baby," she coos, her tone soft and gentle. "I don't want to do this the hard way, but you've left me no choice."

My teeth grind together, and my eyes narrow. "You just murdered my dad in front of me. What could be worse?"

Ignoring the gruesome sight of my dad's body, Susan swiftly steps over it and reaches for the doorknob. "You have twenty-four hours. Get with the program, Ignatius, or she fucks you until you fall in line."

"I don't want to make love to you under these conditions, darling, but if you don't get on board, I will." Nancy kisses my cheek and follows her mother out of the garage, leaving me in this fucking chair with my dad's corpse only a few feet away.

# *thirty-one*

## STEEL

THIS IS TAKING TOO LONG. As time passes, my frustration intensifies. Being the leader of an MC was supposed to keep things like this from happening. If it did, my connections and brothers should have been faster.

My eyelids feel heavy with exhaustion. They have betrayed me a few times and closed while I was at my desk or the bar. Cracking open an energy drink, I hear the satisfying fizz as I lift it to my mouth and chug. I refuse to sleep until Iggie is back where he should be—with me.

Shank is on call, waiting for me to ring when he's needed. He's one of the members who doesn't live on the compound. His place is just a few blocks away, but he always shows up when we need him, and that's all that matters.

"It's not your fault."

I turn to my left and see Iggie's best friend. "Sure feels like it. I should have been able to find him by now."

"Yeah. But you also had people working against you from the inside from what I've gathered. Don't beat yourself up. You didn't take him and from what I've seen, you're working your ass off to find him."

"I won't stop until he's safe." I stare deep into his eyes so he knows just how serious I am. "We haven't known each other long, but Iggie is mine. I'll do whatever I need for him to come back safe."

"Steel!" Hawk shouts, his voice carrying into the main part of the clubhouse.

I throw my empty drink into the trash can behind the bar and head to my office. Trucker meets me at the intersection of the hall that separates it from the first-floor bedrooms. "I heard Hawk holler. Did he find him?"

"Headed to find out now." I nod my head toward the bar. "Draco is out there alone. Keep him company, yeah?"

His lips curve upward in a small, subtle smile. "Yeah. I'll entertain him."

Seems like Trucker has taken a liking to Draco. I'll dissect that later. Right now, I need to see what has Hawk so excited.

Before I can close the door behind me, Hawk starts talking, his voice filled with urgency. "I got 'em. I'm pretty sure I got 'em. It's too much to be a coincidence."

"Show me." I cross the room and stand over his shoulder, staring at the screen.

He takes a moment to gather himself, exhaling loudly. "So, remember how Draco said to look into Doug and gave us the burner phone number? Well, I was able to pull some records for it through the pre-paid company. Not everything, but enough to see that he calls and texts one number more than anyone else. I searched that number and it pulled up a Susan Credla. Susan works at Howards. That can't be a coincidence."

"It sure the fuck can't," I grit. Stalking to the door, I rip it open and shout for Draco.

"While you update him, I'm going to do some checking on Susan's phone. See if anything stands out between her number, Doug's, and Iggie's."

Draco comes jogging around the corner with Trucker right behind him.

"Did you find him?" he asks anxiously, his voice filled with desperation.

"Maybe. Does the name Susan Credla mean anything to you?"

Draco's top lip curls in disgust, and a choked sound escapes his throat.

"Who is she?" I push.

"She is... or was Iggie's manager. Nancy, her daughter, has an unsettling obsession with Iggie. He always brushed her off and said it was a harmless crush. The other day, though, when we talked, he said she was getting weirder. He was going to speak to his new boss about keeping her off the corporate office floor."

"Doug has been calling and texting Susan for months," I tell him. "Do you think she or her daughter are capable of this?"

He rubs his temples. "I don't know them. I just know they made Iggie uncomfortable. But you know how he is. Always wants to see the best in people and just goes about his business."

"Wait!" A sudden outburst from Trucker interrupts us, and as I turn to look, I see him fixated on the laptop screen, engaged in a hushed discussion with Hawk.

"What?"

"That phone number the Susan lady's been texting and video chatting with. It looks familiar."

Hawk's fingers dance across the buttons, the soft clicks filling the room before he leans closer to examine the screen. "Hoooly shit."

"Spit it out, Hawk. What is it?"

"That number looks familiar because it was Combo's."

Got him. Tonight, I'm going to get my man back and send those cunts and Iggie's shitbag dad to hell where they belong.

What kind of dad goes along with or helps plan his son's kidnapping? According to the records, they've talked, texted, and video chatted a lot. He has to be close to the bitch who made it happen.

It doesn't matter because they won't be an issue as soon as I get that address and my men gathered. Howards will be two employees short and I'll be reunited with the man I love.

"Get the address, Hawk. I'll call the guys back, and we'll leave as soon as I fill everyone in." I leave the room, heading to my bedroom to get more weapons.

"What about me?" Draco calls after me. "I wanna go with. He'll need me."

The pounding of blood in my ears matches the intensity of my glare as I spin on my heels. "He'll need me. He's mine."

"He's yours... I'm not discounting that, but he's my best friend. If they hurt him, he might want someone he's known longer. You know what I'm saying?"

His words make me involuntarily bare my teeth, emitting a low growl. "Fine. But you stay with Trucker."

"Thank you."

"Draco, if they touched him like that, I'll rip their hands, tongues, eyes...whatever dared touch him, from their bodies."

"You have my full support." He returns to my office and I step into my room, closing the door.

There is no room to fuck this up. These are not your typical hardened criminals or even low-level drug dealers. The Manager, or so she likes to be called, must be completely insane, off her rocker... or off their rockers.

I know Iggie is very open and proud of his identity, so it's impossible for anyone at Howards to be unaware of his dating preferences. Especially if this cunt has made advances toward him in the past and he rejected her.

She just doesn't wanna take no for an answer and that won't fly with me.

This is one of the problems in the world: the media tells you that men aren't or can't be assaulted. But I assure you they can. Forty-three percent of victims of sex crimes are male, shedding light on the often overlooked experiences of male survivors.

One percent of perpetrators are female. Because one percent is a small number, it's often disregarded as insignificant, making it a topic nobody wants to address.

Iggie won't be silenced... if they hurt him, that is. I don't want to put that on him if he escapes unscathed in that way.

What I know for sure, three people are dying tonight and I'll spend the rest of my life making sure no one ever hurts Iggie like this again.

I can't dwell on that now. I need the club here, so when we get the address Hawk is pulling up, we can leave.

Like my fingers are on fire, I urgently text all members of Hell's Mayhem to return immediately. As I sit on my bed, I can hear the sound of my own breathing and feel the thumping of my rapidly beating heart.

A knock on my door rips me from my thoughts. "It's open."

Pistol pushes the door open. "You look like dog shit, brother."

"Fuck you."

"Everyone is back and waiting for you. Let's go get your man," Pistol says with a smirk, his voice filled with determination. I can't help but silently thank the universe for orchestrating our fateful encounter years ago. I couldn't ask for a better brother or VP.

Standing tall, I stride toward my dresser and jerk the top drawer open, snatching up an additional firearm and my trusty duo of blades. I slide the blades into my boots effortlessly, feeling the cold steel against my skin, then tuck the gun in my cut.

"Age before beauty." I smile.

"Ugly fucker," Pistol murmurs, and heads out to the main part of the clubhouse.

The moment I step through the doors, I am met with the sight of every brother eagerly waiting, exactly as Pistol said. All heads snap in my direction, and the array of emotions on their faces ranges from sympathy to anger.

I know that each and every man standing here is prepared to join me in the battle.

"Listen up! We are pretty sure we know who Combo and Pepper were workin' with and who took Iggie. Hawk has their home address. It's the only property registered in the bitch's name. The information should be hitting your phones any second. We park a block away and walk the rest. I don't want them gettin' spooked and doin' anything crazier than they already have. Circle the property. Pistol, Zero, and Viper, you're coming with me. Same for you, Rubble, Tex and Zombie. The rest of you stay here, but keep your eyes and ears open. We'll call if we need you. Hawk, you stay here and keep searching in case we missed anything."

"What about me, Prez?" Trucker asks.

"Draco is coming, and he stays with you. When we find Iggie, I'll holler and you bring him to his friend." I look at the man in question.

"You remember to stay on Trucker's ass. If you step a toe out of line, I will have him bring you back here, no questions asked. You hear me?"

"I understand."

"Good. Head out." I walk through the clubhouse and out the door, sucking in a breath of crisp night air.

I'm teetering on the edge of sanity, ready to plunge into the abyss of despair. If he remains lost to me after this, I will take the leap. Iggie is it for me. I can feel it in my bones, my heart, my fucking soul.

# thirty-two

## STEEL

RIDING to the house has my temple throbbing and my heart pounding. We've put all our eggs into one basket and I'm praying we're right. If not, I'm right back at square one and I doubt knocking on every door in town searching for him will go over well.

The train of headlights in my mirror has me subtly nodding and a small smile crossing my lips. While I'd prefer to not be in this situation at all, I'm glad I have my brothers at my back.

Every possible outcome of tonight rushes through my mind like a movie on fast-forward. There's, however, only one outcome I will accept, and that's Iggie being safe and back to a normal life. Well, as normal as it can be after being kidnapped.

This is it. We're a block away and going on foot the rest of the way to the house. As I park along the curb, I tap the brakes and turn the key, shutting off the engine. I exit my truck and wait for my brothers to do the same. Once we're gathered by my cage, I reiterate the plan and take the lead.

When we're two houses down, I halt and raise my fist, signaling everyone to stop. I face my men and blow out a breath. "This is it. All evidence leads us to believe Iggie is inside. If he's not, we're about to traumatize two ladies. Not the worst we've done, but still, if that's the case, let Pistol and I handle it. Remember the plan and if you find Iggie, I'm told immediately."

Zero and Rubble move to the side of the house where there's a sliding glass door. They're not to make entry, just stand sentient in case anyone is inside and tries to make a break for it.

Viper, Pistol, and I head up to the front door while Zombie and Tex cover the yard so no one can sneak past us.

Pulling my gun from the inside of my cut, I point it toward the door and motion for Viper to kick it down.

My enforcer lifts his leg and slams the bottom of his boot against the door, directly under the doorknob. The second kick sends the door flying open and hitting the wall behind it, the frame and trim splintering from the force.

Pistol moves inside first, and I follow behind. "Viper, go up."

With careful steps, Viper creeps up the stairs, while Pistol steps over the small gate blocking the stairs to our right, and begins his descent to the basement. I move further into the house. The first door on the left is a bathroom... and it's empty.

Moving through an archway, I see the living room, kitchen, and what looks like a home office are all connected with an open floor plan. The whole lower level is clear. The kitchen counter has two places set up with candles and a box of condoms. The food is cold and hardened. At least a day old, if not more. It looks like someone was planning for a good night, but it was interrupted.

"Basement was clear. A lot of drawings that said Nancy *hearts* Iggie. And I found these." Pistol holds out a hand and his fingers are wrapped around more pictures from that night in the alley. A night that seems like forever ago.

I grit my teeth and can feel my heart rate pick up. "They are definitely who took him and who our rats were working with. But where are they?"

The creak of the stairs has me jerking my head in that direction. Viper looks pissed as he strides over to us. "Upstairs is clear. For sure, this is the place, though. One room looks like a ten-year-old girl lives in it. It's all pink ruffles and dolphins. The only thing that told me a child didn't really live in it was the pictures of Iggie everywhere. And the printout of how to force an erection."

"I'll fucking kill her if she touches him," I hiss.

"Let's go see if the guys saw anything." Pistol claps me on the back and I crack my knuckles as I follow him to the sliding door where Zero and Rubble are waiting.

Rubble steps aside and lets us leave the house. "No one was in or out but you guys. The cars are still here, though. I called Hawk, and he ran the plates. One car is Susan's and the other is Doug's. He said Nancy doesn't have a car registered in her name, so they have to be here somewhere. Right?"

"You'd think. But maybe they had someone pick them up? I don't know." I lean against the siding of the house.

The atmosphere is tense, the air thick with anticipation. My guys are standing in a circle, their expressions a mixture of determination and apprehension.

"Alright, listen up. We've cleared this house, but there's

still no sign of him. I've got a feeling there's more to this than meets the eye."

Their nods of agreement display their unwavering resolve, even in the face of uncertainty.

Stepping forward, Pistol's voice resonates with a low and urgent tone. "Steel's right. We can't leave any inch of this place untouched. Did anyone check the garage?" With a gesture, he draws attention to the detached garage adjacent to the house.

I lead the way, my heart hammering against my chest. It looks dark and the cars are in the drive so they can't use it to park. I motion for my brothers to follow me cautiously, the crunch of our footsteps resonating through the quiet winter night.

Upon closer inspection, the garage is dark because someone has covered the windows. Gathering my resolve, I grip the doorknob and twist, feeling the resistance before the door opens. Stepping into the garage, a wave of stale air greets us, mingling with the scent of piss and something more sinister.

Then, suddenly, there it is—a body, lying motionless on the cold concrete floor. My stomach churns with unease as I observe the gaping hole in the back of the guy's head. It's not Iggie, so that's good, but who the hell is it? And why are they dead on the garage floor?

It hits me like a ton of bricks, leaving me breathless. One of the vehicles in the driveway is registered to Doug, Iggie's dad. This must be him.

"Who the hell are you?" a voice cuts through the silence, her tone laced with malice. She's a stout woman with glasses, her gray curly hair framing her face. I am completely oblivious to her presence. Looking behind her, I see Ignatius tied to a chair with some cunt straddling his lap... his naked lap.

As I squeeze the bottom of my cut, a wave of fury courses through me, causing my jaw to clench tightly. We found my man, but this is exactly what I was worried about and is far more horrifying than I could have imagined.

"You shouldn't be here!" the strawberry blonde, dead woman walking, screeches, clambering from Iggie's lap.

His eyes meet mine. I can see the unshed tears pooling in his eyes, on the brink of spilling over.

"He is mine!" I demand, my voice a low growl. "And you two crazy bitches are gonna pay for what you've done."

Both women stare at me before laughing. "He's Nancy's!" the older one snaps. "She's loved him for years. You were supposed to be taken care of. Frank assured me that he and Arthur would take care of you and that other little bitch who dared touch my daughter's lover."

"Frank and Arthur are dead. And you're going to join them. No one takes from Hell's Mayhem and lives. You took what is mine and hurt him. That can't be tolerated." My voice drips with fury.

My blood is boiling at the sight of Iggie, bound and helpless. Without any hesitation, I swiftly retrieve my gun from inside my jacket and fire a shot, hitting Susan in the shoulder. She lets out a piercing scream as she collapses to the ground, clutching her injured shoulder.

"Tie her up. I want her in the shed for later." I signal to the guys behind me, my eyes blazing with determination.

The garage erupts into chaos, the sounds of Nancy screaming. "You filthy convict! You shot my mom!" In a frenzied rush, she sprints toward me, her arms flailing wildly. I swiftly withdraw the blade from my boot, and in an instant, she inadvertently impales herself on it.

Her breath catches, and she stares up at me, blood seeping from her wound and trickling out of her mouth.

"Don't worry, it's just your belly. We'll patch you up so you can die the right way." I pull my knife from her gut, and Viper catches her before she can fall.

"I'll put her with Mommy dearest and get them to the shed."

Looking at Iggie, I cross the room to him and cup his face. "Are you okay?" It's a stupid question and I don't know why I ask, but it just came out.

"I don't know," he whispers, his voice barely audible.

"You will be. I'll do whatever I have to do to make sure of it. I got you, baby." I cut the zip ties that bind his hands behind the chair.

When I'm back in front of him, he rubs his wrists, I'm sure they're sore from being restrained, and then wraps his arms around my neck.

"Can you get them to leave?" He flicks his eyes at the men remaining in the garage. "I'd like to get dressed."

His arms fall from my body and I spin around. "Get out!" With a nod of understanding, the guys quickly exit through the same door we came in. Grabbing my phone from my cut, I send a text to Trucker and pocket it again.

# thirty-three

## IGNATIUS

I HOPED and prayed Steel would come, but when Susan shot my dad, and then Nancy stripped me of my pants and removed the makeshift catheter, I lost all hope. She was going to rape me. There isn't a doubt in my mind that she planned on carrying through with her promise to fuck me.

She told me if my dick didn't get hard while she ground against me, she'd shove pills down my throat to force an erection. At the thought, a wave of nausea hits me and I'm filled with gratitude that Steel arrived just in time.

Yes, this still messed with my head, but it could have been far more devastating. He came in the nick of time. Steel should have killed them on the spot. He showed remarkable restraint and I'm glad he did. The fact he didn't let them have a quick death fills me with glee. They'll wish they were dead by the time Steel is done with them, though, of that I have no doubt.

The look in his eyes when he saw me told me everything

I needed to know. This man would burn the world down for me and I almost threw that away because of fucking Nancy.

My jaw drops as Draco bursts into the garage while I hastily put on my pants. What the hell is he doing here? My dad's lifeless body on the floor in front of him causes him to freeze. In a rush, he covers his mouth with his hand, his face contorting in disgust as he gags. He looks up at me and I can see the sorrow already, the apology ready to fall from his lips for something he doesn't need to be sorry for. Regaining his composure, he rushes over to me and hugs me so tight I feel like he might squeeze the air from my lungs.

"What are you doing with Hell's Mayhem? How did you get here?" I ask and he smirks, looking over at Steel.

"He sent someone for me to see if I could help with any leads or information to find you. We pieced it together, and I demanded to be here in case they found you. I wanted you to have a familiar face besides this possessive alphahole."

Steel's determination knows no bounds, evident in his efforts to locate and reach me by tracking down my best friend. Thank God for him. Thanks to his relentless obsession, I am now reaping the benefits and feeling grateful.

"You need to be seen by a doctor. And your dad, Iggie? Oh, my God... your dad. He knew? He was helping? I'm so sorry." His voice is frantic as he jumbles sentences together in a flurry.

I tightly shut my eyes and vigorously shake my head. "He helped, but not in the way you think. Not even in the way he thought, from what it sounded like. To him, it was supposed to be an intervention since I was seeing a gang member." My eyes dart to Steel, and he winces.

"He tried to talk them out of it... to let me go. Then they told me to choose my dad or being with Nancy." My voice cracks and a sob leaves me. "I killed my dad!"

Steel pulls me close, his arms enveloping me in a comforting embrace. "Listen to me, Iggie," he says, his voice gentle but firm. "You didn't kill your dad. They did. And I won't let you shoulder that blame. They made the choice together, and they pulled the trigger. It's not your burden to bear, and I won't let you think differently for even a second. We're in this together, through thick and thin. You're not alone, Iggie. We'll get through this, side by side."

A small smile crosses my lips, a sense of relief flooding through me as I think about Steel's words. He's right, but I'm gonna need time to process my dad's final words and I'm not ready to share them with anyone yet, not even Draco.

"We should get you out of here. Take you to a hospital and then, if they release you, you can come back to my place," Draco offers.

"No!"

With adrenaline coursing through my veins, I hold Steel's forearm with an iron grip. "I mean, no thank you. I wanna go with Steel." I look at the man in question. "Can I go to the clubhouse with you? Please."

He nods, smiling. "I planned on it. I have a doctor on call waiting for you. There's no way you're leaving my sight for a while. Hope you're not still mad at me, baby. I'm gonna be on your ass like glue."

"Okay," is all I can say. What else can one say to that?

Steel swoops me up like a strong gust of wind and carries me effortlessly to his truck. He parked really far away and I don't understand why. I have to be getting heavy and am capable of walking, but he doesn't put me down until he gets to the truck. With one hand, he opens the door and gently places me inside before quickly moving to the driver's side and taking his place behind the wheel.

Steel grips my hand, brushing his thumb over my

knuckles as we drive in silence. It's exactly what I need right now. I just have to focus on getting my thoughts in order and accepting that I'm finally rescued. No more Nancy and Susan.

When we get to the clubhouse, he parks his truck and carries me inside, straight to his bedroom. It's odd to find the clubhouse completely deserted, with not a soul in sight.

He gently places me on his bed before retrieving his phone and pressing it against his ear. "We're here."

Minutes later, a large bearded man strolls into the room with a black medical bag. He sets it on the bed and holds out a hand. "Iggie, I'm Shank. The club doctor and yes, I have a real medical degree, but I'm also a member of the club. Is it okay if I check you over?"

"Yeah. That's fine," I assure him while nodding my head.

Shank pokes and prods me everywhere. Before taking my temperature, he thoroughly examines my eyes, ears, and mouth. As he puts the stethoscope back in his bag, I can see the nervousness in his eyes as he looks at me.

"I hate to ask, but I have to. Did she... they... or, umm, anyone assault you?"

"No. She kissed me and ground against me a few times, but that's it, minus when she put the sketchy catheter on my penis," I tell him honestly.

Despite nodding, his attention keeps shifting to the pacing, growling president in the corner of the room. "Then we won't do a rape kit. I'll give you some antibiotics just for the cuts; it's better to be safe than sorry. Otherwise, just rest." He digs in his bag once more before pulling out a business card. "This is a friend of mine. Her name's Holly. She's a therapist but works from home, so it's all telehealth. You should make an appointment."

"I will."

The moment he exits the room, I quickly abandon the comfort of the bed and make my way to the bathroom.

"Where ya goin'?" Steel asks.

"Taking a shower. I haven't showered since the morning of my abduction and I'd really like to clean up." I strip before getting into the shower.

Turning on the water, I jolt when the cold water rains down on me, but it quickly switches to hot and I lean my head back, letting the warmth beat down on me. The door opens, and when Steel steps in front of me, I tense. He can't think we're going to be intimate, right? I'm not ready and we still aren't together. Although that seems trivial now that he searched and came for me.

"I don't expect anything, Iggie. Relax." He places his hand gently over my heart, prompting me to take a deep, calming breath. "I just wanna take care of ya, baby."

Grabbing a cloth, he squirts some soap on it and slowly runs it over every inch of my body. As promised, he sticks to washing me and doesn't venture into anything more. The cloth glides over my cock and balls, devoid of any sensual or tender touch, purely mechanical.

As I rinse off the soap, I twirl around to wash the suds off the front of my body. Steel takes that opportunity to lather my hair in shampoo, and I can't help but let out a soft moan as his strong fingers work their magic on my scalp. After thoroughly rinsing my hair, I turn off the water, feeling the droplets slowly trickle down my body.

Steel quickly steps out and wraps a towel around his waist before grabbing another one. He holds it open, waiting for me. As soon as I get out, I feel his arms encircle me with the cozy towel, and then he silently departs the bathroom.

"I'm gonna get you some clothes to sleep in. Do you want pants or just some boxers and a shirt?"

"Shirt and boxers are fine," I reply. Nodding, he walks over to the dresser, quickly grabbing both and passing them to me.

"Get dressed and I'll do the same. Then we'll go to bed."

After I dry off, I slip the shirt over my head and pull the boxers on. I flick off the bathroom light on my way out, making my way to Steel's bed. Snuggling into it with the blanket wrapped around me, I sigh softly and close my eyes, surrendering to the peacefulness of the moment. The bed dips as Steel slides in behind me, his presence bringing a comforting warmth. He pulls me close, his arm holding me tightly. "Sleep, baby. I got you."

WITH A RACING HEART, I jolt awake, startled by a scream that escapes my lips, shattering the silence. Rocketing up in the bed, my eyes scan my surroundings, taking in the familiar sight of Steel's room and the comfort of his bed.

"Shhhh, Iggie. It's okay. Just a bad dream. You're safe here with me. Nothing and no one will hurt you again. I swear it. Go back to sleep. I'll watch over you." His calloused thumb rubs small circles on my biceps and I lie back down.

As I take a deep breath, my heart rate starts to slow, and I find solace in closing my eyes, shutting out the world around me.

I'm safe. I'm with Steel. I'm at the clubhouse. Nancy and

Susan can't hurt me here. I recite this to myself over and over again in my head until I pass back out.

When I wake again, it's nine in the morning and Steel isn't in the bed anymore. Where did he go?

My question is answered when the door opens, and he appears holding a tray. "Morning, Iggie. I went and grabbed us some breakfast."

He hands me a plate overflowing with a delicious feast of eggs, bacon, sausage, and toast.

"Thank you." I take a bite and hum at the buttery goodness of the toast.

As I'm savoring the taste of the crispy bacon, the bedroom door violently swings open, causing a loud thud when it slams against the wall. Kiki hobbles in, her face lit up with an enormous grin and Marni trailing behind her.

"Long time no see, Iggie." Kiki sits on the bed next to me and snags a piece of sausage from my plate. I look over at Marni and she takes a seat in the chair by the door.

"What happened to you?" I ask, turning back to look at Kiki. She looks like she went through a meat grinder.

"Same thing that happened to you. The bitch's plan went awry, though, and I fought back. My attacker is dead. What about yours?"

I wince. "Not sure. I'm not ready to know yet."

"Fair enough."

Steel rises from the bed, balancing his plate in one hand. "Well, I have to call church to go over last night. The girls are gonna keep you company and I'll be back, okay?"

"We'll be fine, boss man. Go on." Kiki waves him away.

# *thirty-four*

## STEEL

THE RUMBLE of voices fills the air as I enter the main part of the clubhouse. "Church! Let's go." The urgency is evident in my tone. My brothers all grab their drinks and head to the church meeting room. I leave my plate on the small table by the door before entering. Taking my place at the officer's table, the comforting scent of leather and the sense of brotherhood puts me at ease.

Once everyone is inside and settled, Viper locks the door, then takes his place at the back of the room.

"We need to talk about Ignatius' rescue." I look around at each member, my eyes meeting theirs. "He's here and safe. Shank examined him thoroughly, and fortunately, he was unharmed. More emotional than anything else. He's gonna be here for a while and I expect him to be treated with respect."

"He yours, Prez?" Rubble asks. "I mean, I know he is... but you saying he's your old—"

"He belongs to me. That's all you need to know for now. Anything beyond that, I'll wait for him. He just got back."

I'd love nothing more than to tell everyone in this room Iggie's my old man and give him a property patch. But I just got him back and before that, we were on the outs, so I'm not rushing him. He needs to recover from his ordeal, not worry about me and my titles.

"The cunts are in the shed. Viper, I just need you to do the minimum necessary to ensure their survival until I find out what Iggie intends to do. Seein' them ended might help his healing. So until then, they're at your mercy. Don't give a fuck what you do, but don't kill 'em."

With a menacing glint in his eye, my enforcer cracks his knuckles. "It's done."

"Now, let's address the next matter at hand. I'd like to propose patchin' Nate and Chad in." Prospects aren't allowed in church since they're not patched. So this will be a surprise.

I have no doubt that this is about to go in their favor, as evidenced by everyone nodding and smiling. "We vote. All in favor of Nate and Chad patchin' in, say, aye."

"Aye!" the room erupts.

"Alright. Anyone opposed, say no."

Silence.

"Alright, it's unanimous. Hawk." I look at my secretary. "Get their patches."

"It's already taken care of, Prez." Hawk smirks. "I had a feelin' they'd make the cut."

"Then we just need names, any ideas?"

With some laughter, we name Nate "Barbi" and Chad "Polar Bear," a fitting tribute to their newfound brotherhood.

"Anything else?" I look at my officers, making sure we don't need to cover anything else.

"Yeah," Tex calls. "I didn't bring it up before because of everything going on, but we've hired the bouncer for Element, but he has a friend who I'm hiring for the Cockpit. We'll keep an eye on him, but I think he might be good for the club, too."

We lost members, so our numbers are slightly down. Nothing I'm too worried about since we've always been a midsize club, but enough that I might take a personal interest in scouting this Zion guy and his friend.

"Where are we with openin'?" I ask.

"Everything is good to go. Just need to plan a grand openin' party. Zero is getting a budget, and I thought we'd let Barbi and Polar Bear handle the party. Their first real responsibility as patched members." Hawk smiles.

"Do it." I nod, liking this idea. "I also will see to gettin' a replacement in for Cody. I know some of you have needs the ladies can't meet, so bear with me as I find someone new."

The meeting adjourns, and we head out to tell our prospects about their new promotion. Both of them are working at the bar, cleaning and restocking.

"Prospects!" I shout. They both spring up and quickly move around the bar to position themselves in front of me.

"Yeah, Prez," Barbi asks.

A mischievous grin spreads across my face as I reveal the "member" patches to them. "I think it's time we removed those prospect patches. What about you?"

Nate's eyes widen to the size of saucers and Chad beams from ear to ear. "Fuck yeah."

"Well then, let's get you patched in officially and then party. Take off your cuts and repeat after me." They do as asked, and I hand their cuts to Rubble, who will pull the prospect patches off and get the member ones on.

"Raise your left hand." Both of their left hands shoot up.

"I pledge my loyalty to the never-ending brotherhood I stand with today. I love my club, the Hell's Mayhem, and with my brothers, I will honor what we stand for. I will honor the code of brotherhood and shall let no other stand between us. I am Hell's Mayhem, now and forever. If my brothers fight, I fight alongside them for this."

Both repeat our oath and I smile. "I officially declare you both brothers of the Hell's Mayhem. Barbi and Polar Bear, may the brotherhood be strong and the holes be tight."

Chad smiles at his road name, but Nate's mouth drops open as he spins on Tex. "That was one time. You swore you'd never say anything!"

Tex bursts into a deep belly laugh, filling the room. "You got drunk and humped a Barbie doll that one of the guy's kids left here. No way was I lettin' that shit not be your road name."

"Fuck you." Nate laughs, swinging at Tex, but he wraps him in a brotherly hug and heads to the bar.

"That's it then. Let's party!" I shout and a round of cheers goes up.

Beers flow freely as we toast to brotherhood and new beginnings.

Amidst the loud music and laughter, I decide to slip away from the party, my mind filled with thoughts of Iggie. Heading back to my room, I find him asleep in the bed and Kiki stroking his hair, watching TV.

"He's only been out a little while. You got a good one, Prez. Keep him this time." Kiki smiles, sliding from the bed.

"Thanks, Kiki. We patched in the prospects, so tell Gabe and Daria, would ya? And let Gabe know I don't want him trying to pick up the slack from Cody. I'm gonna start looking for a replacement."

"Sure, boss." She leaves the room and I take her spot on the bed after slipping my boots off.

SOMEONE SNIFFLING JERKS ME AWAKE. I hadn't meant to doze off. Opening my eyes, Iggie is sitting in the bed, tears streaming down his cheeks.

I sit up gently and instinctively wrap my arm around his shoulders. "What happened? You wanna talk about it?"

"Thinking about my dad. I have a mixture of feelings. I'm confused," he confesses.

"Tell me," I whisper, feeling the soft warmth of his temple against my lips.

After wiping his eyes, he raises his gaze to meet mine. "Susan pointed the gun at him and told me to choose. Be with her daughter or my dad. I didn't want to choose. I told them I couldn't. He was an ass to me about being gay and we didn't talk. But he's my dad." He takes a deep breath.

"He looked at me and told me to choose myself. Then he went on to say he didn't understand my life or agree with it all, but he loves me. That he hadn't been a good dad, but he could do this. I did what he said, and she shot him. Right in front of me. Fuck, Steel, what am I gonna tell my mom?"

I stroke his back softly, providing solace and a sense of security. "I'll call in an anonymous tip on the house and ensure the authorities handle the body and break the news to your mom."

268

With a grateful smile, he takes a deep breath and whispers, "Thank you".

Before long, a sharp knock on the door breaks the silence, and it slowly creaks open as Trucker and Draco enter. Despite my anticipation, I'd ended up losing track of time due to my impromptu nap. I'd sent them on an errand to get some things for Iggie.

Draco hands Iggie a new iPhone and a bag of clothes from his house. "Steel asked if I'd get you a few things from your house. He had your phone, but it was cracked, so he insisted you get a new one."

"Thanks, Draco." Iggie smiles.

"Don't thank me. I only did the picking up. Steel paid for it and set it all up."

"Still, thank you. I wanted some of my things so I could actually get dressed, but I'm not ready to go home. Nancy and Susan admitted to being inside the house before. I was clueless, but it creeps me out even if they can't get inside again."

Our eyes meet, and I can see a whirlwind of emotions reflected in Iggie's deep gaze. The weight of the world is evident in the way his shoulders sag and his posture droops. But I also see resilience, a glimmer of strength shining through the shadows. And I know that he'll find a way through the storm.

"Iggie," I whisper gently, feeling the warmth of his hand as I intertwine my fingers with his. "You don't have to face this alone. We're here for you, every step of the way."

A tear escapes Iggie's eye, tracing a path down his cheek as he nods in silent gratitude. At this moment, I feel a bond strengthen between us, forged in tragedy and fortified by the unyielding love I have for this man.

# *thirty-five*

## IGNATIUS

TODAY, as I prepare for my first appointment with Holly, a wave of anxiety washes over me. Which I guess is the point of having a therapist, but I've never done this whole counseling thing before. I don't want to reveal too many details and risk causing trouble for the club... or for Steel. Nevertheless, I have some issues that I need to sort out.

It's been a few weeks since Steel found me and brought me here. While I've started exploring beyond his room, I still haven't ventured outside the compound except for short walks. Even then, Kiki or Steel has been with me. Both have played a significant role in my recovery, and I'll forever be grateful to them. Especially Kiki, since she was attacked because of me.

Tonight will be Kiki's return to whoring, and she is over the moon. I can't blame her. I'm missing Howards, but I'm also terrified to return. It's where I met Susan and Nancy. Where I thought Nancy's advances were harmless. She was pushy and a tad sketchy but never gave me deranged lunatic vibes.

Steel is out at the shop, cleaning up my car since we're going to sell it. I don't want it. I made an effort yesterday to sit in the driver's seat and park it outside, instead of taking up a spot in their shop. However, I was unexpectedly hit by a wave of panic, making it impossible for me to move. Steel had to carry me to the bedroom, and he spent the rest of the afternoon rubbing my back, reassuring me I was safe, and reminding me to breathe.

After much thought, I ultimately chose to part ways with it and put it up for sale. Pistol actually suggested it. He asked if I thought I could drive a different vehicle and I wasn't sure. But this morning I sat in Kiki's Mustang with no racing heart or gasping for air. So I told Steel to list it. Get what he can for it and I'll buy another when I'm ready.

Lifting the lid of the laptop Draco brought from my house, I open the web browser and type in the website I need. With a deep breath, I log in and get settled, ready for my session. On the hour, the screen fills with a pretty redhead, her hair in a bun and green eyes staring at me.

"Nice to meet you, Ignatius. It's obvious, but I'm Holly. How are you today?"

I can't help but smile, feeling a sense of relaxation wash over me as I listen to her soothing voice. Even with just one sentence, she gave off a warm and friendly vibe. "I'm good. A little nervous, I won't lie. How are you?"

"Living the dream." She laughs. "And being nervous for your first session is normal. We're going to work through that and give you some coping skills to help with your nerves. Sound good?"

"Sounds good." I nod.

"Okay, so first off, why don't you tell me about yourself

and what happened that led you to my screen?" She winks and I really like this woman.

I tell her where I work, and about my parents and my hobbies. But now the hard part. "My coworker and her mom abducted me. They tied me up in a garage and kept me there. Nancy, the daughter, was obsessed with me. I thought it was a harmless but kinda creepy crush, but I was obviously wrong. She and her mom concocted this whole idea that they could force me to love her and they planned for her to rape me."

"How did you get out?"

"My... well, I don't know what he is at the moment. But this guy I was seeing found and rescued me. I'm staying at his place. It's where I feel safe for the time being. But while I was in that garage, my dad showed up. Turns out he had been having an affair with the mom and while, according to him, he thought they were hosting an intervention, they weren't."

"And where is your dad now? How is your relationship since you've been back?"

I struggle to hold back the tears that are on the verge of streaming down my face and hastily wipe my nose with the back of my hand. "She shot him. Susan, the mother, had a gun. She pointed it at him and told me to choose between my dad or being intimate with her daughter. I chose myself and she shot him. I watched as she murdered him."

She nods, her fingers dancing across the keyboard as she types. "That's a lot, Ignatius, for anyone. We're not going to dissect and work through everything in one session. I think we should meet weekly, if that works for you. I have a few more questions, so I know how to better help you."

"Okay."

"Are these women now in police custody? What came of them? Will there be a trial we need to prepare for?"

I'm at a loss for words. I can't tell her that Steel and his club took them and have them in the shed; wherever that is. I'm not sure if he even kept them alive or if they're now dead. I haven't mustered up the courage to ask yet.

Looking around the room, I scramble to find something interesting to say, desperately trying to avoid an awkward silence.

"That's okay, Ignatius. You don't have to tell me everything. Everyone is entitled to a secret or two, right? Give me a simple yes or no. Will you have to testify at a trial?"

"No."

"Perfect. Well, not perfect, but that helps me make a treatment plan. We won't need to work on a plan for you to handle seeing them or testifying."

Thank God she let it go, because I won't betray Steel, not after everything he's done. I'd rather endure my suffering in solitude, without therapy, than betray him.

"What about your mother? How is she handling the news? Your relationship with her. What does that look like?"

"I couldn't tell her he was dead, so once I was rescued, we called the police with an anonymous tip and they handled his body and told her. She called me a few days later and told me he was gone. The funeral is tomorrow. We had to wait for his body to be released because his death is under investigation."

"How do you feel about attending? Are you going?"

Isn't that the million-dollar question? This morning, though, with the help of Steel, I made my decision. "I'm going. We may not have had a good relationship, but I think it will give me closure, and in the end, when it mattered the most, he proved he loved me."

"Do you have someone going with you? That way, if you have a panic attack, you're not alone?"

"Yeah. Steel... that's the guy I was seeing. He, my friend Kiki, and my best friend, Draco, are going with me." I'm so glad they agreed to go with me so I don't have to do it alone. I say agreed like I had to beg or negotiate, but Draco was going no matter what. Steel said yes as soon as I mentioned it, and Kiki refused to let me go without her.

"So when you go tomorrow, I want you to try two things. If you have a panic attack or feel one coming on, I want you to close your eyes and take slow, deep breaths. If that doesn't help, pick a category, it can be anything. I used to always do baby names because it was easy. Start at A and work your way through Z. It will take your mind off whatever has you panicked."

"Sounds easy enough. What if those things don't work?" I ask because while they sound simple, they also don't sound foolproof.

"This is a marathon, not a sprint, Ignatius. If they don't work, be honest with your friends so they can help you. Next week when we meet, we can discuss alternatives. It might come down to you needing medication, and that's okay. I don't want you feeling a certain way if you have to take anxiety meds. Fun fact: more than ninety-two million prescriptions are filled each year for anxiety."

"I can do that." I smile at her, feeling good about getting through tomorrow and while I hadn't thought of taking medication, I'm not against it. But I'm glad she told me the statistics, only so I know it's not uncommon to feel how I do.

"Alright then. Our time is up. But let's schedule for next week. Does the same day and time work for you?"

"Yeah, that works."

"Perfect. I got you on the calendar and I'll see you next

week. Ignatius, I'm going to email you my cell. If it gets too bad and Steel can't help you relax, you call me, okay? I want to be a last resort, though. You can do this."

I nod again, and by this point, I feel like a bobblehead. But she's told me so much yet so little all at once and I'm trying to process everything.

"Bye, Ignatius." She waves, and the screen reverts to the homepage of the website.

Immediately, a notification pops up on my screen, reminding me of the weekly appointment I have with her. I hear a soft ding from my patient portal and quickly click on the message. Along with a reminder of what we talked about for coping skills, she included her phone number just like she said.

I close the computer and step out of the room, ready to head to the shop. I need to find Steel and update him on how it went.

## thirty-six

IGNATIUS

THE WEIGHT of my grief presses down on me as I stand by my father's graveside, flanked by Steel, Kiki, Trucker, and Draco. Marni wanted to come, but Steel and Pistol insisted she stay back at the clubhouse since it's still unsafe for her to be out and about. The wind gently rustles through the trees, bringing the aroma of damp soil and the bitter hint of sorrow with it. It's hard to believe that he's gone, that I'll never hear his laughter or see his face again.

I glance over at my mother, her eyes puffy and bloodshot from crying, and my heart fills with an overwhelming sense of guilt. She's been doing this alone, and I've been too wrapped up in my own pain to truly see it. As she approaches me, her footsteps slow and hesitant, I can see the unsaid words swimming in her eyes.

"Iggie, I'm so sorry. I know I haven't been the best mother," she murmurs, her voice choked, and filled with regret, "but I want you to know that I love you. You should also know that there's nothing left for me here. Next week, right after Christmas, I'll be making the move to Florida. I'll be staying with my friend Clarice."

Like a punch to the gut, her words knock the wind out of me, making it hard to breathe. She's leaving, just like that. Starting over somewhere new, like my dad didn't just get murdered and her son doesn't still need her. Overwhelmed by panic, my chest tightens and my eyes well up with tears, struggling to contain my emotions.

Steel's hand landing on my shoulder calms me, his touch warm and reassuring. He's been my rock throughout all this when I felt like I was drowning in sorrow. I manage to nod at my mom's words. "Sounds good, Mom. Do you wanna do anything for Christmas? Get together before you leave?"

Her watery smile tugs at my heart as she reaches up to gently push a strand of hair behind her ear. "Thank you, Iggie. And no. I do not want to celebrate the holidays with the news we've received. I'll just spend the day packing. You go on and have fun."

With one last hug, she turns away, disappearing into the crowd of mourners. My anger swiftly overshadows my grief. How can she act like she lost her son and her husband? She apologizes, but then says she's moving and doesn't want to get together for Christmas. Has she no heart? I know she had to have known about Dad's affairs, but to treat me so coldly as well?

Steel's hand is still on my shoulder, his presence a steady anchor in the storm that is my life right now. I let out a sigh, using it as a tool to clear my mind, and then shake my head to refocus. Holly is gonna have her work cut out for her. I do feel a lot better about coming today to see my dad off. I needed closure, to make peace with what happened.

Leaving the gravesite, we walk in silence toward where

we parked. The air is heavy, our steps measured and solemn.

A chorus of car doors slam shut, we start our engines and navigate our way back to the clubhouse. When we arrive and step out of the vehicles, Kiki lets me know she'll see me later before Draco turns to me, his gaze soft. "I need to go home," he says quietly, his voice tinged with regret. "But first I have news, too."

My heart lurches in my chest, fear tearing at the edges of my mind.

"I took a slight demotion," he admits, his gaze meeting mine with a mixture of uncertainty and determination. "I'll still be with the same company, but I won't be traveling anymore. I want to stay close to my best friend and put down roots, maybe meet a nice lady."

Trucker winces at those words, his body tensing up as if he's been physically struck. Unspoken emotion causes his jaw to tighten. Does he have feelings for Draco? It wouldn't surprise me, but Draco is straight, so this will only end with Trucker getting his heart broken.

As my unease grows, Steel grips my shoulder again, offering silent support. "That's great news, Draco."

Draco returns the smile, albeit somewhat hesitantly. He wraps his arms around me for a brief, tight embrace. "I'll text you later. I'm excited to be home for good. Traveling was fun, but being here full time is what I want."

"I'm happy if you're happy. Hey, since I'll be bumming it solo for Christmas next week, you wanna come here and we can do something, the two of us? Maybe get drunk and watch *Christmas Christmas*?"

"I'll be here with bells on." He smiles and turns, heading to his car.

Trucker's eyes never leave him until his car disappears

from the compound property. With an annoyed huff, he stomps toward the clubhouse, his steps heavy and purposeful. Yup, he's got it bad.

Steel breaks the silence. "Iggie, you wanna have dinner with me?"

I hesitate for a moment, torn between the comfort of his company and the overwhelming fear of being in public. Today was enough for me. I'm not ready for the bustling of a restaurant.

"I can't, Steel. Not yet."

"Just the two of us in my room. I promise."

The allure of being alone with him is too strong to ignore, and before I realize it, I find myself nodding in agreement. "I'd like that," I say, a small smile playing on my lips.

Dinner with Steel is a much-needed escape from the overwhelming pain and sadness that's consumed me throughout the day. He has the room set up with candles and soft music, the atmosphere warm and inviting. And as we sit down to eat, a sense of peace settles over me.

For the first time in weeks, I feel like myself again, free from grief. Our eyes meet across the table, and a mischievous smile spreads across Steel's face, reminding me of the deep connection we share. He's more than just a friend; he's a lifeline, a beacon of hope in the darkness.

I reach out to take his hand, my fingers trembling slightly. "Thank you, Steel," my voice barely above a whisper. "For everything."

He squeezes my hand in return. "Anytime, Iggie."

The soft flickering candlelight lights up his face and casts dancing shadows on the walls. I can see the truth in his eyes. With Steel by my side, I can face whatever challenges the future may bring, knowing I have someone who cares for me deeply. And for now, that's enough.

# *thirty-seven*

## STEEL

IGGIE HAS BEEN ATTENDING therapy sessions for a full two weeks. He has an appointment later today and I hope it's as good as their first. He seems to really like this Holly woman Shank recommended.

While he's in his session, I have some business to attend to. Tomorrow is Christmas Eve, and while most people are preparing to celebrate with loved ones, I'm preparing to end the two cunts who dared touch what's mine.

Susan and Nancy.

"What are you doing today?" Iggie asks as he slides on his t-shirt and jeans.

He deserves my honesty, especially after what happened the last time I withheld information from him and put him in danger. Though it's not my fault, I refuse to be the source of any more pain for him. "I don't want to go into the holiday with those cunts still breathin'. Today is the day. Viper and I will deal with them while you're talkin' with Holly."

"You can't do that without me! I want to be there." His teeth are clenched as he speaks, and I know I've upset him.

This is for his own good, though. He doesn't need to see me murder someone. Watching his dad get shot has already affected him so much. I was waiting for him to see if he needed that closure. But now that his anxiety is so bad, I don't think watching another life leave this world is the right thing for him.

"No. You don't need to see them again. Plus, we aren't together. I still have hope we will be again one day, and watching me take a life might ruin that. You'll see me differently. I'll be a monster."

He takes a step toward me, his hands firmly planted on his hips, and shoots me a piercing glare. "I deserve to face them. To confront them on my own terms. I won't interrupt and if it gets too much, I'll leave, but please don't just tell me I can't."

Goddammit. This man has me by the balls. It's safe to say that they are essentially his. "Fine. I don't like it, but I don't want to hurt you or be the cause of any more issues. You can come. But, Iggie, I'm serious. If you start feeling overwhelmed or can't handle it, just leave."

"I promise."

I cup his face and stare into his haunting eyes. "Promise me that when you see me in there—when you see what I'm capable of... you won't think less of me. I may be a monster, Iggie, but for you, I'll always be the hero."

"I know, Steel. You're not going to scare me."

"Okay," I whisper before leaning in to plant a gentle kiss on his forehead. "After your session, come find me and we'll go together."

I step out of the room, leaving him alone to get ready for his appointment and gather his thoughts. Our argument cut it close to his time, so I head out, sliding my cut on in the hallway. Walking to the bar, I take a seat next to Pistol and shake my head. "Get me a drink, Daria."

"Sure thing, baby." She bats her lashes at me, but I ignore her. Daria is harmless, but she's always so strung out on blow, she can't remember who actually wants to fuck her or not. If I didn't owe her cousin a favor, she wouldn't be allowed to be a whore for Hell's Mayhem.

I prefer our whores to be drug free. They want to get drunk and party with us, cool. As long as their shit gets done and they do what they're here for, I don't mind. But I don't like when they partake in the harder shit. We sell it but don't do it. And I'm hoping with Element opening soon, we won't have to sell it much longer.

Iggie finds me an hour later, still at the bar, my fingers tracing the condensation on the cold glass as I slowly nurse my drink.

"I'm ready."

Without a word, I nod, get up, and head out to the shed.

He follows me through the backyard to the hidden shed shrouded by trees in the back corner of our property. Holding the door open, I let Iggie step inside and then shut it, moving in front of him so I can investigate the scene first.

Nancy and Susan dangle from the rafters, their limp bodies swaying gently in the air.

Iggie gasps and freezes next to the wall. "Are they even alive?"

Viper emerges from the shadows. "That's my specialty. Best you don't ask questions you don't really want answers to."

Viper's eyes glint with sadistic pleasure as he approaches his helpless victim, his footsteps a slow, deliberate cadence that echoes through the silence.

Susan's wrists are bound tightly above her with fraying rope. Her breath comes in shallow pants as she hangs there, eyes closed. Blood trickles from the cuts and bruises that mar her skin, evidence of the brutality she has endured.

Viper circles Susan like a vulture circling its prey. With a flourish, he produces a gleaming knife from the folds of his cut.

"One... two... Viper's coming for you." Viper's voice is a low growl, dripping with venom. "Three... four... you're a delusional whore."

Without warning, he strikes, the blade slashing through the air with deadly precision. Susan's piercing screams fill the shed.

Viper's movements are methodical, each cut a deliberate act of cruelty. Blood flows freely from her wounds, pooling on the floor beneath in a macabre form of art.

"Please," she coughs and blood pours from her mouth.

Viper only smiles. "No thanks. You touched what wasn't yours. Tried to force your daughter on someone who doesn't even like pussy. She ain't even that good lookin' to turn a man straight."

"Doug maa—"

He cuts her off. "Don't lie to me or I'll cut your tongue out. You killed Doug 'cause he couldn't get on board the crazy train. Turns out that pussy wasn't quite good enough to get him to turn on his son. Go to hell, you psycho cunt."

And then, with a final, fatal stroke, Viper delivers the killing blow, the blade plunging deep into Susan's chest with a sickening thud. Her cries fall silent, her body slumping against her bonds as the last signs of life slip away.

I turn to check on Iggie, and he's leaning against the back wall. One hand over his mouth, the other holding his stomach. "Remember what I said. You can leave."

He stays rooted to the spot, determined to be brave. "I'm okay. Go on."

It's my turn now. Viper may have gotten to play with Susan as his reward for caring for them over the last two weeks, but Nancy is mine. Viper steps back next to Iggie in case he needs someone, and I loom over Nancy, my face a mask of cold determination.

I slap Nancy once, causing her to slowly open her eyes. "Wake up. It's time."

"Mom?" she asks, turning her head slowly.

"Mommy is gone." Viper laughs.

A pathetic sob leaves Nancy and I withdraw my belt from the loops of my pants, the metal buckle glinting ominously in the dim light. Nancy's eyes widen in terror, realization dawning on her like a bolt of lightning.

"I only wanted him to love me like I loved him."

Without warning, the first blow falls, a savage strike that has Nancy crying out.

"He's not yours to love. He is mine!"

I strike her again, each blow a cruel reminder of her powerlessness. Blood flows from the wounds where the buckle hits her instead of the leather, staining the floor beneath her.

But I'm relentless. There is no mercy.

It's time to send her straight to hell. I draw my gun from my cut and pull the trigger. The deafening roar of the gunshot shatters the silence. Nancy's body jerks violently as the bullet tears through the flesh of her chest, her screams echoing through the shed like a banshee's wail.

She gurgles briefly before her head lolls forward.

I sheath my weapon and move to Iggie. "Are you okay?"

"I'm good, actually. It wasn't as bad as I thought. The blood made me queasy, but I'm okay. They deserved worse."

My cock hardens in my pants. What a little secret psycho I'm in love with. We took it easy on the bitches because he's right; they did deserve worse. But I didn't want to scare Iggie more than necessary.

"Viper, can you take care of them?" I ask, nodding to our deceased guests.

"I got it, Prez."

"Thanks, man." I grab Iggie's hand and lead him out of the shed toward the clubhouse.

The night air is cool against our skin, a stark contrast to the heat of the shed. As we enter the dimly lit interior, I guide him to my room without a word.

Iggie flops down on the bed and scrolls his phone while I head to the bathroom.

Peeling off my blood-stained clothes, I step into the shower, letting the hot water wash away the grime of my deeds. With each drop that cascades down, I feel a sense of purification—a cleansing of both body and soul.

Once I'm dried off and dressed in fresh clothes, Iggie and I head to the bar. The familiar scent of cigarettes and alcohol envelops us as we take a seat, ready to unwind after the night's events.

We discuss our plans for Christmas Eve tomorrow as we sip our drinks. With no family obligations weighing us down, we decide to spend the day at the club, surrounded by our fellow members who, like us, have no family ties to attend to. It may not be traditional, but it's our own version of holiday cheer.

Kiki blasts out of the kitchen with two plates in hand, setting them down in front of us. "I prepared you a Christmas Eve Eve dinner."

"Hey!" Marni shouts as she comes from the kitchen with two more plates.

Kiki rolls her eyes. "Fine, *we* made dinner."

We sit at the bar in a line, eating the chicken and dumplings the girls made while chatting amongst ourselves.

"Kiki." Iggie wipes his mouth with a napkin. "Can you take me to town tomorrow? I want to get Steel a gift, and a few others, too."

"Duh." Kiki shakes her head, laughing, like Iggie has lost his mind.

I reluctantly agree to let Iggie go without me, but I'm sending Trucker along to keep an eye on the two of them.

As we finish our meal, I look at the man to my left and feel a glimmer of hope. Maybe, just maybe, there's a chance for us to find happiness together, despite all the pain and darkness that surrounds us.

# *thirty-eight*

## IGNATIUS

IT'S CHRISTMAS MORNING, and I'm lying in bed wondering how this became my life. I'm waking up in Steel's bed, but we're not together. I have no plans with any family and that's what today is supposed to be about. Instead, I'll be spending it with my newfound family: Hell's Mayhem MC.

Are they really even mine if I'm not Steel's?

Last night, Kiki took me into town to get a few gifts, and I can't wait to see their faces when they open them. I was even able to sneak something in my bags for her without her knowing. Being in town made me realize how much I miss my job. I ended up texting Barron when we got back to the clubhouse, asking if I could come back after New Year's Day.

Of course, he was thrilled I'd be returning and told me the timing was perfect. I'm so thankful that Steel updated him on everything that went down and Barron was understanding.

As soon as I put my phone down, a cold sweat rushed

over me and my throat felt like it was closing up as I second-guessed my decision.

Remembering what Holly said about listing something, I picked Christmas items and started at A.

However, that didn't work. Neither did Steel's soothing words and touch. Finally, I decided to call Holly and have her work through it with me. She didn't even bat an eye that I was calling her on Christmas Eve.

We worked through my panic and got my breathing back under control before having a small session to figure out what triggered me.

That is how I came to my decision, and now I need to tell Steel. It will have to wait until after our small gift exchange, and definitely when we're alone, because while I'm hopeful, I don't know how he will react. But it's time I stop leading him on, even though that's never been my intention, and tell him I want to be with him.

The clubhouse is lit up with the flickering glow of Christmas lights, casting a festive atmosphere over the bar and seating area. Steel and I sit sideways across from Gabe, Marni, and Kiki—the few left at the clubhouse on this fun holiday morning.

Steel reaches into his pocket and pulls out a small velvet box, a mischievous glint in his eye. With a dramatic flair, he hands it to me.

"What's this?" I ask, a grin spreading across my face as I accept the box.

"Open it and find out," Steel replies, his voice tinged with playfulness.

My fingers tremble slightly as I lift the lid, revealing a silver chain with a pendant attached. My eyebrows shoot up in surprise as I look at the necklace, noticing a small button on the back of the pendant.

"A GPS tracker?" I question, not positive that's what it is, but I have a good hunch.

Steel chuckles, his gaze softening as he meets my eyes. "Yeah. No matter what happens, if you need me, I'm there. Always."

A lump forms in my throat as I look at Steel, my heart filling with gratitude. "Thank you," I whisper as my breath hitches.

It's my turn to play Santa. I pull out four wrapped gifts, one for each of my new friends. I hand Kiki hers first, and she tears into the wrapping paper with a huge smile on her face. Her eyes widen in surprise when she sees a tentacle dildo. She lets out a delighted squeal.

"Iggie, you're a legend!"

Handing Marni her gift, I watch eagerly as she slowly unwraps it.

"I've not gotten a gift on Christmas in years." She rolls the paper into a ball and sets it on the table. "This is too much."

"No, you've mentioned you might want to go to college. This will help you apply and do homework." She holds the new laptop to her chest and smiles at me as a tear rolls down her cheek.

"Thank you."

Next up is Gabe, who quickly tears into his present, revealing a Funko Pop figure of his favorite *Walking Dead* character. His face lights up with excitement as he holds the figurine up, a grin spreading from ear to ear.

"Dude, this is awesome!"

Finally, it's Steel's turn. I watch as he unwraps his gift, a sleek black leather belt with a silver buckle, along with a new knife. His eyes widen in appreciation as he examines the craftsmanship, and a wide grin spreads across his face.

"Damn, baby, this is amazing!"

As the festivities continue, my phone buzzes with a text message. I glance down at the screen.

> Draco: Raincheck on today. My cousin is having her baby, and my mom wants me to take her up to the hospital.

> Me: Okay. No problem. Merry Christmas!!!

THE GIRLS and Gabe excuse themselves to put away their gifts and call their families. Well, Marni is going with Kiki to call hers because she's not in contact with the family she has left.

I'm left alone in the main part of the clubhouse with Steel. Knowing it's now or never, I take a deep breath, readying myself for the conversation ahead.

"Hey, I need to talk to you about something."

Steel looks up, his gaze searching my face for clues. "What's on your mind, Iggie?"

"I'm going to sell my house. And before you ask, I've spoken to Holly, and she agreed it's a good move for me."

Steel smirks. "It's your house, babe. You can sell, rent, or burn it down. Whatever makes you happy."

"I'll need a place to stay when it sells. The market is hot right now, so I have no doubt it will go fast." I worry my bottom lip, hoping he asks me to stay or more like tells me I can stay longer.

"That's a predicament." He rubs his chin. "Do you know if you want to buy another house or rent? Draco will be here full time so maybe you two can get a place together."

My heart beats faster in my chest. Did I overstay my welcome? Has he rethought his feelings for me? Or maybe he just doesn't want to assume I'm asking to stay since I didn't come right out and say it? I also haven't told him where we stand since I've been back and he's always worrying after me. I need to just lay all my cards on the table.

"I'm not sure. But I know that before I make a decision, there is someone I need to talk to about my feelings for them."

"Oh, and who would that be?" he asks, one side of his lips turned up cockily.

"Just this guy I met selling jeans a few weeks back."

He smiles at me and stands up suddenly, holding a hand out to me. "Take a drive with me."

━━━✦☠✦━━━

THE TWINKLE OF Christmas lights shines as Steel and I cruise through the quiet streets.

As we drive, the weight of unspoken words hangs heavy between us. I take a deep breath, steeling myself.

"Steel," I begin, my voice soft. "Our relationship... It can only work if there are no secrets or lies. Everything has to be out in the open, no matter how dark or fucked up it is."

Steel nods, his expression serious. "I understand and agree," he says, his voice firm. "So you're saying there is an us?"

Relief flows through me as I reach over and grab his hand, bringing it to my lips, pressing a gentle kiss to his knuckles. "Ashton Steel," I say his legal name, a smile spreading across my face. "Will you be mine?"

Steel's response is immediate and filled with warmth as he growls, pulling me into a heated kiss. "Yes," he murmurs against my lips.

I can't help but laugh. "Keep your eyes on the road, Biker Boy," I tease.

We continue to ride in comfortable silence, just holding hands and enjoying the time together. Eventually, Steel turns off the main road into a quiet neighborhood not far from the clubhouse. He parks the truck on the side of the road and turns to me with a grin.

"I have a surprise for you."

My brows draw together, curious about what's going on and why we're here. "Where are we?"

"Well, Baby. It was a huge leap and you could have told me to shove it... hell, you might yet. But I took the leap anyway, knowing how I feel about you. This is our home, if you say yes."

My mouth drops open in complete disbelief. "What about the club?"

"I don't have to live there and you shouldn't have to, either. Move into this house with me. Our house. Better yet, be my old man."

My lips curl automatically. "Eww. No. I can't use that term. It's even worse than old lady." I laugh.

Steel rolls his eyes and looks at me, his mesmerizing brown eyes locking on mine. "I don't care about the term. Just be mine."

"Yes."

Steel closes the distance between us, his hand reaching out to cup the back of my head.

I lean into his touch, my breath catching in my throat as

I feel the warmth of his hand wrapped in my blond locks. His lips crash against mine in a devouring kiss. It's possessive and eager, an exploration of each other's warmth and sweetness.

Time stands still as we lose ourselves in the heat of the moment, our hearts beating in perfect rhythm.

When we finally break apart, breathless and puffy-lipped, I know this is just the beginning of a love story waiting to be told.

Steel reaches into the backseat and pulls out a black leather jacket that matches his. Only it says Iggie and 'Property of Steel'.

I take it from him and sniff the rich leather before looking at him. "So, when can we move in?"

## *thirty-nine*

### STEEL

I SIT on the edge of the bed, surrounded by the familiarity of what used to be my room. I can't help but feel a pang of nostalgia. It's been a month since we moved into our new house, but being back here brings back a flood of memories.

Lost in my thoughts, I feel Iggie's presence before I see him. He steps between my thighs, his arms wrapping around me tightly. The warmth of his body against mine makes my cock twitch and I will it to stay down. I'll deal with him in the shower later tonight.

Iggie, though, has other plans. He lifts his leg gently and rubs against my dick, his green eyes staring into mine.

"Are you sure about this?" I ask softly, my voice barely above a whisper.

Iggie's response is simple but resolute. "As sure as I am of anything."

His words wash over me, filling me with desire. "Tell me how you want it. This is on your terms, Iggie. You want it soft, or should I fuck you like I did before? Own you like no one else has?"

"Own me, Steel. When we leave here tonight, I want to have a reminder of who was inside me and who owns me."

"Strip." I stand up as he takes a step back and we both undress.

My cock is already hard and leaking pre-cum as I take Iggie's hand, pulling him toward the bed and pushing him down.

He's bent over the bed, his perfect little ass on display for me.

"God, I missed this ass," I growl, spanking his left cheek.

Dropping to my knees behind him, I part his cheeks and, without hesitation, dive between them. Using just the tip of my tongue, I flick back and forth on his perfect star. "Such a tasty little hole," I murmur.

"Oh," he groans.

I use my left hand to rub his taint and balls with my thumb as I eat his asshole. When he's good and wet, I push my tongue inside as best I can, causing him to cry out. "I've missed your tongue."

"You never have to miss it again, baby. I'll eat this pretty ass whenever you want."

My dick is hard and pulsing and I know if I don't get inside of him soon, I'll cum on the floor. It's been weeks since we've been together and I've respected him, giving him the time he needs to heal. But my right hand can only do so much and it sure the hell doesn't feel as good as my man.

"You ready for me to fuck you?" I ask, shoving my index finger into his hole and curling it against his prostate.

"Please."

I stand up, stroking my shaft as I position myself at his

entrance. I ease into him gradually, allowing him time to readjust to my presence.

Reaching up, I wrap my hand in his hair and pull him backward slightly as I begin to drive into him faster and harder.

"God, I've missed your slutty hole."

He doesn't reply, just whines as I pound into him, my hips slapping against his ass. I'm not going to last long since it's been a while.

I let go of his hair and reach around to grab his cock, jerking him in time with my thrusts.

"I'm gonna come, Steel," he moans, burying his face in the mattress.

That's good because I can't hold off any longer. With a bellowing roar, I drive into him once more before stilling. Rope after rope of my hot cum fills his ass. There's so much it seeps from his hole and around my cock.

I don't pull out. I leave him stuffed as I jerk him until I can feel him tense, and his back arches as he finds his release. He empties himself, his cum covering my hand and the bed under him.

Good thing that when a new brother takes this room, we'll replace the mattress.

When he stops quivering and his breathing returns to normal, I pull my cock from him and head to the bathroom to grab some toilet paper since we've taken all the towels and rags to the new house. I do a half-ass job of cleaning myself up and then head to the bed to clean my love up.

"Thank you," he whispers when I finish.

"You're welcome, babe. And thank you for letting me have you again."

He stares at me and I let the three words I've felt for a while, but been too worried to say, slip free. "I love you."

His face splits in a huge smile as he stands and kisses me. "I love you, too."

A bang on the door startles us, interrupting our confessions. Pistol's voice comes from the other side. "You're missing your own moving-out party!"

We exchange amused glances before getting dressed and deciding to join the festivities. I grab drinks for us as soon as we get to the party, and we prepare to take on Kiki and Marni in a game of pool.

The game lasts a little while until Marni's precision nails the eight ball into the corner pocket, sealing the win for her and Kiki. We laugh and tease, trying to psyche them out as we rack the balls to play again. But our fun is interrupted again when Barbi bursts in from guard duty, looking freaked out and worried.

"What the fuck is goin' on, Barbi?" I ask, concern lacing my tone.

"Prez, there's a woman at the gate," he says urgently. "She doesn't look good, and she's askin' for you. More like beggin'."

Without hesitation, Iggie and I, along with Viper and Pistol, follow Barbi to the gate. Standing on the other side is a very beat-up, very pregnant woman. She turns to face us as we approach, desperation in her eyes.

"I didn't know where else to go. I had no other options," she cries, her voice trembling with emotion.

Iggie shoots me a questioning look, confusion swirling in his eyes.

"Brielle, what the hell is going on?" I demand, my voice tight with worry and apprehension.

# afterword

Thank you to every single one of you who made it this far. I appreciate every page turn! You're helping me live my dream.

If you loved my spicy little story please consider leaving a review! It would mean the absolute world to me!

REVIEW HERE

# words from cassie

I wrote this book because Iggie and Steel lived in my head and wouldn't stop talking to me. Their stories needed to be told and while I loved every minute of telling it this book also scares me. I touched on things that I don't see a lot in books or media in general.

I have this very small platform and I'd be doing a disservice if I didn't use it for something other than smutty stories. I wanted to show that not all perpetrators are male and victims can be anyone.

Sexual assault can happen to anyone, it doesn't matter your age, sexual orientation, or gender identity.

Perpetrators can also be any gender identity, sexual orientation, or age, and they can have any relationship to the victim.

If you or someone you know has been assaulted please call the police. YOU ARE NOT ALONE!

If you need to talk to someone call 800.656.HOPE (4763) to be connected to a trained staff member from a local sexual assault service provider in your area.

MALESURVIVOR.ORG: THIS RESOURCE CONTAINS GENERAL INFORMATION AS WELL AS A THERAPIST SEARCH SPECIFICALLY DESIGNED FOR MALE SURVIVORS OF SEXUAL VIOLENCE

# *acknowledgments*

First I have to thank Chad my husband for supporting this dream no matter what. You were there from beginning to end supporting me and pushing me to keep it going. To our kids' Faith, Ro, Mario, Marshon, Sutton, and Georgia. (Ya'll probably thought I was kidding about six kids huh?) Thank you! Thank you for letting me type away while you entertained yourselves and I said a billion times I'm working. Thank you for helping to wrangle your younger siblings when I couldn't. I love you all so much!

To myALPHA/ BETA readers, you all are the bomb! Loving this story as much as me and really making it what it is today.
My ARC readers, what can I say you guys rock. I'm blessed to have each and every one of you. The majority of you have been with me since the beginning. Here are too many more books together.
To my Street team, Thank you all for sharing my books and pimping me out. It means the world to me and I love each and every one of you.
Lastly, to my readers, I appreciate all of you. Without you, I'd still be just playing these stories out in my head. It is your support and enjoyment of reading our work that keeps me going.

## about the author

Cassie resides in Northern Illinois on a farm with her husband and six kids. When not writing, she can be found reading, chauffeuring her kids around, or showing pigs. Cassie is a huge advocate for foster care and adoption. Enjoys a good horror movie, dark romance, and alcohol. Lots and lots of alcohol. You can find her sitting on her front porch enjoying watching her kids play while she writes. She has an English bulldog named Daisy, a Huskies named Sky, a barn cat turned satanic kitten named Pumpkin, along with Aurora the ferret who she will go to war for. Let's not forget a ton of chickens, 2 goats, and 3 horses.

Cassielein.com

https://books.bookfunnel.com/cassieleinauthor

# also by cassie

Check out all her books here

Shattered Omega

Anthologies

Knotted at First Sight

Standalones

Up In Smoke

Wild Child w/ Alisha Williams

Scarlett w/Alisha Williams

Trapped By Beauty w/ Alisha Williams

Kindlevella w/Bre Rose

All on the Field

Shattered Omega

Under the pen name G.P. Darling (Cowrite with 2 friends)

Unknown

Exposed

Collapsed